A TOWN NAMED NEWRY

ALIX CRAWFORD CARNEY

LYSTRA BOOKS
& Literary Services

ISBN 979-8-9921363-3-3 paperback
ISBN 979-8-0021363-4-0 e-book
Libary of Congress Control Number: 2025917762

Cover photograph used with the kind permission of Fud Cater.

Book design by Kelly Prelipp Lojk.

Author's photograph by Stephen Carney.

Published by
Lystra Books & Literary Services, LLC
391 Lystra Estates Drive, Chapel Hill, NC 27517
lystrabooks@gmail.com

To my mother,
Ann Holland Hoagland Crawford,
who always pushed me to be more.

Greenland
Iceland
Canada
U.K.
NEWRY
Ireland
United States
CHARLESTON
Atlantic Ocean
Africa
Carribean Sea
South America

Chapter 1
March 20, 1898

"Lady! Let's get a leg on, now. You're holdin' up the line."

Bridie Murphy nearly jumped out of her skin. Jaysus, did he have to yell right in her ear? It wasn't like she was going anywhere.

She was standing in an endless line of passengers at the Irish Port of Newry, waiting to board the ship *Newry*, set to sail to the Port of Charleston in America. Never had she expected to be in such a line. Until three days ago, she had never even heard of Charleston.

She sighed and adjusted the bag hanging on her shoulder. It wasn't a real bag. Just an old potato sack with a rope strap she'd sewn on. There were two more at her feet. When the official yelled at her to move along, she heaved them over her other shoulder and bent to pick up the tattered carpetbag at her feet. The movement made the baby strapped to her chest whimper, but he thankfully stayed asleep. She looked down at Finn, her six-year-old, who smiled bravely up at her. Already he was trying to become the man of her family. Tears threatened again. Would they forever be so close to flowing?

"Soon, Finn. Soon we'll be on the ship," she said, leaning down to give him an awkward kiss on his cheek hidden under the too-large blue cap covering his head and forehead. It was a wonder he could see anything. He was tied with a rope, waist to waist, to Rory, his four-year-old brother, looking like a ragamuffin, as usual. His bags dragged on the ground, his shirt hung out, and his face and hands were grimy. Bridie's threatening tears were replaced by irritation.

"Jaysus, lad. Look at you. You look like one of our lost lambs." They shuffled ahead, ten feet, and stopped. Again.

She and her fellow passengers stamped their feet, turning in circles to stay warm. It looked like the other passengers had done as she had with her family and dressed in extra layers of clothing. They looked like fat bears. Some muttered and swore amongst themselves; others snapped at children or whisper-yelled to their spouses. More than a few men nipped at flasks. Her boys swatted at each other and whined about how hungry they were.

"Come here, luvs," she said, giving them each a bite of potato and a bit of bacon from the stash in one of her bags. "It shouldn't be too much longer," she lied. "I wonder what our cabin will look like?"

"I hope it's warm," said Rory.

"I hope we have one of those little, round windows so I can look outside," said Finn.

Bridie took out her father's pocket watch. Three hours already, standing in line, and they seemed no closer to the gangplank. She knew they had moved, but it was in small fits and starts. God in heaven, how much longer?

The baby, Brendan, really awoke this time, his whimpering growing into inconsolable cries of hunger. Each cry made her overburdened breasts leak into her clothes. She had hoped she'd have the privacy of being in the cabin by now; she had never nursed one of her babies in public. Must she lose every bit of herself, including her modesty? Some of her neighbors looked angrily at her, increasing the hysteria bubbling in her heart and brain. Jaysus, Bridie, she told herself, don't lose your head now. It can't be much longer.

An older woman a few people back bustled her way through the line to Bridie. "I know exactly how you feel, deary," she whispered in Bridie's ear. "This happened to me once with my son, waitin' for a train. There's nothin' else to do but just sit yourself right down here and start feedin' that little one. I'll stand in front of you and hide you with my skirts."

Grateful, Bridie sank to the ground, loosened her clothing, and began nursing Brendan, a fulfillment for them both. When he was through, she put herself back together, which, considering the many layers of clothing she wore, took a bit of wrestling. She changed his reeking, soaked nappy, putting it into the waterproof bag she'd made from Charles's old macintosh. She hoped it worked.

The lady sat down beside her with a sigh. "I'll sit a bit with you, if you don't mind."

"Ma'am, I can't thank you enough." A catch in her throat and the impending tears surprised her, yet again. Is it any wonder? It had been a long time since anyone had shown her any kindness. "My name's Bridie Murphy. Did you see where my boys went?" she asked.

"I'm Aileen. The little one said he had to piss, so the older one took him over there by the wall."

The line began to move again, and the two women groaned themselves up. With relief Bridie saw Finn rushing towards her through the crowds, the rope taut from the weight of Rory lagging behind, looking everywhere but ahead. Rory would be the death of her yet, always dashing away into trouble. Even though he was her most irritating child, there was a devilish sweetness about him that touched her heart. She knew it was wrong for a mother to have a favorite (and she'd never admit it to anyone), but he was hers.

At least she didn't have to worry he might wander off someplace while tied to Finn, already acting older than his years. Strange how Finn slid so quickly into the role of elder child and her helper. Still a boy, yet now with a grown-up air. They both wore their blue Milford Football Club jerseys and caps that their da had given them last Christmas. The caps fell over their eyes, and the shirts hung below their knees. But no matter, the boys loved them, and the bright royal blue would help her to keep track of them.

The agent yelled to the crowd, "Get your paperwork out, ready to show me."

Finally! For one sick moment, Bridie thought she'd lost the papers and dug frantically through two bags before finding them exactly where she had put them in the first bag. God, what if they're not in order? What if they aren't allowed on the ship?

They gathered their belongings and moved on to the agent. He shook his head. "Pull over here and untie them, lady. It's awful tight quarters gettin' on the ship, and they'll tangle everyone up."

Jaysus. It took her some time to untie the boys, she was shaking so. The impatience of everyone around her made it worse, and tears threatened. Finally, the boys were free from each other. After stuffing the rope into a bag, she handed the agent her rumpled papers. The man gave them a quick glance and waved her forward to the gangplank. So much for her panic.

"Come on boys. Finn, you go first. Take Rory's hand, and Rory, you hold my hand." She grabbed the rail with her free hand and stepped onto the gangplank. The two boys were agog and giggling ahead of her. She looked only at her feet and prayed she wouldn't faint, or worse, vomit from the height.

Once, when her husband was away, *again*, she'd had to repair a leak around the chimney. At the time, she couldn't decide which was worse, scaling the ladder or climbing the roof. This gangplank was far steeper and longer. She was almost grateful for the mass of people behind her; they kept her moving.

Once at the top, an officer glanced at the papers and punched the ticket. The slow-moving crowd was funneled across the deck into a narrow, dark passage. Abruptly, all forward movement halted.

A deckhand struggled up the gangplank, pushing and shoving through the crowd. "Out of the way. Move for God's sake. Some arse is blocking it down below."

A few of the passengers muttered. One yelled, "Whatya think we are? Cattle or something?"

Another scoffed, "Nay, mate. They treat cattle better than us."

The bottleneck unjammed, and they began to move again, still in the dark, then onto a narrow stairway going down to a dim light at the bottom.

Bridie pushed her boys in front of her. "You two go ahead of me. Hold the railing and be careful. It's terrible steep."

At the bottom were more crewmen, one with a megaphone. "Single men to the right, single women line up on the left, over there with the matron. Marrieds and those with children go straight into the room behind me."

They entered an enormous echoing room of bunks. Row after row of iron bunks, five across and three tiers high on each side of the room, running fore and aft. How many bunks are there in this one room? Someone had told Bridie there were more than a thousand steerage passengers on a ship like this. She subtracted the single men and women. Maybe three hundred? Could that mean seven hundred in this one room? Jaysus, Mary, and Joseph.

Curtains between each mattress were now rolled up and could be let down later for privacy. Privacy? Bridie gave a small laugh that came out like a sob. On one side of the room, running the length of the cabin, was a wide area with long tables and benches, lit poorly by light bulbs hanging from the ceiling.

A steward punched Bridie's ticket again and aimed her to a row of bunks. "There you go, ma'am. Oh, but you're a lucky lady. You're over there, the three bunks on the bottom next to the hull. That's a good spot. You won't have to climb up and down with the lads." He lowered his voice. "And you'll only have strangers on one side of you."

"Thank you, sir," she said over the lump in her throat. It appeared as frequently as the tears. Would she ever be able to accept a simple kindness without crying? Well, it was only five days since she'd become a widow. And as soon as this ship set sail, she would be an exiled widow. She allowed she could be a little weepy.

"All right, boys. Toss your bags up there on that side. We'll keep all our bags right here in bed with us. Don't leave them lying around or someone will steal them for sure." She slid her voice down to a whisper. "We're on our own here, and we have to watch out for each other."

The mattresses were straw ticking, like home, and came with three scratchy blankets and three pillows.

She prayed they were clean. Each bunk had a plate, a tin cup, and cutlery. All just as described by the matron in the police station. That woman might have been a Brit, but she was charitable, and Bridie was learning to savor all kindnesses shown her. She hoped they would help her morale during the hard times she knew were coming. As if she hadn't already gone through enough.

She puttered around unpacking, making their bunks into their home. For how long? Ten days, they had been told. Maybe twelve, if there were problems.

She felt movement on her other side. An older couple were beside her, fussing about in their bunks. Oh, blessed day! It was Aileen, the lady who had helped her.

"Oh, my, it's you," Aileen said. "This is my husband, Patrick Collins."

"How do, ma'am? Nice to meet you and your lads. Excuse me while I try to get our bags sorted."

Aileen chose the inside bunk near Bridie. Lowering her voice, she said, "I didn't want to be on the other side. Even with your three babes, I'd rather be beside you than the edge," she whispered. "No offense to you, dearie."

Bridie smiled and nodded conspiratorially—nor did she want to sleep beside Aileen's husband.

"How come there's no little windows, Mam, like the ones I saw outside?" Finn asked. "I wanted one to look out of."

Patrick Collins hoisted another bag onto his bunk. "This is steerage, lad. We're below the waterline, and windows would leak," Mr. Collins said, ruffling Finn's dark head of hair, the same shade as his mother's.

Bridie's stomach fluttered. *Below the waterline...leak.* Chilling.

"Where do you come from?" she asked Aileen.

"Loughgilly, my dear. And you?"

"From Newry," Bridie said.

"Fancy that," Mr. Collins said. "We're only six miles north of Newry. We were practically neighbors."

∾

Two hours later, while there was still some daylight, the passengers were on the deck for the medical inspection. Two surgeons inspected the men and two matrons inspected the women.

Bridie noticed they were not all thorough. The passengers only had to remove their hats and gloves, allowing their faces, hair, and hands to be glanced at. Lastly, an eagle-eyed man stared at each of them, then punched their tickets before they were allowed back to the cabin.

Who was he? Could he be a detective? Were there other reasons for the inspections? The paranoia she'd been living with ever since her husband Charles had been arrested was still with her. Three people were pulled out of line; for what, no one knew.

By now it was evening, and while they were on deck, a supper had been delivered. It was simple fare, but oh so welcome—bread and butter, tea for the adults, and milk for the children.

Bridie sat on the end of her bunk in a daze, sipping her tea. It was the first moment of calm she'd had all day. This ship would be in control of her life for the next ten days, and after the recent chaos of her life, there was nothing to do but sit. Brendan, fed and cleaned, played with his toy truck on the bunk, while the other two ran around finding other children. Funny how little ones can make friends in an instant. She nodded off, then woke with a start looking for her boys and dozed again. She hadn't felt this safe since ... when? Before Charles's arrest almost eight months ago.

Some of the passengers began grousing about why they had not yet left the dock. A crew member came into the cabin and told them it would not be until after midnight. "I know that's late, but it is a Friday. And every sailor knows it is bad luck to set sail on a Friday, so we wait until just after midnight. That's not too long, now."

There were grumblings, but no one was going to argue about sailors' superstitions.

"The ship's bell will ring three times, fifteen minutes before we untie the lines, so if you want to watch as we leave, come up then. The long whistle will mean the gangplank is being wheeled back to the dock, the lines will have been cast off, and the tug will have us underway."

Brendan fell asleep, and Bridie continued sitting, her sleepy eyes on the boys. Suddenly, the bell's three tolls roused everyone.

The boys rushed back, squirming with excitement and demanding to go up on deck.

Bridie saw there would be no rest now. Her fellow cabin mates were scrambling around as they pulled on their heavy layers. She bundled the boys up again, strapped Brendan to her chest with the shawl, and arrived on the steerage deck, teeming with passengers. She found a quiet spot back against the deckhouse, but the boys kept pulling at her, begging to stand near the rail. She clung to their hands tightly, shaking her head no, but they continued their pleadings.

Reluctantly, she let them pull her to the rail, where she kept a tight hold on them. She could only stare straight out. The one time she dared glance down, all she saw was a shadowy, moving throng of people calling out to the ship. A wave of nausea overtook her. The ship was even taller than the Newry Hotel. She remembered Kathleen laughing at her whenever they had to wash the windows on the top floor. "Good Lord, Bridie. It's only four stories up."

A tugboat idled in position behind them, smoke puffing from its stack, a low light glowing in its wheelhouse.

She looked at the gangplank, about ten feet away to the right and still bustling with confused activity. Panicked late passengers shoved themselves up the gangplank against visitors elbowing themselves down to exit. All were at odds, irritably jostling each other, some yelling and swearing.

"Typical lads, aren't they? Always wanting to get up close to see how things work. Like me, I guess. I still do that." A young man stood beside Bridie. She guessed he was around seventeen. Well, that's not that young.

After all, she was fifteen when she married Charles. A lifetime ago, it seemed now. Twenty-two she was and felt like an old lady. She nodded briefly back.

The gangplank lights were disconnected, leaving the last visitors exiting in semi-darkness, clinging to the handrail as they continued struggling down. Shouts from the dock workers down below echoed up. On deck, the sailors yelled to each other and down to the men on the dock, making ready to disconnect the gangplank from the ship.

Bridie stepped backwards, holding her boys by their jerseys. A bitter gust of icy wind tore at her coat and scarf, startling the baby into a wail. She let go of the boys to re-cover herself and re-secure Brendan, then went to grab the boys' hands.

They were gone! "Finn! Rory!" she yelled. She felt a flood of panic in her chest and thought she might faint. Oh God. She mustn't faint. There. Over there. A blue hat. Rory? Finn?

"Please, mister," she cried to the lad beside her. "Over there! The little one in the blue cap and shirt. Please, can you catch him?"

The noise of the whistle set her mind screaming in panic, yet she stayed glued to the spot, paralyzed. The gangplank was released from the deck and rolled backwards into the darkness. At the same time, she felt the jolt as the tugboat edged the ship into the river.

"Jaysus! Merciful Mother of God! Stop! Where are my boys?" She shoved against the other passengers, but it was impossible to move through the mob. She had to get to the gate. She heard screaming and realized it was her, accompanied by Brendan's wailing. All their noise and no one paid them any attention. She expected the boys to materialize out of the darkness—waiting for her at the gate. But there was only one sailor, reconnecting the railing where the gangplank had been.

"How could you not see two little boys on a ramp, you stupid, stupid man?" she yelled. Finn suddenly appeared just as she slumped to the deck.

"Mammy. Mammy. I'm sorry. It's not my fault," he cried, falling in a heap beside her. "I tried to hold him back, but he just ran off. I was holding his hand, and he pointed to something. 'Look at the flowers. I'm going to get them for Mammy.' You know how he is. He took off running, and the next thing he was gone… I tried following him, but it was too crowded, and I couldn't get through… and then I couldn't find you. Please don't be mad at me, Mammy. Please." Snotty tears streamed down his face, and he shook as if he had the ague.

She pulled him to her, trying to stop his cries and stifle the screams rising in her throat. Little Brendan, crushed between them, wailed even more. "Hush now. Hush, Finn. I know it's not your fault. It's mine. I should never have let go of you both. I should have tied you together again. Let's get up and find someone." She couldn't resist screaming at the seaman still standing nearby. "Someone who might do something except stand there staring like a damned eegit."

All this time, so much time, fellow passengers passed them, some offering to help, most just walking around them. She stood up shakily with Finn clinging to her and Brendan still crying on her chest. Just then the lad came back with a sailor, an officer. She knew by looking at them there was nothing that could be done.

The officer was kind, at least. "Once we're under way, ma'am, once we're being pushed by the tugboat, we can't turn back. We have no way to control our movement, and we could cause untold damage to the ship, the harbor, the pier, other ships … It's way too dangerous. And a crime."

"Dangerous? But what about the danger to my son?" Her voice trailed as she sagged to the deck again. The officer and the lad grabbed her arms and helped her over to a bench.

"I'm sorry, ma'am. There's nothing I can do."

He took out a little notebook and pencil. "Give me your son's name and particulars, and I'll give them to the captain on the tugboat, and he'll let the port authority know. They might even have him inside now, nice and warm. They'll make arrangements for him to be placed in a home or something."

"A home? Or something? He's only four! How can you let that happen? Everyone knows what those orphanages are like. They're as bad as the prisons." She knew about prisons—her husband had just been murdered in a prison.

"Ma'am, it's all we can do right now. When you get to Charleston, notify their port authority to contact the Newry Port Authority for information about your son.

I'll give you a letter describing what happened that you can give to them."

The officer wrote down Rory's name and a description, then her name and the family's destination. He closed up his notebook and said, "Now, I'm sorry, but I must be on my way."

Someone had her arm and helped her up. It was the lad. He was still here? God bless him. How would she ever thank him?

He led her and Finn to the passageway down to the cabins. "I'm so sorry, ma'am. I wish I could have done more. But you and your boys need to go below and get warm."

"Sir? Will I see you again?" a sniffling Finn asked.

"Sure, lad. I'm stuck on this ship just like you. My name is Ian. Ian McManus."

Bridie somehow remembered her manners. "Thank you for everything, Mr. McManus."

Twenty minutes later found Bridie in her bunk, lying still, somehow holding back her screams. She kept an arm wrapped tightly around each of her boys, who slept the sleep of the exhausted, one of them still hiccuping from his tears.

The ship rocked gently as it moved through the water, the engines droning steadily, a thrumming lullaby.

The ship must still be in the Newry River … it would never be this calm again … too bad it's not during the day… it would've been fun to see everything …like when they traced it on the map … she nodded off … Rory would have loved …

She startled, her heart racing at the vision of a small, lost Rory. Did he drown? What if he was hurt? What was he doing right now? Crying? Was someone holding him, soothing him? Was he even alive? If he were dead, would they find his body? Where would they bury him? A pauper's grave, surely. Would a priest bless him at least? If she ever came back to Ireland, would there even be a marker for her to find?

Stop it, Bridie told herself. Stop stirring the pot; it's only increasing the torment. There was nothing that could be done now about poor little Rory. Maybe she would never know what happened to him. But she had to go on. She was still a mother to Finn and Brendan. They needed her more than ever now.

She had been so hopeful when she realized she was being given a chance to start over in a new country. Included in the envelope with the tickets was a pamphlet about the ship, including a chart that showed the course it would take to America. Those last three nights at home, in the dim light of the lantern, they sat at the table and traced the route over and over, the boys' stubby fingers leaving greasy streaks on the paper. In a singsong voice, Bridie had crooned, "Here we go, down the Newry River, then into the Carlingford Lough, then into the Irish Sea, then to the Celtic Sea, and then into the Atlantic Ocean, and then ..."

"To *Charles*ton!" Finn and Rory would shout out, little Brendan chortling with them.

Had she been foolish to tell them that Charleston was named after their da? And that was why they were going there? It was just a silly, white lie. She so hoped it wasn't a bad omen. But she wanted to keep the memories of their da alive. For herself too …

Charles. He of the lanky, strong body, the shocking red hair, the keen, green eyes that pierced her heart. Even now, bereft and crushed within this group of outcasts, penniless and homeless… even now, she felt her face flush, and her heart leapt remembering when she first laid eyes on him. The feckin' fool. Or was she the fool? Would she ever be able to forgive him?

Chapter 2
1890–1891

Bridie Cleary and her father, Jack, lived in a small apartment on Rosemary Street in Newry. Bridie's mother died when she was four, and Jack never remarried, raising her alone. Jack was the bartender at Madden's Pub. It was a living and paid better than most jobs available to a Catholic Irishman. They were poor but not starving.

At fourteen, when most children stopped going to school, Bridie and her best friend Kathleen begged their parents to let them go to the new school for girls that had just opened in Newry, the Domestic Science Centre. In addition to general housekeeping, Kathleen and Bridie learned home management and bookkeeping. The only work for most Irish Catholic girls was as domestics, but with a certificate from the school, a girl could get a better job, possibly in a wealthy household or in a hotel.

The following year, after graduating, Bridie and Kathleen were both hired at the posh Newry Hotel as chambermaids. Recently renovated, its four stories of newly cleaned granite stood out from its dark and grimy neighbors.

Within three months, outgoing Kathleen was working in the restaurant. Bridie, after suffering a case of height fright while cleaning the windows in a room on the top floor, worked in the office helping the bookkeeper. On busy nights, she helped in the restaurant and bar.

One night when Bridie was working cleanup in the bar, three men came in for a late drink. One of them, a good-looking redhead, started flirting her up, but she'd have none of it. Not to be deterred, the man showed up the next evening and offered to walk her home. Nervously, she agreed, and soon he became a regular sight waiting for her outside when she got off work.

Charles Murphy was twenty-one, educated, worldly, and from a once-wealthy family. He was poor now, with only one small farm—all that was left of his family's once-large holdings, the rest confiscated by the British, he told her in clipped words. He was obviously upset by this, and she did not ask him for details.

She had never hidden anything from Da before, but she held off telling him about Charles. She knew he would disapprove and not just because of their age difference. When Charles told her he was a Fenian, she *knew* Da would be against them being together.

Many a night she listened to Da go on about the Fenians. "You know I want an independent Irish Republic as much as the next fellow—what Irish-Catholic doesn't? We all want to be rid of these Brit maggots. But not by violence. All that does is piss off the Brits even more."

No, Da would not approve. Though, maybe he'd feel different when he found out Charles played football for Milford?

Bridie and Charles took long walks in the countryside, away from prying eyes, places she hadn't been to since playing with her friends as a little girl. Charles had the gift of gab and was well versed in the ancient myths and legends, having immersed himself in Irish history when he was in college. His good storytelling brought the adventures dramatically to life. She was dazed by his knowledge and embarrassed at her ignorance. It was a relief when he finally mentioned a character she knew.

"Oh, finally, a name I recognize. Queen Maeve. She was my favorite. I liked to pretend I was her and lord it over the boys." God, that had to have been the stupidest thing she had ever said. She'd ducked her head to hide the blush crawling up her neck. How could someone so smart, who went to college, who was so much older, be interested in her?

"Well, you're not the only one with a favorite. Mine was Finn McCool, a truly legendary giant. It was he who threw the Cloughmore Stone across the lough. Now, on Easter, the townsfolk gather at the rock and hurl down eggs. Not quite the same, but I like the nod to history. If I ever have a son, I'm naming him Finn." Then it was he who looked a bit abashed.

When Da did find out, he was spitting mad. "Him? Damn it, Bridie, he's a feckin' Fenian! He and his ruffian friends come into the pub, put their heads together, and whisper. If it was up to me, I'd throw their asses out, but Madden's a big supporter." He stared hard at her. "And don't think just because he's the best player on the Milford team and the reason they won the cup back in '88… Well, don't you even dare to think that will make a damn bit of difference. I forbid you to see him."

Furious and hardheaded—she was his daughter after all—Bridie continued to see Charles. When she found herself pregnant, Charles was unruffled.

"Oh, my sweet *chailín*, my lovely darlin'. We're up the pole now, aren't we? But I knew from the beginning that we'd be together. You don't even know how remarkable you are. You might be young, but you're not only beautiful, you're smart and funny and tough. And you're wily; you'll handle anything thrown at you. Besides, I can't live without you. So, I'll face your da and ask for your hand in marriage. But you need to stand by me and hold my hand. I fear he'll tear me apart limb by limb if you're not there to protect me."

Bridie did hold Charles's hand when he asked for her hand in marriage—it was the only time she ever saw him even slightly nervous. She knew Da was sorely disappointed in her choice of a husband, even if he was a football star. And she knew Da knew she would never change her mind.

"I can't stop you, Bridie. You're my daughter, and I love you, but I fear that his politics will lead to disaster, and it will be yours and your children's burden to bear. I know you think love conquers all, but love can only do so much. Love won't help you if the stupid bugger gets killed."

They married on Halloween in 1891. She knew Da thought it another bad omen, but he didn't say anything. The ring Charles put on her finger had been his mother's. It was silver, with the same Celtic knot that was sewn on the green velvet bag hanging on her shoulder. Mam's bag, the same one Bridie had slept with every night when she was little, after Mam died—a talisman of love.

The two men never became friends, but they tolerated each other for Bridie's sake, bonding over the babies and football. Da died before Charles was arrested, a blessing, really. It allowed him to miss seeing his words come true.

Chapter 3

1898

There were some good things about being crammed into an iron box on the ocean. Bridie had no responsibilities other than watching her babies and keeping order in her little corner of the giant cabin. No farm, no sheep, chickens, mule or cows, and no potato fields to maintain. No cooking nor endless cleaning of the tiny house, smoky and dusty from the peat fire. She tried not to think about what she was leaving behind. To do that, she had to think about her missing boy, though he was at the forefront of her brain already. Every time she saw a boy with red hair, or a blue cap, her heart leapt, only to fall with a thud within her chest.

The weather had been good, except for one stormy day. Luckily, Bridie was not prone to seasickness and became the unofficial nanny to the fifteen restless and irritable babies in the cabin. She welcomed the work, the plight of her fellow passengers allowing her to step out of her own misery for a bit as she helped them in theirs.

On fair weather days, she strapped Brendan tight to her chest and paced the deck. He was growing like a weed and already taking steps. Her marching exhausted her body and her brain, which swirled with anger and guilt about Charles and Finn. Anger at Charles who had abandoned his family for his cause, and guilt about her anger at Finn. He was just a six-year-old boy. He didn't push Rory off, for God's sake. He didn't deserve her ire. When she wasn't stewing about them, she anguished about poor little Rory. God in heaven!

And why was she calling on Him? If, there was a God, why was He testing her with so much? Why did He take her boy? And Charles? It'd only been a few days since she had become a widow. How much could one person handle in a lifetime, never mind all at once? She fretted about Charleston. What if she couldn't find a job? Where would they live? Who would watch the boys when she was at work? How could she be a good mother?

Thankfully, most days Finn spent with Ian, who had taken him under his wing. Ian was a godsend. He answered Finn's hundreds of questions and took him along to explore the ship and the other decks. He had even snuck into the first-class cabin and somehow managed to have them served tea.

Bridie marveled at the lad. It was as if he had a sixth sense about how Finn felt and what he needed. Maybe he had gone through something awful too. Sometimes she'd come upon them talking seriously, Finn looking ready to cry. Ian could take Finn away from his pain with a joke or play, yet he could listen too. Something she wasn't able to do for her boy.

Occasionally Ian took Brendan on walks, strapping him to his chest with her bright red shawl. The first time, the sight made her laugh out loud. It shocked her, that laugh. It was her first real laugh in months. When she took back the baby, her hand accidentally brushed his neck. He drew back awkwardly and rushed off. She stared at her fingers. She had never touched any man, except for Charles.

Would she ever touch a man again? Would she ever feel the touch of a man's fingers on her again? Of lips on her lips? On her body? She ached with the loss.

She and Charles never seemed to get enough touching, and the farm offered many places for them to stop, drop their clothes, and make love. All it took was a look, a smile, a brush of a hand and the flame lit… and the babies were born. After each birth, Charles wrote their names into his old family Bible, adding them to the long list already there.

"For two-hundred-some years, my family of Murphys has lived and died on this land. I might have stopped believing in a God, but this Bible is special. Inside its cover are all the names of my family with their births and deaths, who they married, where they lived, and what they did. It's all I have left of them. So, luv, if something happens to me, you must keep it for the boys. They need to know their history."

She had shivered and eyed him nervously, her father's words of warning echoing in her head. Charles felt her worry and smiled ruefully. "Well, enough of all this maudlin talk. Don't you worry about me. Come here, let's make another one to add to the book. Maybe a girl this time?"

Oh, how she had adored him. And thank God for that because she had tired quickly of farmwork. She was a girl from the city, and rural life was an abrupt and exhausting change—even when Charles was home. None of her school courses had prepared her for the drudgery. Add three babies and a husband away on increasingly long absences, doing God knows what? She was in a constant pool of worry.

It was a small farm, all that was left of the Murphy family's original, large landholdings. "My family may not have been the best stewards of what had been handed to them on a silver platter, but it was the fecking Brits that took it all, leaving me this one shitty farm. They're the real culprits. I won't rest until every last one of them is gone from Ireland.

"What I really miss are the horses. We had a few, all Irish Hunters, truly the best horses in the world. Riding through this countryside was a delight. And racing them? Especially in the steeplechase? Well now, that is something I'll miss for the rest of my life."

The sadness that crossed his face touched Bridie's heart, and she took his hand. She worried about his devotion to the cause, but a part of her was captivated by his daring to fight against how things were. Like a knight in shining armor rescuing his country.

Three months after Brendan was born, Bridie's da died. Charles was away, so Bridie hooked the mule, Samuel, to the wagon, bundled up the babies, and drove to town. A pang of longing flooded through her when she entered her old home. It looked just as when she had left it six years before, neat and tidy.

Bridie had money to pay the undertaker. She'd taken it from the secret cache Charles showed her when they married, hidden behind a stone in the fireplace. "I've put money in there for you, for when I'm away. In case you need something for an emergency." A loaded word, considering what he did during his absences.

She took only a few things from her father's apartment. The brass oil lamp in the parlor, the one they used to read by after supper, some linens, a few knick-knacks, and a small porcelain dish decorated with shamrocks. "Your mam treasured that dish. I gave it to her for a wedding present," Da always said, tearing up, "Along with that green bag you love so much."

Da's old carpetbag easily held everything she took from the apartment. The undertaker had given her Jack's pocket watch, which was in her pocket. Having something of Da's on her person made her less bereft. When she drove back to the farm, Charles was still absent.

Anger overwhelmed her. Just thinking of the chores that awaited her sent her into a binge of crying. How would she do it all without him? It's his damn farm. He should be tending to it and her and his bloody children.

He finally came home in July, full of apologies and hugs and kisses for Bridie and the boys. But he was different—quieter, almost melancholy. A strange aura surrounded him, as if he were waiting for something or someone. He settled back into the life of hardscrabble farmer. Bridie hoped, as she did every time, that it was for good. Her hope was not long lived.

"Jaysus, Charles. You just got home," Bridie said. He was leaving in three days, for how long he didn't know. They had just made love, and she tried to keep her voice affectionate, but anger could simmer only so long before it bubbled over.

With a sigh, she jerkily sat up, covering her breasts with the sheet. "Just go off and play your war games and leave me here with three babies. Your babies, in case you forgot. And on your fecking farm. Shearing time is coming up, and I'm sure as hell not going to do it."

"Bridie, Bridie," Charles said. "I've already told the Thomas boys to come over and shear them in two weeks. And I added money to the cache to pay them."

His voice was so annoyingly calm, she thought she might scream. "How nice of you to plan ahead. They'll need feeding, won't they? And now you want to clear out the woods for more sheep? You really are a selfish bastard."

She wrapped the sheet around her and began pacing the room. "Why do you think it's fine to leave it all to me? The farm, the house, the babies—all of it. Jaysus, Charles! Even you complain about it. How can you say you love me and do this to me? If you really loved us…"

Oh, it went on and on. Da was right. Love could only do so much.

In the dark hours of August 10, 1897, British soldiers crashed through the door, yelling orders, brandishing rifles. Was this why Charles was acting strangely? Did he know they would come for him? God, if he did, that meant he brought the fecking Brits right into their house! What if they had shot one of the boys? What kind of man did that? She seethed at him and the Brits.

One of the soldiers read an official looking paper out loud. She stopped listening when he said Charles was accused of being the mastermind of a plot to blow up the British courthouse in Belfast.

Bridie looked at Charles, praying he would deny the accusation. He just sat there, defiantly staring back at the soldier.

Could he do that? Blow up a courthouse? In Belfast? In addition to everything else she had to do on this shitty, feckin' farm, how could she ever defend him if he did that? People would have been killed—innocent people. She was horrified. She took a deep breath, as if to speak, but she knew it was useless.

The soldiers went through the house, tearing it up, guns in hand, looking for accomplices and evidence. A shout went up when a soldier found the loose stone in the chimney and pried it out. Bridie somehow kept from gasping when she saw the cache behind it was empty. Where was the money? God almighty. He couldn't have stolen her money, could he? What else was he capable of?

As they shoved Charles out the door, he turned and looked directly into her eyes. "I did it for you and the boys and for my family and all the names in our Bible. Take care of it," he yelled. "I love you, Bridie."

When she finally got the children settled down, it was midnight. Jaysus, what in the hell was she supposed to do now? No husband, no father for her babes … and no money. Had he used their money in the cache to buy guns? That would be an unforgivable sin.

As she crawled exhaustedly into bed, she noticed the Bible on the table. He had surprised her the other night, joking, "I think it's time I start to look for meaning in the Good Book." They had both laughed. He never read from it, only prized it for what it represented: the history of his family, to which he was able to add.

It opened naturally to the page listing their names. There was a new name right after Brendan's: Samuel Murphy, with a recent birth date and no death. Who was that? The only Samuel she knew was their mule. Was this a joke?

In the morning, feeling like a fool, she went to Samuel's stall. His wooden feed bucket lay where the soldiers had tossed it. She righted it, then looked at it more closely. It was Samuel's bucket, but it was different. Charles' voice echoed in her head. *You're a wily one, Bridie.*

She smashed the bucket with the axe and found an envelope stuffed into the false bottom. Inside were a letter and some bank notes—fifty pounds of Bank of Ireland pound sterling! It was a small fortune. Bridie fell into a new fit of weeping. She wiped her eyes and read the letter.

Bridie, love. If you've found this, you need to go see my solicitor George Taylor in Belfast immediately. His office is opposite the Crumlin Road Gaol. Go there and wait for him and he'll see you as soon as he can. He promised me.

He's a Brit, but a good bloke. We went to college together. You can trust him. I love you, Bridie dearest. You are the love of my life and you and our boys are the best things to ever happen to me. I'm sorry I've ruined your life. It's going to be difficult for you and the boys.

Difficult? Jaysus.

She begged her nearest neighbors to take the boys for two days, the husband driving her into Newry, where she met Kathleen at the Newry Hotel.

"God, Bridie. You look awful."

Bridie nearly snapped back, but seeing the humor and sympathy in her dear friend's face, she smiled ruefully. "Yeah, well you try looking good when your husband gets arrested."

Kathleen took it upon herself to primp Bridie up. "After all, you are going into the big city, to meet with a solicitor. You can't go there looking like a dirty bogtrotter. I'll lend you my hat and coat and your mam's bag will finish it off nicely. You've always been a looker, Bridie, so make them remember who you are."

With Kathleen's help, she bought a roundtrip ticket to Belfast—it was her first train ride.

A looker, Kathleen had said. Charles used to say that also. Bridie almost had a bounce in her step when she got off the train. Until she got to the Crumlin Road Gaol—its imposing exterior and size terrified her. The building across the street was only slightly less forbidding. Inside, she easily found Mr. Taylor's office, where a kindly clerk told her to take a seat and that Mr. Taylor would return in two hours.

When she met him, Mr. Taylor seemed kind and knowledgeable, but what did she know? She chose to trust him because Charles did. Hah. Like he was such a trustworthy person? Not that it mattered; the news was not good.

"I'd hoped they'd let you see Charles, but he's not allowed visitors. The evidence against Charles is strong, and he is not making it any easier for himself. He has not denied what he has been accused of, nor will he ask for mercy or give up the names of his collaborators. It is a serious crime with severe penalties."

"What about us, his family?" Bridie interrupted, trying to keep her voice controlled.

His gaze showed sympathy for her. "I don't know what I can say or do to make it easier for you. I am shocked at how he has changed. He was always hardheaded, but this is beyond the pale. He has veered totally away from the rule of law. And, it seems, he has decided to die a martyr."

"My father warned me," Bridie said. "He said marrying Charles would be mine and my children's burden to bear."

"It appears he was right." George Taylor said.

"And I'm just supposed to wait for him to die?" Bridie stood up suddenly. "Thank you for seeing me, but I have to leave."

She knew it was rude, but she would have fainted or screamed if she stayed another minute. She had nothing to say to Charles. Ever. He could go straight to Hell. It's what he deserved for what he did to his only family.

Despite the warnings from her father and her own knowledge of Charles's involvement with the resistance, she had lived in her own little world, never fully understanding the consequences for her and the children if he was caught. In the beginning, it was because of her infatuation with him. But mostly it had been because of Charles himself. It was hard not to be pulled into his fearless belief in himself and his cause. She realized that she had been complicit in the delusions of a misguided revolutionist. How could she have been so stupid? Love can't conquer a damn thing.

Now, alone, she had to make a life for herself and her boys.

Once back on the farm, her life didn't change much over the next seven months. She had been doing all the work anyway, though now she had to also take care of the finances. At least Charles had been a neat and methodical recordkeeper, and thanks to her training in bookkeeping, she was able to get a clear picture.

Charles owned the farm outright. It was only fifty-five acres: thirty acres of potatoes, ten acres of flax, and fifteen acres of pasture for the sheep, two cows, chickens, and one donkey. The largest income came from the potatoes, followed by that from milk and eggs. Bridie sold the sheep; they were too much work. If she worked eighteen hours a day, she and the boys might just survive.

The two older boys had witnessed their father's arrest and handled their feelings in different ways. Finn retreated into himself but surprised her with his sense of responsibility. He took on as many duties as his six-year-old body could handle, determined to fill in for his da. Rory, at three, attached himself to the donkey, Samuel.

Samel, Rory called him. When the animal wasn't doing field work, he was Rory's pet. They followed each other around in the yard, Rory chattering nonstop, while Samuel's big ears twitched in apparent response. Sometimes, Bridie came upon them standing head-to-head, Rory on tiptoes, his arms around Samuel's neck and pressing his forehead against the lowered head. It was as if they were communing somehow. It was supernatural, like the faeries and all the other mystical lore of this God-forsaken country.

When Bridie had to hook the donkey up to the plow, she plopped Rory on top of Samuel, and the lad continued his lengthy conversations, while Samuel's ears moved in response. It was a wonder the animal ever heard her commands. He must be going on rote like her. She smiled. Maybe she should try whispering into Samuel's ears. It seemed to help Rory.

Chapter 4

1898

All the walking she did on deck tired her out, and when sleep came, she slept well—a small mercy she was thankful for. But before she slipped into blessed slumber, the image of Rory running off in his blue hat and shirt always came to her, making her weep silently beside her boys. Often, she'd feel Finn shuddering beside her, sniffling as he held in his tears. She would wrap him in her arms to calm him, calming herself as they lay together, rocked to sleep by the ship's movement, the ship's engines a noisy lullaby.

On the night before their arrival to Charleston, she lay awake, her mind racing with thoughts and dread of what was to come next. Nightmare stories circulated amongst the passengers of relatives who had written harrowing stories about getting through customs and how arbitrary the process was. What if they didn't let her into the country? Were Fenians considered criminals in America? Would she be considered a Fenian?

What if that detective, the one who checked them after boarding the ship, had somehow sent a message to a compatriot in Charleston? Would she be followed? Would she and her boys be threatened? Where would they live, what kind of job could she find, how long would her money last? Oh, how her mind spun with the worries.

And above all, she had to get the authorities to help in the search for Rory. The officer who had spoken to her the night of Rory's disappearance found Bridie on their last day at sea.

"You understand, I can't promise you anything, Mrs. Murphy," he said. "Here are two copies of my letter. Keep one for yourself and give the other to the agent inside the customs building. It describes your situation and tells them who to contact back at the Newry Port Authority."

He pressed her arm kindly and added, "I have a young lad myself, and I don't know what I would have done in your situation. My heart goes out to you, my dear."

"Thank you, sir. You're very kind." She went back to her pacing; Brendan patted her face and squirmed inside the red shawl, ready to bust out. *Not yet, little one. Just stay small for another day.* Her mind returned to Charles.

∽

Seven months after Charles was taken to prison, on March 15, 1898, there was another banging on her door. Again? What now? Charles' trial wasn't due to begin for another two months.

This time it was the police. The sergeant informed her that her husband, Charles Murphy, had taken his own life by hanging himself in his cell. An officer would come by later in the day and take her to the station in Newry so she could speak to the police. Mr. Taylor, Charles's solicitor, would also be there. The two policemen left as abruptly as they had arrived, leaving Bridie slowly sliding down the back of the closed door to the floor in sobs, the two older boys trying to comfort her.

After she put the lads to bed, she put more turf in the stove—the peaty, earthy aroma filled the room but hardly warmed her; she was cold to the bone. She made herself a cup of tea, added the last of Charles's Scotch, and wondered what the hell was coming next. At twenty-two she was a widow—with three babes. Da was right. She was bearing her cross.

The farm was now hers, and she could dispose of it as she wanted, which she most definitely wanted. She remembered her life with Da in their apartment. It seemed like heaven: a normal life in a town, in a warm house with her boys happily going to school while she kept a clean home and cooked them good food. Not just potatoes with an occasional slab of bacon.

She wondered about Charles. What had he thought of, alone in that cold cell, knowing it was his own fault he was there. Knowing he had abandoned his family to a life of uncertainty and poverty. Over the past months she had inured herself to his absence. Would she ever feel affection for him again, now that he was dead? How had he felt when he had put that twisted sheet around his neck?

She sat up with a start. The man she knew would never have killed himself, and not just because of his Catholicism. No. He was too certain of his place in the resistance, too proud to give the Brits the satisfaction of caving to their pressure.

Everyone heard the rumors of how prisoners were treated in prison. Especially the Fenians. She knew in her bones he had been murdered. He was just another mick to them. Something to be gotten rid of, like vermin.

❧

At the Newry police station, a matron took the boys, while Bridie met with George Taylor, who paced the small room and spoke to her in a quiet, angry voice. He agreed with her suspicions.

"If it's any consolation, Charles suffered sorely about what he'd done to you and the boys."

He stopped his pacing and sat close to her. In an even lower voice he said, "Charles suspected his captors would kill him, rather than put him on trial where he could publicly spew his accusations. That was the last thing they wanted. I happen to know exactly how he died."

Bridie cringed, as if he was going to strike her. He continued. "Don't worry, I won't give you the details, but he was definitely murdered.

"And there is more bad news. The farm has been confiscated by the state and with no payment to you."

Bridie shuddered and let out a long moan. "No! God no. Not the farm. It's all I have. They won't even buy it? They're just going to steal it?"

She jumped up. "Those bastards. How can they steal my home?" Then she collapsed back onto the chair, tears streaming down her face.

George Taylor gave her his handkerchief and sat down beside her. He ran his hand down his face. "They say it was an illegal place of treason. Forgive my language, Bridie, but that's horse shit. We could fight it, but it would take years and money."

He took a nervous breath and leaned in closer, his voice now a whisper into her ear. "Bridie, I might have overstepped my bounds, but I had to quickly present something that might offer you a decent future. I lied to the authorities. I told them you knew how he had died and that you were going to go public with the information. I took liberties about your future without asking you.

"I suggested it might be in their best interests to offer you a way out of the country. Perhaps passage to America? For you and your boys to begin in a new country. Away from Fenian influences and the press. Remove the thorn in their side, so to speak. And they have agreed. All the arrangements have been made."

"America?" Bridie whispered dazedly. "A foreign country? Across an ocean?"

"Bridie, you will live a life of misery if you stay here

in Ireland. This will at least give you a chance to start anew."

Bridie was stunned, but she knew he was right. If they stayed in Ireland, their lives would be even worse than now. But exile? Jaysus, Mary, and Joseph. Would this nightmare ever end?

He looked ready to cry himself. "I am so very sorry about everything, Bridie. At times like this, I'm embarrassed to be English. I pray you are able to make a new life for yourself."

She was then taken to an office where a priggish policeman told her that her ship sailed in three days.

With pursed lips, he said, "You're allowed to stay in the house for that time." He handed her an envelope. "Inside, are your papers. Passage for four, one way from Newry to Charleston, South Carolina. And five pounds, for necessities and fees."

Bridie accepted the envelope and the terms. What else could she do? But, for the first time in a very long while, a glimmer of hope surfaced in her overwrought head and heart. She slipped the envelope into the bag on her lap—her mother's bag, still a symbol of hope to its owner.

A second police officer, kindlier than the prig, delivered them back to their little farm, saying he would be back to pick them up at five in the morning on their day of departure for the drive to the port. She did her chores, made a dinner of potatoes, and fell into bed, the three boys snuggled in with her. She had her first full night of sleep since Charles had been taken away.

The next morning, she set to packing. It didn't take long. She emptied Da's carpetbag, placing Charles's Bible on the bottom along with two six-inch candlesticks, Murphy family heirlooms. She had no use for them, and they were heavy, but they were sterling silver and would surely come in handy someday. And she added her mother's bag—if anything happened to it, she'd come undone. She placed the bundle from Da's house on top and added as much clothing as would fit. She then tucked everything in snugly with a feather pillow, a luxury for herself.

At the last minute, she remembered *Mrs. Beeton's Book of Household Management* and stuffed it in. It was the required textbook when she was in school and considered the bible of domestic science. It was beat up and old when she bought it, but if ever there was a time for its use, it would be in her new country.

It was the middle of March and bitter cold. They would dress in layers, not just because of the cold, but to bring the extra clothing she had no way to pack. The boys scrounged up old cotton potato sacks onto which she sewed lengths of rope for straps. With a good soak in soap and water, they were more than serviceable as shoulder bags.

On the last day, she did what she could for the animals. She wanted Samuel, the cows, and the chickens clean and fed. Samuel gave her a small nicker and nuzzled her when she came into the barn. It was almost as if he was saying goodbye to her. She put her arms around him and sobbed. What would happen to him?

She had a sudden idea. She left Brendan with Finn, climbed up on Samuel's back, pulled Rory up to sit in front of her, and trotted over to her nearest neighbor.

She told them what had happened and that they would be gone the next day. "Please take Samuel. He's part of our family, and he'll be a good addition to your farm. I'll be damned if I'll let those maggot Brits have him."

Then she had another thought that made her break out in maniacal laughter. The couple looked at her oddly. "I know I seem crazy but hear me out. No one has been out to do an accounting of what is on the farm, so I don't see how they could know what we have in property. Take what you want. They're picking us up tomorrow at five in the morning, so with luck you might have the whole day before they take it over." They joined in her laughter. "And tell the other neighbors too."

Good Lord, she was turning into a revolutionary; Charles would be proud.

After a small meal of potatoes and bacon, the four of them fell into bed. The boys slept the sleep of young, weary babies. Bridie nodded off, dreaming of a future different from the one she had been living three days before…

She awoke with a start and reached for her father's watch: three thirty. She had time to make a cup of tea. In the light of a candle, she stirred the fire to life and heated the pot. When her tea was ready, she sat in the rocking chair with the cup, her mind whirling. Despite

the enormity of what was to come and all the possibilities of disaster, she felt almost calm. She could leave
this country that took so much from her.

She woke the boys and dressed and fed them potatoes and bacon. God, perhaps in Charleston they'll
have something else to eat?

"Remember I told you to think about what special
things you wanted to add to your sacks? There's still
room for a few toys in with your clothes." The boys
returned with their favorites, carefully adding them to
the sacks.

"This is what I'm bringing special," said Bridie,
showing them the lantern packed in the carpetbag.
"It was your Granda's." She had emptied and cleaned
the base, giving the brass a quick rub to make it shine.
Even if she never found a chimney for it, having it near
would be a reminder of him.

She still had thirty-five pounds remaining of the
money Charles had left in the envelope, now sewn into
a sash she was wearing under her clothes. Da's watch
was in her pocket.

They were ready.

Chapter 5

1898

It was April Fools' Day, and Charleston was beginning to appear in the distance. Bridie sat on the deck box, leaning back against the deckhouse with Brendan against her chest. It was still dark, though a paleness was sneaking through the sky in the east. Ian and Finn stood at the railing in front of her, pointing at city lights beginning to appear in the distance.

How Rory would have loved to be with them. He'd have been running back and forth, reporting on what he saw in the distance. "*Charles*ton, Mammy. It's really there!"

Later, after breakfast, and using a clean nappy dipped in a bucket of water, she washed herself and her boys as best she could. "Finn, stop your squirming. Just get dressed, and you can join Ian on deck. And don't go getting all dirty. If he's not there…"

"I know Mammy. I know. I'll come right back," he said, jerking around.

"I'll be up when I've finished packing, in time to see us come into port."

She finished dressing herself and Brendan and put the dirty clothes in the carpetbag, on top. Maybe customs won't want to go through dirty laundry. She had all her papers, including the letter to the customs agent, in her potato sack.

Brendan had turned one just before they left Ireland, and he and three other little ones aboard had begun taking steps. Now they tottered about the cabin like drunken sailors. He had gained weight, and Bridie worried he might burst out of the red scarf. It only had to last through today. By tonight they would be somewhere where she could just let him crawl and toddle and not be wrapped to her chest. She refused to think about any alternative.

The women chatted amongst themselves, exchanging their relatives' names and addresses. Bridie was one of only a few staying in Charleston. Most were off to other parts. Aileen and Patrick were going north to a city called Charlotte, where their son lived.

"It's funny, ain't it?" a teary-eyed Aileen said. "I've only known you eleven days, but I feel like I've known you all my life. Like a sister, you are. Don't you lose that address I gave you. I want to hear all about what happens to you and the lads."

When Bridie went back up to the deck, Charleston was aglow in the morning light. The city appeared enormous…and shining. The only cities she knew were Belfast and Newry, large too, but dark and forbidding in their gloominess.

Ian and Finn, still at the rail, watched as the city beckoned them. Ian turned and waved her over. "There's room here between us. I think I can see the Custom House over at that end of land."

With Brendan strapped on her chest, she moved closer but stood behind them. "I'll stay back here, If Brendan tears through the scarf, better it happens on the deck." She could not say out loud, *than in the water.*

"Mammy, look how pretty it is," Finn said. "Do you like it?"

"It is pretty, and it's warmer. I really like that."

Ian laughed. "I do too. Though everyone I've talked to says it's terribly hot in the summer. That I'll be sorry to have chosen carpentry."

Rory zipped before her eyes. She startled, but it was just someone's blue jacket. She was becoming used to him showing himself to her. As upsetting as it was, it was also comforting in an odd way. She would never want to lose the ability to see him, even if it was just a vision.

A mile offshore, the ship slowed to an idle, and two small steamships came to the side, dropping off two groups of men and women in uniforms: doctors and matrons to do the final health inspections on each passenger. The steerage passengers were ordered to meet on deck, where they would be inspected.

They formed two lines: women, children, and boys under fifteen gathered forward, and all the men and the older boys, aft. In addition to dangerous and contagious diseases, the officials said they were checking for eye diseases, skin disorders, and heart disease. Those passengers found with those ailments were marked with chalk marks on their backs—E for eyes, S for skin, H for heart—and taken aside where they would be examined further. Passengers who cleared had their tickets punched yet again.

Still fearful from her last days in Ireland, Bridie worried there might be detectives, looking for Fenians. How would she know if someone was a detective? He certainly wouldn't be carrying a sign. Would he wear a badge? Carry a gun?

"They're doing the same with the first and second classes on the upper decks, but they get to stay in the salons. They're having tea, and some of the men are at the bars," Ian said. He had taken a final, quick walk to the upper decks.

Once the exams were finished, the ship powered slowly to land and tied up to the dock. In contrast to the pushing and shoving when they boarded the ship back in Ireland, disembarking was more civil, with the passengers filing into the back of the Charleston Custom House. It was slow going, but orderly. And noisy. Voices ricocheted in the cavernous main room. Passengers yelled back and forth, officials answered questions, and instructions were repeated endlessly through megaphones. Surprisingly, despite the racket, everything seemed to move at a steady pace. Most passengers were civil and just glad to be off the ship.

Ian had disembarked with them but bade Bridie and Finn goodbye almost immediately. He was met by an employee of Charleston Lumber who whipped him right through the lines.

Bridie worried herself sick. If the agent saw three children listed on her ticket and counted only two, how could she possibly explain Rory's absence? Would it be considered a crime? Was she at fault in some way? Who would believe it? She wouldn't, if someone told her such a tale.

It took an hour and a half until Bridie, with a squirming Brendan at her chest, stood in front of an agent. He was smiling at her. How could he smile through all this? Finn stood on his tiptoes to peek over the counter edge. She gave the agent her much-punched ticket, which he read quickly. He said, "But ma'am where is…" Without a word, Bridie gave the ship officer's letter to the man.

He scanned it, looked at her, and reread it. "Ma'am, this is a terrible thing that happened to you. And your boy."

Bridie nodded at the man mutely.

"I don't know what we can do now, but I will give the letter to my superiors and will keep following up on it. You'll have to return here, maybe every week, to check on any progress. Ask for me. I'm usually at this spot, but sometimes they switch us around.

"Now do you have anything to declare?"

His kindness almost moved her to cry again, but she bit her lip and held back the tears.

She bent down and unwrapped the candlesticks and Da's pocket watch. Was this kind man going to steal them or make her pay?

"No, ma'am. Those are fine. Family heirlooms aren't declarable." He punched her ticket yet again. "That's the last time, ma'am," and handed it back to her. He gave her an official map of the city and a list of rooming houses nearby who took in immigrants.

"The boarding houses let us know every morning how many rooms they have. This one here, on Hayne Street, is only six blocks away. She has two rooms available. It's clean, they don't mind kids, and the landlady is Irish. Actually, she's my aunt," he said in a whisper. "Here's the route. I'll draw it in for you," which he did on the new map.

"I'm also giving you a list that includes all the domestic agencies. Welcome to America, Mrs. Murphy. And you, lad," he said with a wink. "Take good care of your ma." Finn nodded seriously.

The next line was the money changer, where after another hour, she exchanged her pounds for $165. The number of bills made her feel rich. Careful, Bridie. It's got to go a long way.

She was in a state of shock. Compared to how she had been treated in her own country, this was paradise. Surely, not all of America was so kind.

Less than four hours after they entered the customs building, the little Murphy family found themselves standing on busy East Bay Street.

She checked the map. "Off we go. Finn, hoist those

bags again. The man said it's only six blocks. We can do it. You lead, and I'll tell you when to turn. You're the man in this family now," she said with a catch in her voice.

"Follow me, Mammy," Finn said, proudly taking his first steps on a street in America.

True to the man's word, the rooming house wasn't far. But with the crush of people, the strangeness of the city, their baggage, and their uncooperative sea legs, it seemed much longer.

The house loomed large in front of them. Bridie and Finn lumbered up the stairs to the front door. Her timid knock on the door was answered by a large lady, standing with her arms folded across her ample chest and a severe look on her face. "Well, well, well. Look what the ship has brought me today. A whole damn family, and on April Fools' Day, no less. Don't just stand there gawking. Let's get you settled."

Bridie took a deep breath and bent to pick up the carpetbag. She sure wasn't going to look anywhere else. "Finn, help me with the bags now and wipe your feet before you go in. And don't touch anything." She was reminded of Rory. He was the one who always got into stuff. Not Finn. The lady led them into a large entrance hall with a grand, curved stairway leading upstairs.

Bridie tried not to gape. This was too grand to be a rooming house. Her money would be pissed away in two days. Doors to the left and right of the entrance hall led into parlors where she glimpsed chairs and settees with tufted velvet seating arranged in groups. This was almost as fancy as the Newry Hotel. She could hear voices and kitchen noises from the end of the long hallway.

"My name is Mrs. Millbury," the woman said. "I have a big room available that will fit the three of you, since two of you are little ones. It's my nicest and biggest room, but people complain about the three flights of stairs, so it's the same price as the other rooms. Three dollars a day, four with meals, or twenty for the week. Are you wanting to rent by the day or the week? Breakfast and dinner both start at six, except on Sundays when we eat dinner at noon."

"I'll pay by the day, with meals," Bridie whispered. She dug out four dollars of her newly exchanged money and handed it to the outstretched hand. What if she had to stay here for days—or weeks? She almost gagged. Would she have any money left over? What if Mrs. Millbury had to throw them out?

"Do you have a place where I could do my laundry? All those days on a ship stank up all our clothes."

"Don't worry. Most all my roomers have come off some ship or another. I'm used to it. You can do the wash yourself, or I'll do it for a dollar. Let's get you up to your room. Here, give me that carpetbag. You can carry those two sacks, and you, young man, can carry the rest. Help us ladies out."

Mrs. Millbury carried the carpetbag like it was a toy as she led the way upstairs. Bridie had to stop to catch her breath when she reached the third floor. Even Finn was panting. Mrs. Millbury, unfazed, continued to the end of the hall where she opened the door.

The room was enormous, with two beds made up with clean linens, a dresser, a washstand, a table, and chair. And mother of God, two glorious windows overlooking the city below. Tears came to her eyes. "Thank you, Mrs. Millbury. This will do us just fine."

"Here's the key. You have soap and towels over there on the washstand. There's a toilet at the end of the hallway, marked WC. The other door beside it is marked BATH, and there's a sign-up sheet. It is the only bathtub in the house, and it gets quite popular, especially on Friday evenings and Saturdays. I have to pay for the water and heating, so there's a fifty-cent charge for a bath. If I were you, I'd use it now—most everyone is out working. I do this floor's sheets and towels every Friday. Just bag up the dirty linens in a pillowcase and bring it downstairs on that morning."

Bridie gave her two dollars. "One for the laundry and one for the bath. There's three of us, and I'm sure we'll use more water than one person."

Mrs. Millbury turned to leave, her face now kindly. "You can't hardly tell, but I'm Irish too. Came here as a lass around the same age as your older one there. I can still remember my mam breaking down in tears when she finally got all of us little ones into a real room and not on the ship anymore. You'll do fine, lassie."

Bridie was glad to have a key to the room. She wanted to hide the valuables, but there wasn't any place. She'd just keep them in the bottom of the carpetbag. The cash she would continue to keep in her money belt. She grabbed the towels and soap, scooped up Brendan, shoved Finn out the door, locked it, and almost ran to the bathroom. She bathed first, luxuriating in the feel of hot water and soap on her body and her hair while the boys waited in the warm, steamy room. Afterwards she refilled the tub and washed them, Brendan screaming, though he hushed up when he saw how much his brother liked it. Before leaving, she scrubbed the tub; no one need know how dirty they had been.

A bell rang at six, announcing dinner. Bridie arrived, nervous and shy, carrying Brendan, with Finn close behind. Mrs. Millbury greeted them at the door.

"When everybody settles, I'll introduce you, Mrs. Murphy. Take this seat, dearie." She put a hand on Finn's shoulder. "Lad, you sit with the other children at the smaller table."

It was a motley group that filed in and found chairs. Mrs. Millbury gave a little cough. "Before we say grace, let me introduce Bridie Murphy, all the way from Ireland." There were nods and smiles from most, and Bridie, reddening, nodded back.

Bridie was struck dumb by the dishes being passed around. Real meat, real potatoes, real vegetables, bread, butter, milk… She had never eaten this way at home, even when Da was alive. And certainly not after she married. It was a feast, one fit for the Newry Hotel. There wasn't much conversation; everyone was too busy eating.

Bridie counted sixteen adults at the table and five children at the smaller table. Besides herself, there were six other women at the table, one of whom held a baby on her lap. The infant was younger than Brendan, who wiggled on her own knee. Four women appeared married, judging by the comfortable way they sat near the men beside them. One sat alone and looked to be quite pregnant. The rest were men. Most accents sounded Irish, Scotch, or British, though a few were speaking languages Bridie did not understand.

After dinner—dessert was apple pie!—most of the men wandered into the parlor to chat, while the smokers went out to the front porch. Some of the women helped clear the table and work in the kitchen. Mrs. Millbury insisted it wasn't necessary, but she didn't refuse the offers.

Bridie took her tired boys and went back to their room. With full stomachs and clean hair and bodies, the three crawled into their lovely clean beds. The boys fell asleep immediately. Bridie lay awake wondering where Rory was sleeping. In a safe place, please God?

The next day after breakfast, another feast, Finn ran off with a new friend, and she sat around the table with the few women remaining. They were all curious about her and very chatty about job prospects, offering opinions on everything.

"The kinds of jobs we get hired for start early and end late. No rest for the weary," one woman said.

"Well, I'm used to that," said Bridie. "No different from what I've been doing back on the farm. And I used to work in a hotel, so I know domestic work."

"Charleston Domestic Services is right down the street, but if it were me, I'd go to all of them. You've got nothin' to lose," offered up another.

Mrs. Millbury joined them with a cup of coffee. She tossed her head towards the kitchen, where the sounds of cleanup carried on. "I try to get most of my help now by word of mouth. I've got a girl comes in at four in the morning to help in the kitchen, two that come at ten to clean, and another at three to help with the cooking and serving."

She lowered her voice. "I'd be wary of Dayton's. The last girl they sent me was sickly and not up to the task at all. And on top of it all, the rotters charged me more than the other agencies had. Never again."

"But the only way for one of us to get a job is through the agencies, right?" asked Bridie. "Didn't you all get jobs?" She looked to the other women.

"We did," another lady said, "but sometimes it takes a long time. And be prepared for how nasty they all are."

The others laughed and nodded. "It'll defeat you if you let it. They're all beastly."

Bridie already felt defeated. "I'd guess it will be even harder to find a place that will let me keep my boys." She looked around at the sympathetic faces. She was filled with dread, wondering what was to come.

"Patricia's Placement got me a decent job. I'll use them again when I go back to workin'," the pregnant one, Shirley Ames said. "If I was you, I'd take the day off. It's Friday already."

Bridie was tempted, but with the weekend coming, that would be three days off. Three days wasted on paying for a room she couldn't afford. She rounded up

Finn and went up to their room. Finn sat on the bed sulking.

"I'm sorry, luv, but I must get a job fast, or we'll be begging in the streets. And you must watch Brendan," she said as she gave him a hug. Poor lad. Six years old and lost one brother, and now he must care for the other.

At four o'clock, Bridie slowly climbed the stairs to the room. She tried not to let Finn see how defeated she felt. He endured her hug then raced out of the room so fast he probably didn't notice a thing. She had visited three agencies, each of which dismissed her quickly and rudely. It was all she could do to get them to give her directions to the next agency on her list.

The next day, Saturday, she and her boys took a walk around their new neighborhood. Both Newry and Belfast were old and dreary, their tall buildings built closely together, blocking out the light. Charleston was open and airy. And warm, far warmer than Newry. The buildings didn't darken the sidewalks like they did in those other cities. Most of the buildings were made of brick, but some were wood, painted white. Most had wide porches in front, just inviting visitors to sit back and relax. They gave the city a festive air, not grim like back home. The cobblestone streets were narrow, crowded, and noisy. If not for a kind passerby who alerted her to avoid the tracks, they probably would have been run over by a trolley car.

They found a park nearby where Bridie let Brendan toddle around while Finn listlessly kicked a rock around. "You remind me of your da. Whenever he was idle, he'd kick something around too."

"I miss Rory. Even if he is only four, we could kick it to each other."

Bridie's heart broke. "I know, Finn. I miss him too. Soon you'll find some other lads to play with."

On Sunday, they, along with about half the other boarders, went to mass at St. Mary's Catholic Church, a five-minute walk from the rooming house. She hadn't gone to church often after she was married. The farm was too far from town, and Charles wasn't a keen churchgoer. Being in a church again with its rituals and fellowship eased her mind and gave her a sense of hope towards the coming days of job searching. Would her prayers for Rory's well-being be better received in a house of worship?

Her hope for work vanished quickly. The next two days brought the same dismal results. As soon as the agencies found out Bridie had children, she was rejected. Bridie considered lying, but she needed a job that would take her and her children. She wouldn't be able to live in the rooming house much longer, and she couldn't keep leaving her boys alone all day. She was so depressed that she swung by St. Mary's on her way home to get on her knees and pray. The priest, Father James, sat with her a bit, offering her some comfort.

On Wednesday, her last stop was Dayton's, the agency Mrs. Millbury warned her against. It was the largest agency, and its agents were the rudest of all the people she had yet encountered. It was all she could do to not burst into tears as she left, weaving her way through the long line still waiting to get in. Outside she had to lean up against a building for support. A small, beady-eyed woman sidled up to her.

"Are you seeking a job?" she asked in a whisper. Bridie nodded hesitantly. The lady crooked her finger. "I might be able to help you, but we can't talk here. Follow me."

Bridie had seen her when she walked out and assumed she was a jobseeker like everyone else in line. She was dressed in grey and had the same worn and tired look as the other women in line, a look Bridie knew she herself was fast approaching. Maybe the lady looked so worn out because she was old.

Up close, Bridie noticed the woman's dress was a fine material and she carried a parasol, though the dress was worn and the parasol's trim drooped. She flashed back to school, when she and Kathleen laughed about carrying a parasol; that was only for rich people.

Paranoia reared up again. Could she be a spy? Looking for…what? Fenians? Jaysus,

Bridie, stop looking for trouble. Look at her, she's ancient. She followed the woman down to a small park, bursting with bushes blooming pink, red, and orange. They sat down on a bench.

"Maybe we can help each other," the woman said. "I need a housekeeper and a caretaker for my sister." She looked ready to cry and wrung her handkerchief through her fingers. Bridie was taken aback. Why, she was a wreck.

"We've fallen on bad times, and we need help. But I won't pay these agencies another cent. They're all thieves, and I never get anyone good. Dayton's is the worst. Last time I complained, they accused me of spreading lies about them. They said they'd call the police if I came back. I decided I'd show them. I'd stand in their line and watch the applicants and find someone promising myself. I've been watching you, and I overheard you talking to the interviewer. I know you have children, and I can offer you room and board for all of you in lieu of wages."

Bridie pretended to consider her offer, but knew she'd take it. Even if it was terrible, she had to start somewhere.

"All right, Mrs... I'm sorry. What did you say your name was?"

"Miss. Miss Mary Fleming. And my sister is Miss Elizabeth Fleming. We live at 12 Guignard Street. You can't miss it. It's a big, red brick house. Where are you staying?"

"The Hayne Street Rooming House."

"That's not far at all, only about half a mile. Can you come by tomorrow?"

"I guess so, Miss Fleming. Is ten o'clock all right?"

Bridie ran home to the rooming house and up the two flights of stairs and took Finn's hands and spun around the room. Then she swung Brendan around and fell onto the bed, still laughing. The crotchety man in the room below theirs began banging on his ceiling.

"With luck, he won't have to hear us anymore and we can sing and dance as much as we want. Come here, Finn, and let me give you a big hug. You've been a good boy. I think I got a job, laddies. She's a funny little lady, but she says we can live there. I don't even care what it looks like."

Caution set in, though, and during dinner, when someone asked, Bridie just said she had a prospect and no more. She wasn't sure about the Fleming woman. Her idea of picking out her own help from the line outside the agency was a little crazy. Maybe the lady and her sister were insane.

If it didn't work out, Bridie didn't want to look the fool in front of everyone. She'd seen how gossip spread amongst the lodgers, and she did not care to be the subject of it.

Chapter 6

1898

Bridie stared at the front of the old shack and then at Miss Fleming with disbelief. "Do you really mean for us to live here? For God's sake, it's a shack! I have two wee children." Her anger was going to make her cry, and she turned to leave before it happened. Don't cry in front of this witch, Bridie girl.

"Wait, Mrs. Murphy. Wait until you see the inside. It's not as bad as it looks. I cleaned it up myself," Miss Fleming said, taking Bridie's arm. The old biddy led her onto the porch and through the door.

It was dim inside, with only one window to allow in light. A huge, brick fireplace took up one wall with some shelves and cubby holes built in on each side. Cupboards and a sink stood against the back wall, and a large table with a bench and chairs took up most of the room. Bridie was surprised to see a pretty china cabinet with intact glass doors and a decent amount of crockery on its shelves.

She moved towards the opening at the left of the fireplace, the little lady following. It led into another room: a bedroom with two beds and a dresser. It also had one window and another fireplace, the backside of the one in the main room. Well, they would be warm in the winter anyway. That's *if* she took the job.

"Back in the old days, this room was the laundry for the big house," said Miss Fleming. Leading Bridie back to the front room, she said, "This room was the kitchen for all the servants. They slept upstairs, but the second floor blew off in a storm ten years ago. We only replaced the roof."

Bridie had to ask. "How many servants lived here? And they all slept upstairs?"

Miss Fleming looked down and began fiddling with her handkerchief. "Well, I'm not sure. I was just a girl back then. But I guess about eight or nine before the war."

Bridie shuddered. Nine people sleeping in one room? Men and women? And children? *Slaves?* They had to have been slaves. Jaysus, she was going to live in a slave shack. God save us all.

Miss Fleming took Bridie outside and showed her a brick outhouse behind the cabin. These past days at the rooming house, Bridie had become accustomed to big windows letting in light and air—and a bathroom down the hall.

"No one has lived here for years, so there was never a need to turn it into a real bathroom," she said, looking down at the twisting, ever-present handkerchief.

"If you take the job, we can discuss that later. On another note, if you need more furnishings, there is much to choose from in our attic."

If Bridie was honest, the cabin wasn't that bad, despite its history. It was not unlike their little cottage back home. It too had been dark, but this one smelled of wood smoke, not peat.

She looked back to the porch. The cabin and outhouse were located, along with an unoccupied stable and other buildings, behind the main house. She imagined what it must have been like back in the day, with servants (*slaves!*) bustling, horses in the barn, maybe a cow or two, chickens... How Rory would have loved the barn, even without animals. Though he'd probably be pestering her to get a mule.

Now the sad yard was dirt and weeds. She followed a path leading to an overgrown, weedy garden plot. Kneeling, she grabbed a handful of dirt and held it to her nose. Loamy and damp, the smell brought her back to her garden on the farm. With this mild weather, she could grow wonderful vegetables. Not just potatoes.

She would stay. What else could she do? If slaves could do it, so could she.

"Well, Miss Fleming. I will work for room and board. Whatever food I cook for you and your sister will be shared with me and my boys. Now take me to the big house and let me see what I'll be dealing with."

Miss Fleming, fairly skipping, led them from the cabin to the mansion's back door and into the kitchen. Bridie gaped in awe.

"Back in the old days," Miss Fleming said, "this was a separate building called the kitchen house. Back then, they were all detached because of the fear of fires. But when fireplaces stopped being used for cooking, Mother had a hallway built to connect it to the house."

Bridie was trying to compose herself. The kitchen was four times larger than the shack she had just left. There was a black cast-iron stove with four burners *and* a huge fireplace with hooks for hanging cooking pots. She counted two sinks, multiple counters, cupboards, and cabinets, many with glass doors displaying a majestic array of crystal and china. It reminded her of the Newry Hotel. But how could one home have need for such an enormous kitchen? And how could one person manage it all? The Newry Hotel had a head cook giving orders to ten workers.

Miss Fleming rattled on, apparently oblivious to Bridie's misgivings. "Cook always complained she couldn't see what she was doing, it was so dark in here, so Mother had the windows installed. And gas lights later, of course. It is a bit large for just the two of us now. But back in the day… well, you just wouldn't believe all the hustle and bustle going on in here. Elizabeth and I haven't entertained in years."

Bridie nodded. Thank God. She'd be dismissed immediately if she had to prepare for a party.

She jumped at the sound of a bell ringing insistently.

"Oh dear," Miss Fleming said. "That's my sister. Sometimes, she can be so impatient."

Bridie's eyes followed the sound to the back wall, where there was a row of brass bells with little signs underneath. What in the world? She moved closer. The sign under the vibrating bell said "Mistress Fleming's Room." Well, it looked like the ladies would never have a problem alerting her.

"Let me take you upstairs to meet her." Miss Fleming touched Bridie's elbow and led the way back to the front hall. "Ordinarily, you'll use the servants' stairway behind the stove, but I can't use them anymore. They're too steep for my poor old knees."

Bridie followed the woman up the immense, curved stairway and down a hallway with many doors and name tags above them. Did they go with the bells?

"I'm coming," Miss Fleming called, a little out of breath. "Here is the girl I was telling you about." She pulled Bridie into a room. "Mrs. Murphy, this is my sister, Elizabeth Fleming."

In front of Bridie was an even smaller version of Miss Fleming. The little lady removed her hand from the tapestried strip of cloth hanging from the ceiling, within reach of the bed. Ahh, the bell source, Bridie assumed. When the lady moved, Bridie saw she was in a wheelchair.

"I guess she looks healthy enough," the birdlike woman said to her sister, making no eye contact with Bridie. "You made sure, right, Mary? No diseases? She's clean? Bad enough she's Irish."

Miss Mary Fleming whispered, "Just ignore her, Mrs. Murphy."

Bridie needed the job, and it was becoming apparent that the Fleming sisters needed her too. She had to stand her ground now and make it clear to them how they must treat her.

Bridie kept her voice calm. "Yes, I and my boys are Irish. Is that a problem?" The two women stared at her. "I need a job and a roof and food for my babies, and you need a maid. But do not treat me, or them, as trash."

Miss Elizabeth Fleming frowned and stared Bridie in the eye. Even from her wheelchair, she clearly did not feel herself at a disadvantage.

Miss Mary Fleming was flustered. "Oh dear, oh dear." Then she gathered herself. "Mrs. Murphy, please wait downstairs. My sister and I must confer."

"I'll wait for ten minutes," Bridie said, and took herself out of the room and down the stairs.

Five minutes later, Miss Mary Fleming, close to tears, the handkerchief almost crumbling in her twisting fingers, stood in front of her. "Please, Mrs. Murphy. I hope you will stay, and Elizabeth agrees. I know she can be difficult, but she will come around. I'm getting too old, and I need help."

"All right, Miss... Mary? Can I call you Miss Mary?"

Relief flooded the woman's face. "Miss Mary is fine. Though, I'm sure my sister will prefer Miss Fleming."

"All right, then, Miss Mary. Call me Bridie. I'll start tomorrow."

Chapter 7

1898

"Shite! What the hell was that? Did you see it?" a man said.

"Are you startin' up that crap again? God, I hate workin' with you. You're always seein' things or hearin' them. Jaysus!" A different man.

"I saw what I saw. It was small, like a kid, but what's a kid doin' out here and so late at night? And don't laugh, but it was carryin' flowers."

"Ha, now I am laughin', you feckin' eegit. You're tellin' me you saw a feckin' leprechaun with flowers? Next thing we'll be surrounded by dancin' fairies. Oh, and maybe a howlin' banshee for good measure? Jaysus, save me."

"That's just it. I did hear a banshee before I saw the kid."

"You did not see a kid. Get that through your thick skull."

Rory was hiding behind a building, quiet as a mouse. He couldn't understand what they were gabbing about, but they seemed cross. He didn't dare look out until he heard them moving away. He watched them go to the big building and lock it up, still arguing as they walked away. Except for the dim light coming from a window, the night was dark as could be. Finally, when he couldn't hear their voices anymore, he dared to move from his hiding spot. Now was his chance to run back to the ship.

But it wasn't there. There was no ship! Where did it go?

He looked at the flowers he was still holding and started whimpering. He had seen them from the gang-plank and knew Mammy would love them. He fought his way through so many people to get to them, but when he turned to make his way back up the gang-plank, he slipped and got tangled up in all the legs stepping over and around him, sometimes on him. They shoved him down, down, toward the dock, and as hard as he tried, he couldn't get turned around. He screamed like a banshee, but no one paid him any mind. The next thing he knew, he was at the bottom, still caught between feet.

People cursed and kicked him aside. One man sneered, "What's a street urchin doing here? And with flowers, no less. You gotta a little lassie you're giving them to?"

The woman beside him said, "How come you're always so mean?" and looked kindly at Rory. She leaned down to say something, but the man tugged at her.

"Jaysus. Do you have to stop at every little brat you see?"

They disappeared into the darkness, then another man kicked him. That's when he ran. He saw a building where he could hide until the cruel people went away and then he'd climb up the ramp again. He was just starting out from his hiding place, when the two gabbing men came his way, so he slipped back until they were gone.

He couldn't have been hiding long. He was sure it was just a few minutes. But there was nothing where the huge boat had been. "Mammy where are you?" he cried, quietly. He didn't want the men to hear him and come back. Looking around, he saw fearful dark shapes and shadows that sent him into more of a panic.

A hand grabbed him and pulled him to a stop. Through his tears, he saw a face with glasses that glinted back in the meager light. They were more frightening than the darkness. Rory pulled away, now in a frenzy, but the hand gripped his harder.

"Hold on there, lad. I won't hurt you. What's a small boy doing out here in the dark? Calm down and tell me what happened. We can sit here on this bench. Where did you come from?"

Rory whispered, "The boat. I fell on the gangplank, and then people pushed me down it. They kicked me. But now the boat is gone. Da is dead, and Mammy and Finn and Brendan are on the boat."

"The last ship sailed half an hour ago. I saw it leave."

Rory couldn't see the man's face, but his hand was like Da's, soft yet hard, and his voice was kindly.

The man continued. "I can't leave you here all alone. You'll freeze if you stay out here tonight. You can come to my home with me. It's not far, and tomorrow we can decide what to do."

"But, what about Mammy? She'll be looking for me." Rory blubbered. "I can't leave. I got these flowers for her." He held up the battered bunch of flowers.

"I'm sorry, lad, but the ship can't come back, and you can't stay here all alone. My name is Oliver Campbell. What's yours?"

"Ro...Rorymurphy." He said it so fast it came out one word.

"Well, Rorymurphy, you're in luck. I had business here at the port and drove up in the carriage. It's just over here, and there's a blanket you can wrap up in."

Rory perked up some when he saw the horse and asked to pet his nose. The horse lowered his head and snuffled over Rory's hand, then his cap. Rory laughed.

The man smiled. "He likes you. I have many horses on my farm. Here, give me the flowers. I'll put them in the back, so they won't get crushed."

Rory let the man lift him up; he smelled like Da. The man put him onto the carriage seat and wrapped the lap robe around him. The blanket was itchy at first, but it was warm, and in minutes he didn't notice the scratchiness anymore. What he did notice, and what stayed with him, was it smelled like Samel.

Oliver got up on the seat and took the reins. "Get up there, boy. Take us home." Rory leaned up against Oliver and was lulled asleep before the horse passed out of the dockyard.

∽

Poor, wee lad. Oliver should have gone home as soon as his work was done. But no. The man he met with offered him a drink, and Oliver just had to have a few more. Now, he was stealing a child. He blinked his teary eyes and shook his head. What had he done?

Oliver Campbell had been a father once—briefly. After six miscarriages in eight years, his wife finally delivered a beautiful, red-haired baby boy. He lived for two days. It was a shock neither Oliver nor his wife ever fully recovered from. Oh, their marriage survived, if living in separate quarters and communicating only for household business and being politely silent at dinner could be counted as a marriage. Lucille was involved with philanthropic activities that allowed her to host large social events. And he had his horses. But nothing filled the hole in their lives.

Bringing home a lost wastrel was not a good idea. But he couldn't just leave him there, could he? Maybe a child in the house would be just what they needed. A man could always hope, couldn't he?

The closer Oliver got to home, the more he regretted his hasty decision. Lucille would be furious. He could hear himself trying to explain. Lucille, the boy just appeared ... He fell off the ship ... He was crying ... He's an orphan who needs a home, for pity's sake...

God, she would never go along with it. He and his dreams of fatherhood. He was nothing but a fool.

When Oliver drove the carriage into the yard, a groom appeared. Oliver clambered down and carried Rory, still sleeping in the blanket, into the still house.

The help and Lucille were all abed. Rory, his eyes now wide open, squirmed to get down, though he didn't say a word. Oliver sat him in an old rocker in front of the stove. After rustling around in the cabinets, Oliver found the cocoa and made them each a cup. He sat himself down in the other rocker beside Rory, and the two of them drank the hot drinks in front of the stove.

"The flowers look nice there, don't they? How's the cocoa, lad?"

Rory nodded. "Yes, sir. It's very good, thank you, sir."

Oliver smiled. "It is good, isn't it? Nice and warm. Another minute down at the dock, you might have frozen." He paused and looked kindly at Rory. "You don't have to call me sir. You can call me Oliver." The two of them sat in silence, sipping their cocoas, Oliver rocking, Rory's feet sticking straight out in front of him, his eyelids drooping.

At five in the morning, the cook found them asleep in their chairs.

Mrs. McCollough's face had no expression as she gently shook Oliver's shoulder. She, as did all the staff in the household, knew things between the master and mistress were not as they seemed. But despite the mistress's strict and snappish ways, this was one of the best houses in the county to work in. Neither she nor anyone else on the staff was about to disrupt the illusion of a contented couple. Nor show surprise at the master asleep in the kitchen with a strange little boy.

Oliver awoke with a start and smiled sheepishly when he realized where he was. Whispering, he said, "I found this little ragamuffin last night. I had business at the port that ran late, and it was dark when I left. I nearly tripped over him, lost and crying. I couldn't just leave him there."

Rory opened his eyes and stared in alarm at the cook, then at Oliver.

"Hey, little man. Remember me?"

Rory nodded slowly, looking from under his blue cap at the two adults.

"You were wandering and lost, and I brought you home with me. You're safe here. After you're awake and cleaned up and have some breakfast, we'll decide what to do with you. Mrs. McCullough here, will get you something to eat."

He stood up, his heart nearly breaking as he looked at the small boy in the chair, his dirty little legs sticking out, his blue cap covering his hair and forehead. "Mrs. McCullough, get one of the girls to see about cleaning him up and find him some clean clothes. I'll be back later."

As he left, he heard Rory squeak out, "Ma'am. I have to piss."

Oliver had to piss too. And talk to his wife. "Mrs.

McCullough, I know it's very early, but could you send up early tea and coffee to our sitting room? Oh, and better put some digestives on the tray also." He smiled wanly. As if those would help Lucille with the news. "The mistress will let you know if we'll be having breakfast later."

Nothing would have helped Lucille with the news. "Oliver, my God, you are beyond stupid. I should not be surprised anymore, but you still amaze me. You bring home an urchin. A dirty little orphan boy? A Papist, I'm sure. What were you thinking? It's kidnapping, for heaven's sake. No. You'll just have to take him back. Today." She picked up another digestive.

"Maybe if you just saw him, Lucille…"

She stood up abruptly, leaving the sitting room for her own room, crumbs drifting behind her.

Oliver went downstairs to the kitchen, where the boy, now cleaned up and dressed in too big clothes, was sitting at the table eating porridge. He had red hair! It was the first thing Oliver noticed, now that his cap was off. God, just like his dead son. Lucille would certainly feel the same ache. He really was a fool.

Lucille came across Rory later in the day. He had a small rag and was following one of the housemaids around like a puppy as she worked. Lucille gasped. Merciful God. Look at that hair. Oh, Oliver, what have you done? The boy turned towards her, but she looked away before he could make eye contact with her.

"Are you all right, ma'am?" asked the maid.

"I'm fine," Lucille snapped. "Who is this?"

"Rory, ma'am. Mr. Campbell brought…" The maid didn't finish the sentence.

Lucille couldn't help herself and glanced at the boy again. He smiled and looked ready to say something.

"Never mind," Lucille snapped. "I don't want him in the house. And I certainly don't want him to follow you around. He's to stay in the kitchen and nowhere else until the master and I decide what to do with him. Do you understand me?" She spun out of the room. The rest of her day was spent in her bedroom with orders not to be disturbed.

When Oliver returned in the evening, he found the boy happily eating supper in the kitchen with Mrs. McCollough and a maid doting on him.

"This lad can sure eat, sir. He's taken quite a liking to Alice, here. He even helped her for part of the day." Without changing her tone, the cook said, "Until the missus saw him. She requested I keep him here in the kitchen. To tell the truth, he's won us all over.

"The missus said for you to go upstairs soon as you arrived home; that you'd both be eating upstairs tonight. I'll have it brought up shortly. Would you like a bit of sherry too?"

Oliver nodded yes and began to slowly plod up the stairs, hoping Mrs. McCollough would put the whole damn bottle on the tray. Lucille, still in bed, seemed rational at first, but he wasn't deceived. As her anger rose, she got up and began pacing around the room.

"I saw the boy. The shock sent me straight to bed. I am trying to understand you, Oliver. Really, I am. Did you purposely try to hurt me? Have you forgotten what I went through? Six dead babies are more than any woman should have to bear." She let out a quick sob and wiped at the tears roughly.

"Do you want me to have another breakdown? Then you could put me away, marry a young harlot, and have all the sons you dream of…" Her voice changed. "And on top of everything, he has red hair! God, Oliver. How can you be so cruel?"

She broke off abruptly, out of breath.

"Lucille, I never even saw his hair, not till this morning. It was at night, and he had on a cap. He's an orphan, for God's sake. He told me his father was dead, and his mother and brothers are on a ship going to America. I don't even know what ship. I suppose I could find out. But what if they ask questions?"

"You could drop him off somewhere. An orphanage where he'll be cared for."

Oliver had heard too much about orphanages. He paused, hoping to mask the emotion he felt at what he was going to say next. "He could live in the stables with Devlin, as an apprentice. Grooms are few and far between."

"Have you heard anything I've said? I do not want him here, Oliver. You will absolutely have to find somewhere for him to go."

Oliver left the room. If he'd had any hope of a child bringing his wife comfort, of being a bridge between them, well, there was no name for that degree of stupidity. And she said *he* was cruel? He'd be damned if he'd let her win. The boy was already here, and he had nowhere safe to go. Oliver was now responsible for the boy. As long as the boy stayed at the stables, she'd never see him. She never went there.

Chapter 8

1898

As a chambermaid at the hotel, Bridie had only cleaned rooms, and usually empty rooms, at that. There was a simple routine to repeat for each room. But in the Fleming house, she had to tend to a mansion with two individuals, each with their own whims. One prickly and cranky, the other sweet and lonely and both apparently come upon hard times. Well, Bridie too had come upon hard times, far worse than theirs, and she had little sympathy.

It was obvious they were no longer wealthy, judging by the fact they couldn't even pay her wages. But as long as she and her boys were fed and housed, she could swallow her resentment. Getting bogged down in the sisters' arguments and petty rules was another thing all together. It would only hold her back in her work.

She settled into the servant mode, learning as she went along and thankful for her previous education in the domestic sciences. And her *Mrs. Beeton's*, which she read often for tips on the hows and how-nots of working in a manor house.

Miss Mary was grateful for Bridie's help. And her company. The little lady had done all the work before and was not above giving Bridie a hand, especially in the kitchen. She delighted in telling Bridie what each piece of china or cutlery or pot or pan was needed for each meal.

"Miss Mary, for someone raised with a cook and servants, how do you know so much about cooking?"

Miss Mary smiled proudly. "Well, Mother wanted us both to know how to cook. 'You never know when you might need to make a meal,' she always said. Elizabeth couldn't be bothered and only learned the basics. But I loved all the business in the kitchen, and the magic that resulted from following a recipe, and Cook delighted in having a pupil."

She looked at Bridie with doubt. "I hope you don't mind. I don't mean to be bossy."

Bridie laughed. "You're anything but bossy," thinking about the sister upstairs. "No, I'm grateful."

It was obvious Miss Mary was lonely. While Bridie cooked or cleaned, Miss Mary talked about her family. Endlessly.

"Father was a judge, you know, quite famous in these parts. He was the judge for the circuit court. A circuit judge travels around a certain area within a state—a circuit. He traveled often, so he wasn't home a lot." She stopped when she saw the look on Bridie's face. Bridie knew nothing about circuits and judges, but she certainly knew about husbands not being home.

"I'm sorry, Miss Mary. I just remembered some-thing. Please go on," she said as she continued stirring a pot.

Miss Mary resumed. "But when he was home, he and Mother entertained lavishly. When we were little, Mother allowed us to sit at the top of the stairs and watch all the hullabaloo. Oh, it was so grand. Every-thing was so beautiful then," she said wistfully, a far-away look in her eyes.

Bridie enjoyed hearing Miss Mary's stories, her life so different from her own. And it kept her mind from drifting to dark thoughts about Rory.

The bell on the wall rang, and Bridie wiped her hands.

"You don't have to go up," said Miss Mary. I'll go. She's just lonesome."

Two months later, in June, Bridie felt more comfort-able about expressing her opinions. To Miss Mary. She wouldn't dare with Miss Fleming. Her head over-flowed with ways to make the dreary mansion homier. With the heat of summer approaching, Bridie brought up the idea of opening up the house to light and air.

"What do you think about removing the sheets from the furniture and opening the drapes. It will brighten up the place and allow some air to pass through."

"True, but bugs and dust come in too. Are you sure you can keep up with the dusting and cleaning all by yourself? And the cooking? Back in the day, we had a cook, and three house maids."

"Thank you, Miss Mary, for your concern. But I'm young and able. If I can't do something, I'll let you know. And if it gets really bad, we can just close the windows again."

Each dust cover she removed, each drape she pulled open, made Bridie feel as if she was liberating the old house back to its heyday. The warm breeze blew out the dusty, stuffy air and let light shine in, taking away some of the dreariness. Miss Mary followed close behind as Bridie tore off the linen sheets covering the multitude of paintings. Most of them were portraits of men posing with horses and dogs, women in gowns and jewels, perfect little children dressed in finery. Miss Mary knew them all and gave a running monologue of who was who and from which sides of the family tree.

"Watching you dust that table reminds me of Mother. You do it just the way Mother wanted. None of the house maids did it right, and she always complained about them. She would have liked you," Miss Mary said.

Bridie doubted that. She didn't think either of them would have liked each other. Her mother sounded like a finickier version of Miss Fleming.

Miss Mary couldn't stop herself from commenting on each thing Bridie moved, dusted, or cleaned. "Mother always put that there… Oh no, Father would never have allowed that chair to be moved… Gracious, Bridie, you want to do that?"

Bridie knew she was pushing the boundary of good servant behavior. Miss Mary made multiple trips upstairs telling her sister all that was going on. Bridie could hear Miss Fleming's voice, the tone, not the words, responding to Miss Mary's tales. But what could she do? If she waited for the sisters to make a decision, she'd never get anything done.

Bridie's nightmares about Rory hadn't gone away. By now, she accepted that she'd have them forever, like a missing leg, or an ugly scar. She always had them after a trip to the Custom House, when she asked if there was any news about her boy. There never was, except in her dreams, where the agents turned into devils.

The dreams had changed from the event on the ship to fuzzy images of him in an orphanage or begging on a street or slaving in a dank factory. She invariably woke in a sweat, her throat threatening to let out the scream that would wake the boys. She'd go out to the other room and calm herself with a cup of tea.

Sometimes she would be joined by Finn, who had his own hellish visions of Rory. She'd hold him in the rocking chair before the fire and share his misery.

"Mammy? Is it my fault he's dead? Will I go to Hell? What if Rory is in Hell because he ran away?"

Her heart ached for both boys. "No, my sweet. And it's not your fault. Only bad people go to Hell, when they've done something evil. Rory didn't do anything evil and neither did you. It was just a horrible thing that happened. We have to believe that he's still alive and well and that someday he will find us. That's all we can do, luv."

෴

One day Miss Mary, looking worried, asked Bridie to stop what she was doing. "Could you maybe make me a cup of tea? Make one for yourself too. I need to tell you something."

Bridie, hiding her surprise, and worry, brought the tea to the kitchen table. They were going to dismiss her.

"I should tell you something about our father. Needless to say, don't say anything to Elizabeth. She'll have a heart attack if she knows I told you. But now that you're going out and about to the market, I think you should know; in case you hear it from someone else. I was reminded yesterday that some people are just mean-hearted."

Bridie looked at Miss Mary oddly. "How is that?"

"Remember when I told you he was a well-known judge? Well, that made him a target for his enemies, and they accused him of something untrue. The newspapers wrote terrible things about him, using such words as infidelity… unfitting behavior… stepping out. Those were the kinder words used. They were wrong, of course; it was nothing but filthy lies.

"But the stories were out there, and it affected our family, especially Mother. Social engagements ceased; people avoided us and looked at us strangely in town, talking in hushed voices when we went by. It was quite horrible. And it happened to us in school too."

She looked ready to cry, and Bridie reached over and patted her hand. "It's all right if you don't want to go on."

"I've gone this far; I'll just keep on. Our mother, who had a very sensitive nature—Elizabeth is like her—took to her room and just wasted away. The doctors could do nothing. And of course, Father had to keep to his travels, so it was up to Elizabeth and me to care for Mother. She died within two years. Elizabeth was sixteen, and I was fourteen. It's horrible to lose your mother."

A look of understanding passed over Bridie's face. "Oh, Miss Mary. It is. I know how you feel. My mam died when I was four." And Rory was four when he was lost; she would never say die. "It is hard, isn't it, no matter what age it happens? And my da raised me too." Though it sounded like their father wasn't the most caring man, leaving his girls alone. Da was there for her.

"That was the same year Elizabeth was to have come out."

Bridie looked up in surprise. "What does *come out* mean?

Miss Mary looked shocked. "You haven't heard of a debutante ball?"

"I think you've forgotten where I come from," Bridie said with a short laugh. "If there were any balls in Newry, I certainly didn't know of them. And they probably would have been held in the Newry Hotel where I worked, and I'd a been doing the cleaning up."

A flustered Miss Mary apologized. "You're right, Bridie. I keep forgetting you've only been here in America for a few months. I've gotten so used to you, I fail to remember you might not know how we do things here.

"Anyway, Elizabeth was sixteen, and it was her year to be introduced to Charleston society at a debutante ball, to *come out*. She was so looking forward to it, but without Mother, it was not to be. Nor would it be for me, but it was harder on Elizabeth. She already had her gown made, and the invitations had been printed." She wiped a tear and sniffled. "At least they hadn't been sent out yet." She took a sip of tea.

"All that was so long ago. Forty-five years, now. Father continued working, with only occasional trips home, during which he mostly stayed in his library upstairs, only coming out for dinner. Then he died suddenly, four years ago, in that library. That's when Elizabeth took to her room—Mother's old room. Sometimes I worry Elizabeth is just waiting to die up there." She shook her head.

"She's only sixty-five for heaven's sake. Between the two of us we still have a few good years, wouldn't you think? Enough to get out of bed and join the living."

Bell ringing interrupted Miss Mary. "I shouldn't have burdened you with this, Bridie. But I worry about her, and I get frustrated. And she gets lonely." She lowered her voice. "It's like clockwork how she rings at four everyday, isn't it? She told me she can hear us talking. I'll go up and keep her company."

Miss Fleming did seem to ring her bell more often when she and Miss Mary were talking. Bridie wondered if other mistresses talked with the help like Miss Mary did. She guessed not. Certainly, Miss Fleming wouldn't.

Maybe she was jealous, Bridie thought. She probably thinks it's not proper for her sister to be talking to the help, and an Irish servant at that. Well, Bridie wasn't going to let it bother her. Let her ring away.

Bridie was at the fruit stand in the market, her last stop before returning home, when it happened. Out of the corner of her eye, she saw a boy dash between the vendors.

"Rory!" she yelled after him. "Rory, it's me! Your mam." She started to run after him, but he was gone. One minute he was there, the next he was gone, not even a shape in the crowd.

She turned in circles, trying to find him through her tears. Oh, God. Was it him? How could it be? Her panic made her run back to the Fleming house, where Miss Mary was in the kitchen.

"Good gracious, Bridie. What in the world is wrong? You look like you saw a ghost."

Bridie fell into a chair and looked piteously up at Miss Mary. "I did."

Miss Mary made them tea. "Now tell me about this ghost, dear."

Bridie told her about Rory and how he was lost to her. "I never told you because I wasn't sure how long I'd be working here. Maybe you'd fire me. And it's hard to talk about it still. Most of the time I carry on all right. I've imagined finding him alive here, in Charleston, but I've never had a vision before. He was so real looking."

"What a terrible thing to have happen to you." Miss Mary patted Bridie's hand. "You're a brave woman, Bridie."

Bridie winced. "I've never thought of myself as brave. Just dogged, I guess. Plugging along as best I can, bringing my boys with me. What else can I do?" She looked at Miss Mary with a sad smile on her lips, tears welling in her eyes.

Miss Mary, her own eyes weepy, held Bridie's hand. "I guess that's bravery, isn't it dearie? And you're good to your boys."

Bridie sniffled. "Thank you for saying that. Losing Rory has been my greatest failing. Hearing you say I'm a good mam to them is like a salve."

⁓

Early in Bridie's employment, she had asked Miss Mary why the sisters had not moved downstairs to make it easier on themselves. It was hard enough on Bridie's young bones, never mind how little Miss Mary must have felt going up and down the stairs taking meals to her sister.

"Oh, no, Bridie, dear. Only the help sleeps down-stairs." She smiled at the look on Bridie's face. "Well, that's just the way it's always been. And it is most cer-tainly what my sister wants."

Bridie couldn't help but wonder why, then, she and her boys hadn't been assigned the servants' rooms downstairs rather than the slave shack. Though, on second thought, she was grateful for the privacy the little place offered her. She didn't call it a shack or a hut or a cabin anymore. It was a cottage, a proper home. But it could be made better, and she knew the perfect person to help her.

On her walk to see Ian, she was charmed yet again by Charleston, the houses elegant, snugged up beside each other, their fronts close to the curbs, the parks plentiful. She wasn't quite as charmed by the heat and the hu-midity. People had warned her it would get hot in the summer. Little did she know how hot. Her wavy hair had turned into a mess of curls.

Miss Mary was teaching her about all the flowers growing in the neighboring parks that they sometimes walked to. Bridie hoped she might be able to return some of the near dead shrubs around the Fleming house back to bloom. And plant a garden. Though finding the time for that was going to be tricky.

She had only seen Ian a few times since they had arrived in Charleston. They both were busy at their jobs and learning their ways around the city. Ian was

waiting for her in front of Charleston Lumber, certainly the largest business on the street. Bridie had packed a
lunch, and they walked to a nearby park. They chatted
comfortably about their new lives, which were proving
to be mostly satisfying to them both.

"So, the shack is dark and gloomy, and now with
summer, it's boiling. I'm wondering if you could put
in an extra window or two? I don't think they can pay
you, but I'll get them to buy the supplies, and I'll feed
you. It will be good practice for you."

Ian nodded. "Windows will be easy to put in. And
you should feel the difference right away."

"I have another reason for you to come by. I'm
thinking that if the ladies like the work you do, maybe
they'd let you work on their house. There are bedrooms
downstairs that could be rebuilt so the ladies could live
on the first floor. It's killing me running up and down
those stairs to answer that damn bell. I might end up
killing the older one, Miss Fleming."

That afternoon Bridie set up tea for the ladies but
did not leave them to enjoy it as she usually did. She
remained standing by the table. Miss Fleming stared
up at her.

"Is there something else?"

"Yes, ma'am, there is," Bridie said to the two wom-
en. Her heart was thumping so hard against her chest
she worried it might thump out. "We need to do something about the cottage. It is so dark in there, and now
with summer, it's unbearably hot. I don't know how the
former servants ever lived in there. It needs more air."

The two ladies stared at her; Miss Fleming's lips pursed shut. Bridie pressed on.

"Ian McManus, a friend of mine from the ship, is an apprentice at Charleston Lumber. He's one of the best, and he said he can do the work for free, though you'll have to pay for the lumber and glass."

She was going to faint. "I'm sorry, but I have to sit down," she said as she pulled over a chair.

Before Miss Fleming could speak, Miss Mary spoke up. "Bridie, I think that could be arranged." She avoided looking at her sister. "There are three of you in there, and it is dark and close."

Before anything else could be said, Bridie stood up. "Thank you, misses. Me and my boys will be indebted to you," she said. "Ian also said he would be glad to do any repairs here at the house you need done too. Like those shelves in the pantry that you're always complaining about, Miss Mary."

Ten days later, on a Saturday, Ian got to work.

Chapter 9

1899–1900

A year later, Bridie was again looking at what Ian had done to her cottage. The windows he'd put in the back of the house the year before had made the house more comfortable in the summer. But it was still hot and stuffy, and Bridie had begged the sisters to let Ian put in more windows. It had taken time to convince them, then time for Ian to do the work in his few off-hours. Now it was complete.

"Oh, Ian, light and air beyond what I dreamed. And look at what you did to the door. You split it, and now it's a real Irish half-door. If I had neighbors, I could chat to them over the door." She spun around and gave him a hug. "Thank you, Ian. You are such a dear." Ian blushed.

Finn held a squirming Brendan. "Do you like it, Mam? I helped. Even Brendan hammered some nails. Sort of."

Bridie leaned over and kissed the two boys. "Of

course, I like it. Especially because Ian let my two sons help."

She winced inside when she said *two* sons. It was little things like that, that sent her mind straight to Rory. Could he be hammering a nail somewhere? Was there a nice person like Ian teaching him?

"You know, Bridie," Ian said, "This is really quite a well-built little house. I could push out the back and put in another bedroom," Ian said. "Maybe even a bathroom."

"Oh, Ian you are wonderful. Of course, I'd love that, but let's wait a bit for the sisters to get over this project."

Bridie's intention was to have Ian make the downstairs bedrooms into an apartment for the ladies. She had become a bit obsessed over the idea, but it was beyond foolish that they weren't using the whole house. One afternoon, as usual, she carried the tea tray upstairs to Miss Elizabeth's room. What was unusual was the third cup for herself. After pouring out three cups of tea, she calmly sat down with them. Miss Elizabeth gave her a cold stare. Bridie may have looked unabashed, but inside she was a wreck.

"I know it's unusual for the help to have tea with the mistresses. But how else can I talk with the both of you?" she said. "Your house is so lovely, but it's being wasted. It needs you living in the whole house like you did before.

"Miss Mary has told me how it was when you were girls. But I'd like to hear what you have to say, ma'am," she said to Miss Fleming, who was still staring at Bridie in disbelief. "Tell me what your house was like when you were younger?"

It was as if a dam had let loose. Miss Fleming became a bubbling fountain of knowledge. "It was built in 1748 by our grandfather, also a judge and one of the first in Charleston. He wanted a large family and built his house accordingly, but our grandmother never had but one child, our father, and she died when he was young. When he married Mother, they naturally lived here, along with Grandpapa who died when I was eight."

Miss Mary blurted out, "Tell her about when they cut the house in half?"

Miss Fleming's eyes brightened. "Oh, yes, what excitement that was. Mother was thoroughly vexed, wasn't she, Mary? Father wanted the hallway widened and raised, and as Mother always said, 'What Father wants, Father gets.' I was nine, and Mary was only six. We had to rent a house down the street for almost a year while the work was done. They sawed the whole house in half along the hallway's length. Can you imagine?" she said.

Miss Mary jumped in. "Then the halves were moved apart to widen the hall from six feet to twelve and raised the walls to twelve feet, to match the rest of the downstairs. It was quite the structural feat."

Bridie sipped her tea, trying not to choke. How much money does it take to *widen a house*!

Miss Fleming, dabbing at crumbs on her lips, continued. "That's also when they connected the kitchen house to the main house. It was so much easier for the help and Mother. They also put in those bedrooms downstairs for the cook and the house maids. The rest of the sla…" She stopped short. "…servants lived in the cabin. Your cabin." Her voice trailed off.

Miss Mary smiled uncomfortably. "What my sister is trying to say is, we thought you'd prefer to live separately, what with your boys and all. There are a lot of delicate things in the house, and well, you know…"

Bridie knew too well, and she had to admit they were right. Every day she looked at the rubble the boys created in her house.

"You do have a point," Bridie said. "Now that Ian has done such a nice job on my cottage, I think I prefer it to the house."

Bridie stood up and put the dishes on the tray. "Have you ever thought about taking over those downstairs rooms yourselves?"

She left them staring at each other, the new idea floating between them.

❧

In the past year, Bridie felt the relationship between the three of them had warmed. Miss Fleming would forever be reserved, but Miss Mary was a dear. Of course, they were still servant and mistresses, but Bridie was comfortable with that. It was her job, after all. And she was good at it. Plus, she loved returning the tired old house into the mansion it once was. The windows, the knickknacks shone in the new light, and the furniture gleamed from her vigorous waxing.

When she first started cleaning, she had assumed that the fireplace tiles were black. But on closer examination she realized it was soot, under which she was surprised to find white tiles with pretty blue patterned tiles framing the outer edges.

It turned out all the fireplaces had those tiles, though with different patterns: windmills, houses, animals, flowers …

Miss Mary gushed with compliments. "Look what you did! Oh, my dear, I'm embarrassed to say it, but it's been so long since they were cleaned. I couldn't do it anymore and let them stay black, but you've brought them back to life. Those blue ones are Delft tiles, from Holland. They were quite the rage back when Grandpapa had the house built. Wait till I tell Elizabeth what you've done."

In the evenings when Bridie delivered their meals upstairs, she'd hear Miss Mary telling her sister all that Bridie had done that day. "Elizabeth, we really must get you down there. It's like when Mother was alive. Bridie has a similar eye."

"Mary! Listen to yourself. I'm shocked. I know you've become fond of her. And I will admit she has her charms. But she is a maid and Irish at that. And she still makes me wait when I need her. I almost broke my wrist the other day ringing for her."

Bridie always coughed discreetly outside the door before setting them up with their trays. She bet they'd be downstairs in four months if all went according to her plans.

Bridie invited Ian, now a certified carpenter, to come and look over what it would take to give the ladies an apartment downstairs. "I know they still can't pay you, though I'll get them to cough it up for the supplies." She gave him a winning smile. "Could you come on Sunday at ten? Miss Mary will be at church and Miss Fleming will be in her room, so you'll have time to look around and tell me if it's even possible."

That Sunday, after church, Miss Mary was more than a little surprised to see Ian at the kitchen table working on some papers while Bridie prepared Sunday dinner.

She pulled Bridie into the dining room and with a shaky breath whispered, "Bridie. I am a little shocked you invited a gentleman into our house while I was away. Good Lord, if Elizabeth finds out a man was in the house, alone with you, she'd have a case of the vapors for sure."

"I know, Miss Mary. I know it's not exactly proper, but Ian is like a brother. And Miss Elizabeth will meet him shortly."

"How exactly is she going to meet him, Bridie?" It was the first time Miss Mary had ever spoken sharply to Bridie. "What do you mean?"

Bridie took the woman's hand. "Sit down, Miss Mary." Bridie sat down beside her. "I hear you groaning going up those stairs. What will it be like in a few more years? You already told me you think it's morbid that Miss Fleming is sleeping in the room where your mother died.

"Even I tear up thinking of her alone in that room. It's just too awful. And you running up and down to meet her needs? Even I get tired too. It's one thing to go upstairs to clean, but five or six times a day, with trays or laundry is a lot, even for me."

Miss Mary looked down. "I know, but she's so stubborn, and she doesn't think about anyone else. She's always been that way. You're right about that."

Bridie continued, "You know she needs to be downstairs where she can have the whole downstairs to move around in. Where you can sit with her when you want, where you can have your friends in for a bridge game in a proper room. Believe it or not, I am dying to serve you and your guests refreshments at a decent table in style."

She took a deep breath. "Ian would like to go upstairs and talk with you and Miss Fleming..."

"Bridie! You know Elizabeth will never allow a man into her room. Have you lost your mind?"

Bridie sighed in exasperation. "Miss Mary. It's a new century, for goodness' sake. I've set up your father's study as a tearoom. It's a perfectly respectable place for the four of us to have tea." She spoke calmly, but her insides were in an uproar. "You go up and get her ready."

Bridie and Ian went upstairs and waited in the study. She fiddled with a napkin on an imaginary spot of dust. The tiered tea stand, laden with Miss Fleming's favorites, was in the middle of the table. Bridie took a deep breath and looked at Ian, who smiled back.

"It will all be fine, Bridie. This is better than the tea I saw when I snuck Finn into the ship's first-class salon."

Soon, they heard the women coming down the hall, Miss Elizabeth's voice complaining to her sister about this forced removal from the comfort of her bedroom.

When they entered the room, Bridie worried that she might really have gone too far this time. Miss Fleming was so beside herself when she saw Ian standing behind her father's desk, she blanched and started wheezing. Bridie held her own breath. What if the old lady died on the spot? Miss Mary looked ready to cry.

Somehow, Bridie spoke. "Miss Fleming, this is Ian McManus, and he is here to talk with you both about making some changes downstairs. But before he starts, let me serve us all tea. Here, let me roll you to your place. Miss Mary, sit beside your sister, and Ian and I will sit on the other side."

Miss Fleming took a deep breath and seemed to calm herself down, though still with a severe frown on her face. No one spoke. Bridie poured for the ladies and put plates with samples in front of them. "Go ahead and start, ladies. I made your favorites."

She went to the other side and poured for herself and Ian and served them each a plate. She pretended to sip her tea. She looked at Miss Mary, hoping she would speak first, but the woman made no eye contact. God, she was leaving it up to her. The maid!

"Ladies, I think you both should consider moving downstairs."

Miss Elizabeth squirmed in her chair and looked ready to erupt. Miss Mary looked at her plate.

Bridie rushed on. "The servants' quarters down-stairs are perfect for an apartment, which Ian will explain to you in a minute. It's difficult even for me to run up and down the stairs. Miss Mary doesn't complain, but I know it's hard on her knees. And she gets out of breath. She waits outside your room until she's breathing normally again, before she enters."

Miss Mary reached for her sister's hand. "It's not all the time, Elizabeth."

Bridie said, "I worry that you're too isolated up here. What are you going to do when your sister can't get upstairs as often?"

"That's none of anyone's business," said the old lady. She said it gruffly but looked ready to cry.

"Maybe so, but Ian has some good ideas. Please hear him out." Bridie looked at Ian, who smiled politely at both women. Bridie knew he must be uncomfortable, but he didn't show it.

"I think I can make life better for all of you. I can turn those rooms into a nice apartment: two bedrooms, each with a window, a bathroom, and a parlor. Here, look at the plans."

Miss Fleming made him repeat himself several times, which he did patiently. Bridie never said another word. In the end, it was little Miss Mary who convinced her sister.

"Elizabeth," she said. "Please, dear. I can't keep running up and down every time you need something. It's just terrible on my knees." Her voice cracked. "You need to leave that room. It's ghoulish, Elizabeth. We

already had one death in there; I couldn't stand another. What Ian is proposing will be perfect for us. I've
seen what he did to Bridie's little place. He turned it
into a lovely cottage. You'll see it when we finally get
you downstairs."

Three months later, Ian carried a terrified Miss Fleming down the stairs to where her wheelchair awaited
her. He pushed her down the hallway and into the newly created apartment, done just as Ian had described.

Miss Mary hadn't been allowed to watch the apartment being built. "You should see it at the same time as
your sister," said Bridie.

The first thing Miss Mary noticed was the glass
doors leading outside.

"Elizabeth, look. They're etched the same as the
front doors into the house. That was quite clever of
you, Ian."

Bridie promised to plant some flowers the next
spring, wondering how she would ever find the time.
She was hoping to start a vegetable garden, too, behind the house. She still remembered how good the soil
smelled that day Miss Mary hired her.

"I'll help you choose the flowers, dear," said Miss
Mary. "You know how I loved working in the garden."

She and Ian looked on proudly as the two women
sat in their new parlor sipping on celebratory sherries,
discussing how they would decorate their rooms.

Chapter 10
1898–1900

From his first day with Devlin, Rory adapted well to life at Campbell's Stables. There was so much to see and do, he had little time during the days to mourn the loss of his family. He and Devlin lived above the stables in an apartment infused with the sounds and smells of horses.

At nighttime, though, he remembered Mammy, Da, and his brothers and often cried himself to sleep. He was scared he would forget them; they were growing dim, like shadows.

Mammy—he addressed most of his thoughts to her—It's nice here. It's cozy, just like Samel's stable back home. Are you safe too? And Brendan and Finn?

Devlin had been furious when Oliver first brought him the boy.

"Christ, Oliver. I'm a forty-five-year-old bachelor. What the hell am I supposed to do with a little boy?

And who is he? Where did you find him? Will the police come looking for him?"

Oliver's face reddened with anger—and a terrible sadness that Devlin had never seen before. The look shut Devlin up. They had an easy relationship, but he knew he'd crossed a line with that last comment. "I'm sorry, Oliver. But what the hell did you think I was going to say?"

"I know, I know, there's no way you would know. But this is very emotional to me," Oliver said. He told Devlin a brief history of the many miscarriages and the death of the last baby and how devastated he and the mistress had been.

He told how he found the boy. "I didn't know what else to do but bring him home. I couldn't leave him there." He shook his head. "I should have known it wouldn't go over well with the mistress. If I took him to the authorities or the church, they'd just put him in an orphanage. I couldn't do that.

"Then I thought of you. You could teach him about horses, raise him to be useful. And perhaps, I could be part of his life too."

Devlin stared at the man. How could someone so smart and successful be so feckin' dumb? Oliver was a right bleedin' tick, and spineless too, against that wife of his. He was a decent man and a good boss, but Jaysus ...

He took in the boy. What else was he to do?

Devlin had never missed marriage or having children. But once Rory moved in, a space inside him he didn't know was there, filled.

Devlin came from a family of horsemen, all trainers. The first time Oliver had worked with Devlin at Down Royal Race Course in Belfast, he was impressed. For a young handler, he had skills rarely seen even in older trainers, including a talent at calming the more obstreperous horses. Oliver offered Devlin a job which he accepted on the spot.

Devlin had always wanted to be involved with the breeding and training of young horses, before they got bollixed up by bad habits from bad trainers. The fact that Campbell's Stables bred Irish Hunters, by his thinking the best horse in all of Ireland, if not in the world, sealed the deal.

The move served them both well. Oliver got a great trainer and Devlin made a name for himself. The reputation of Campbell's Irish Hunters continued to grow, not only in Ireland but in the rest of the United Kingdom, Europe and the Americas. One of their colts had recently been sold to an Arab prince. Devlin lived in an apartment created at one end of the hay loft above the barn. There was a main room with one window, his bedroom, and a storeroom. A small lavatory with a toilet and a pitiful, cold shower finished off the space.

The kitchen, just some shelves, a stove, a sink and a wood icebox, was located along the back wall of the main room. Devlin was neat and orderly, the dishes always washed and put away on the shelves. Two armchairs and a table with a lantern and his pipe and tobacco, along with horse periodicals and a book or two, faced the wood-burning stove.

That first afternoon, after Oliver had gone back to the big house, the silence Devlin had lived with for years overwhelmed him. He was ignorant about children. What did he know about comforting a child? The boy, too, seemed uncomfortable, fidgeting while he stared down at his feet. When he did look up, his chin was quivering, and Devlin was afraid the boy would soon be sobbing.

Devlin took him by the hand. "Come with me, lad. The horses will cheer you up. They always make me feel better when I'm feeling sad."

Rory indeed perked up. It became obvious the boy came from a farm. He knew to stay clear of hooves and machinery and followed Devlin's instructions, trotting behind him like a small, marching soldier.

And talking. Once he began to talk, it appeared he couldn't stop. It was endless chatter and questions.

"Do you have a donkey? We had one, and his name was Samel. He liked me." Rory again looked ready to cry.

Devlin ruffled the hair on Rory's head. "No, lad. No donkeys. But horses are a lot like them, and they'll let you know if they like you. Don't you worry, they're going to love you just like Samel did."

Rory rushed on with his questions. "Where are the sheep and the cows? Do you grow potatoes? Don't you have chickens?"

"Whoa there, little man. This is a horse farm, not a regular farm. There are two milk cows and chickens up by the big house, but you're not allowed up there yet." Never, probably, after hearing what Oliver had told him. Everyone knew the mistress didn't want any of the groundsmen or stable workers in her house, which was fine with Devlin.

As the head trainer, he had met her a few times on his visits to Oliver in his office. She was polite, but cold, and Devlin always left feeling like a piece of horse dung. There were rumors about her vicious temper, but he had never been the recipient. Even so, unless it was an emergency, he usually waited to talk to Oliver when he came down to the stables.

That first night, Devlin made a mattress from the chair cushions, placing them on the floor in front of the stove in the main room. The boy lay there stiff as a board, his eyes wide open.

The poor thing. He must have been scared silly, but he was so brave. Devlin took his well-worn copy of *Grimm's Complete Fairy Tales* off the bookshelf. "One of my favorite memories is of my mam reading aloud to us kids at night. Would you like me to read you a story?" He wasn't sure what to say next but knew Rory must miss his mother horribly. "Pretend my voice is your mother's. I bet she told you stories, right?"

Rory nodded, his chin quivering again.

"This story is called 'The Town Musicians of Bremen,' and I think you'll like it…"

Rory leapt up. "I love that story! It's about a donkey and a cat and a dog and a rooster and they catch a band of robbers. Da told it to me and Finn, and we got to make all the sounds. I made the donkey sounds." Suddenly the lad looked ready to cry again.

Devlin ruffled the boy's hair. "Well, I hope I can read it as well as your da told it. And you can make the donkey sounds. You can make all the sounds if you want. This was the first story my mam read to me when I was your age."

Rory settled into his cushions, a rapt expression on his face, but by the third page he was sound asleep. Poor lad. He didn't even get to bray. Devlin smiled, wondering if his own mother had ever finished a whole story before he fell asleep.

⚬⚬⚬

Rory was a chatterbox and ran his mouth about everything. Devlin quickly learned to tune him out, interjecting with a mumbled yeah, maybe, don't know… The endless prattle became music to Devlin's ears.

After a month, Devlin told Oliver the boy needed his own room with a bed. "I swear the lad grows an inch each day, and he's outgrown the cushions on the floor, but he never complains." They set about clearing out the storeroom for the boy's bedroom, and Oliver provided the furniture. Lucille was at one of her meetings, and the two men went through the manor house's attic, finding a bed, a chest and another chair. "She'll never miss any of it," said Oliver, a guilty grin on his face.

Oliver needed no excuse to come to the stables—
they were his after all. But now, on Lucille's days
away from the estate, he lingered there. Some days he
brought the boy up to the house to visit with Mrs. Mc-
Cullough, who, along with Alice and the other maids,
had all become fond of the red-headed, smiling boy.
Rory never left empty-handed, always lugging back
a basket from the cook. All the staff seemed to know,
without being told, that their mistress need not hear
anything about the boy.

Two years later, Rory and Devlin had adapted well to
living together. The only thing that bothered Devlin
was losing his reading time in the evenings, always
interrupted by Rory's incessant chatter. One night he
gave Rory paper and a pencil, hoping that might keep
him busy. It was clear the boy had never even held a
pencil before, but after Devlin showed him what a few
strokes might produce, the boy was intrigued and set to
scribbling. Before going to bed, Rory showed off what
he had done.

Devlin was bowled over. He saw recognizable forms,
mostly of horses, pictures he would have expected from
an older child. He didn't think it was possible for a boy
as young as Rory to be able to draw that well, especially with no training.

He looked at the boy anew. He was six now, right?
Shouldn't he be in school? Learn his ABCs? Maybe
someone could teach him to draw too. Well, let's see

if Oliver cares as much as he said he does. He was the one who would have to pay for it.

"Good God," Oliver said, when he saw the pictures. "He's quite good, isn't he? I really would have been a terrible father. Of course, it's time for him to get some schooling. But he can't just go to a school. I mean the boy doesn't exist, right? But a tutor could do. I bet our bookkeeper, John, would be interested. Before he started doing our books, he was a teacher at Banbridge Academy."

John Derick was definitely interested. "Mr. Campbell, it will be fun to do some teaching again. You said he's six, right? I can do it on the days I'm here for you, Tuesdays and Thursdays. I'll teach him in the mornings." He wandered off, happily muttering to himself, "I'll dig out my books ... I'm sure I have a primer and tablets ... I still have a blackboard and chalk ..."

Rory wasn't quite as happy to be in a makeshift classroom, as it meant losing time with the horses. But once he got started, he proved to be an able student. All of Devlin's reading aloud had given Rory a head start in reading and a love of stories, and Rory wanted to learn to read to himself.

It didn't take long for John to see Rory's drawing. Impressed, he went to Oliver. "You know, Rory can draw well for someone his age. With some instruction he might develop into a decent artist."

"Yes, I saw some of his drawings. Devlin brought it to my attention. Pretty good for someone so young. Do you have someone in mind who could teach him?"

"I could. My father was an artist and a cartoonist for the *Belfast Telegraph*. I thought that's what I would do when I grew up, but then I discovered numbers and accounting. I still draw and paint in my spare time. I could do it on Thursdays, after our tutoring sessions."

"I'm all right with it. Better check with Devlin about times and such. He's raising him," Oliver said. "Did Banbridge Academy have any idea of how talented you are?"

John's face broke into a grin. "Why, thank you, Mr. Campbell. I appreciate that."

⚬⚬⚬

At the end of their first art session, John was impressed.

"Rory, these sketches are very good. Are there things you especially want to learn to do? Like trees or houses or buildings? What about people?"

"Oh, yes, Mr. Derick. Especially people. I want to draw pictures of Mammy and Finn." He looked tearful. "Their faces are going away. And Brendan. Can we draw a picture of a baby too?"

"Yes, lad," said John, surprised at the tightness he suddenly felt in his throat. "I think we can. And you can call me John. Though if you ever go to a real school, you will have to call your teachers mister or master."

John was impressed at how quickly Rory progressed. His sketches became distinguishable pictures, horses still his favorite subject. When they showed them to Devlin, he had no difficulty identifying which of the sixty-eight horses Rory had drawn. John thought the boy quite remarkable; this must be how a proud father feels.

Faces proved more difficult and frustrating to the boy. To John, they seemed to be good depictions of people—he easily recognized one of himself and one of Devlin. But Rory was always disappointed with the ones he did from memory, the ones of his family, sometimes angrily tearing them up, stomping around the room in tears.

John talked with Devlin about it. "I don't think it's surprising. He was only four when he was lost, and all he has is his little boy memories of them. That's hard to draw from. I'm guessing he'll probably never be satisfied with them. He doesn't give up though. I think he is very good."

Chapter 11
1900–1903

"Mammy? Don't cry. Why you sad?" Brendan asked
Bridie. They were walking home from dropping Finn
at school. Brendan, now three, trotted along beside
her. One year younger than Rory when he was lost
to her. Would Rory age in her mind, or forever be a
child?

Bridie knelt down and gave him a teary hug. "No,
my sweet laddie. I'm not sad. We don't always cry because we're sad. Sometimes we cry happy tears, like
now. I'm happy that Finn is going to school. And in
three more years I'll be crying again because I'll be
taking you for your first day in school. We're both going to miss him, aren't we? Now, you'll get to be my
little helper."

Finn could have begun first grade as soon as they
arrived in Charleston, when he was six. But she had
needed him to watch over Brendan while she worked.
Finn took on responsibilities in a way that hurt her

heart. He watched Brendan, helped Ian with odd jobs for the Flemings, and helped her with the cleaning. She remembered her own desire to keep going to school and couldn't deprive her children of the chance to learn.

Her oldest was losing his childhood doing odd jobs for people. He needed to be in school with boys his own age, learning and playing with friends. No, she'd just have to manage Brendan on her own while she cleaned and cooked.

And it shouldn't be hard. Brendan was different than his brothers. Calmer, sweeter, and more independent, he was the smartest of her boys, easily able to make up games to occupy himself. And he had become quite an entertainment to the sisters, often trotting the path between the two houses.

Plus, Bridie was no longer as overwhelmed as she had been by all the sudden changes in their lives, beginning when the British soldiers knocked down their door. It's a wonder they lived through it all. No longer living in a state of constant fear was something she was still getting used to.

Thanks to Ian, her little cottage was more than comfortable. She'd found a new chimney for Da's lantern at a shop near the market, and it gave off a cozy light. When she looked up from reading or doing needlework, she loved to see the candlesticks flickering from their spot above the fireplace, and her mother's small dish shining at her through the glass cabinet. Her mother's Celtic bag she had hung from a hook in the bedroom, so it was the last thing she saw before closing her eyes at night and the first thing when she awoke in the morning.

Her mistresses seemed content in their downstairs suite. Especially Miss Mary, who was convinced her sister would have died upstairs. But now Miss Elizabeth, as Bridie was now allowed to call her, took an interest in her surroundings—and in Bridie's housekeeping. Maybe a little too avidly, following behind Bridie in her wheelchair. Bridie became expert at ignoring her more outrageous harping. In the good weather, Miss Mary rolled her sister out to the front piazza, where they waved at passersby.

One day Miss Mary came up to Bridie with a strange look on her face. "Bridie, dear. You know that little hillock beside your cabin? It's from a leftover stump of a tree Father had removed years ago. I don't know why he allowed such shoddy work. It should have been removed completely. Now it looks like there might be a critter of some sort tunneling into there. Maybe Ian could block it up or something, next time he comes over?"

Bridie couldn't stop laughing. "Oh Miss Mary. I'm sorry, but that was about the funniest thing I've heard in a long time. It's not a critter. It's Brendan. He thinks it's a *sidhe*."

"Shee?" asked Miss Mary. "What in the world is that?"

"Back in Ireland, it's a hill or a mound under which the fairies live. It was Finn who told Brendan about them, and now he thinks that's what the mound is. A *sidhe* with the fairy folk. He's been building roads and tunnels into it, hoping to meet one of them ever since."

She laughed at the look on Miss Mary's face. "Who knows? You might have more fairies than you know. That hawthorn tree, out front? They love those trees, and they'll gather to dance under them. Don't worry. They're usually not a problem … if they like you."

She continued to make herself go to the Custom House to ask about Rory. It was more than three years she'd been asking about news of her boy. The original kind agent had left, replaced by various agents, all too busy to worry about a boy lost so long ago. They tried to be kind, but she knew they only felt pity and impatience. She would probably feel the same way if she were them.

Ian, now a master carpenter, continued at Charleston Lumber. "Why leave? I like it there," he told Bridie and the sisters. "All the hustle and the variety of jobs keep me interested, and I love being in the city and working on these old houses. I could look at the architecture all day."

The four of them were sitting with iced teas on the piazza. He had just finished making a ramp for Miss Elizabeth's wheelchair from the piazza to the sidewalk. In celebration, he rolled her up and down the ramp a few times, wearing them both out. He was panting when he sat down at the table and gulped down his drink.

"Ian, that was quite refreshing," Miss Elizabeth gasped, her eyes twinkling, her hair blown askew.

With the sisters happily ensconced in their downstairs quarters, Bridie found she had more time. She had never read for enjoyment. Who had the time? But the sisters both read and encouraged Bridie to read any of the many books in the house.

"Why don't you start with the ones upstairs in our bedrooms?" Miss Mary said. "They're the ones we loved as girls."

She helped Bridie to choose. "If you want to go with a novel, try *Swiss Family Robinson*. I just loved how they made a cozy home out of nothing.

"And if you want something to read to the boys, maybe start with *Grimms' Fairy Tales*. Don't be put off by the words 'fairy tale.' They're still good stories— 'Cinderella,' 'Hansel and Gretel.' You can read them aloud to the boys. I bet they'll like the 'Town Musicians of Bremen' the best."

Bridie smiled. "Oh my goodness. Charles used to tell it to the boys all the time. It was their favorite, and they'd take turns making all the animal sounds." She made herself say the next sentence; she couldn't hide him away forever. "Rory always made the donkey sounds."

That October, when the weather cooled, Bridie finally started work on the overgrown garden at the back of the lot. The barn turned out to be a treasure trove of garden tools.

Miss Mary watched Bridie bring them out and clean them. "You do know, dear, that it's a little late to be starting a garden. It's October already. But because we're so far south, we do have some fall plantings. About the only things you can grow now would be root plants like garlic and onions and maybe some turnips."

"Miss Mary, you continue to surprise me. Not only do you know how to cook, but you can also garden?"

The lady blushed. "Gardening is just another thing we women learned. Maybe we don't all get our hands dirty, but we know when and where to plant, and what works best with our soil and climate. I haven't been to a meeting of the garden club in years, but I could take you there. They're the ones who could really help you."

Bridie didn't think the garden club would be thrilled at having a maid at their meetings, but she was touched by Miss Mary's offer.

"I really just wanted to clear it out, so I can plant in the spring. But now you've put a bug in my ear. I'll plant onions, garlic, and turnips, and see what happens. And we'll have turnips for Thanksgiving. We called them swedes, and in Scotland they call them neeps. Funny how many things are the same but called something else. In the spring you can tell me what to plant."

Bridie suspected the sisters were in a bad way financially. Not only could they still not pay her, but they couldn't pay others either, and bill collectors came by often. Bridie could usually shoo them off, but if one came when she was absent, she'd find a tearful Miss Mary on her return.

She knew they tried to live conservatively. The house was lined for gas, but it was expensive and used only for the kitchen stove. They used kerosene lamps for lighting, as did Bridie in her cottage. Since the women had moved downstairs, the coal furnace in the basement didn't have to be used anymore, and during the winter, Bridie kept the kitchen and the sisters' suite warm with the fireplaces. She closed off the rest of the house with the heavy sheets that once covered the furniture. When she went to market, it was with a small amount of money, usually just coins, given to her by Miss Mary, with which Bridie negotiated mean bargains.

One day, using her favorite form of bribery, tea and scones, she sat with the sisters and brought up the unmentionable subject of money.

"I know I am just a servant, and I should not talk out of turn. But it is obvious to me you have come upon bad times."

Miss Elizabeth was nearly apoplectic. "Bridie. Once again you have overstepped your bounds. You *are* just a servant, as you put it so well. And an outsider. You really shouldn't …"

Bridie cut her off. "You can complain about me later, Miss Elizabeth. Right now, please just listen. There is no reason to hide it from me. I know you're not miserly because of stinginess, despite being Scottish," she said, smiling sweetly.

Miss Elizabeth twitched in her chair but kept quiet. Her sister reached over and patted her hand.

"Even without seeing your books, it's obvious that you are in over your heads and close to penniless. I shoo bill collectors away daily. The only thing you have is this house and the land it's on. Well, it was the same for me back in Ireland, and the government took it from me. They didn't even pay one cent for it. They can do the same here, and your good name won't save you. But being smart might," she said. Both women stared at her.

"Look at you two. I am not the devil. I told you, remember? When I was in school, I took classes in managing the finances of a home. And I worked in the office of the hotel. So, I'm not completely ignorant. You must agree, you need to do something, yes?"

They both nodded and took little bites of their scones, sweet ones this time. They tried not to smile at the sugariness.

"So, here's what I suggest. Miss Elizabeth, you can get around now. We'll all go to the bank and find out exactly what you have."

"Bridie, you cannot accompany us into the bank," Miss Elizabeth said, giving Bridie a stern look over her lorgnette. "It's private."

Bridie tried not to show her exasperation. Would she ever get off her high horse?

"Of course, I would never go in with you for a private meeting with your banker. I can, though, wheel you there and wait in the lobby for you." She couldn't resist. "Is that acceptable?"

Miss Elizabeth nodded curtly. "Of course it's acceptable, Bridie."

～

Other than going to Mass on Sundays and Ian's visits, Bridie had little social life. Her friend Shirley Ames from the Hayne Street rooming house wheedled her to come along to Hibernian Hall after Mass.

"Come on, Bridie. No more excuses. You have to come, and you'll love it. Every Sunday, they have a late breakfast after Mass. They also do a lot of community stuff, charities and things, and they have a baseball team. I mentioned it to Ian, but he already plays for Charleston Lumber. We're all Irish, except for some of the wives or husbands, and we all got here the same way. You've got to get away from those two old biddies. And the boys can make some friends."

The first Sunday she planned to go to the hall, Bridie dressed herself and the boys with care. She felt as nervous as she used to when she and Kathleen went out. But, once inside the hall, with the cheerful, outgoing Shirley leading the way, she relaxed. There were people, including Ian, she knew from the ship, and others she had seen at church or the market. She teared up when she saw her sons in groups of boys their ages. She shouldn't have isolated them so.

～

Tea was now taken routinely in the library with the three women seated around the table.

"I've been thinking of ways we—I mean you—can save money, and maybe even earn some," Bridie said.

"How would we do that?" Miss Mary asked.

"Let me buy some chickens; it's silly to buy eggs."

Miss Elizabeth had to complain. "Now everyone will think we're poor—poor, white trash with chickens in our back yard."

Bridie couldn't resist. "Well, quite a few of your neighbors have chickens. Two even have cows."

A week later, the three women went out to the barn, Bridie pushing Miss Elizabeth, who was particularly contrary this morning.

"Will you just look at that lovely hen house, Elizabeth," said Miss Mary. "Ian made it for us."

"Look at them. They look quite happy, don't they?" Bridie said proudly.

"Humph. You brought me outside on this chilly day to show me that?"

"Elizabeth. Do you always have to be so negative?" Miss Mary said. "Don't you remember when we used to play with the chickens?"

Bridie had bought two grown hens and five chicks from a man in the market for six dollars. The sisters complained about the cost, but Bridie knew she'd soon recover it. After a breakfast omelet, she never heard another complaint about the chickens residing in the back yard.

"While we're down here, let me show you what Bridie did to the garden," Miss Mary said, rolling her sister down the cleared path.

The day Bridie came home with a rooster, his arrival announced three blocks away, Miss Elizabeth about fainted.

"Bridie! What in the world have you done? It's bad enough we have chickens, but at least they're quiet. But a rooster? It's so common. Now they'll think we're even poorer than white trash—that we're as poor as the nigras. They're the only ones who have noisy roosters strutting in their yards. Whatever will the neighbors say?"

"You shouldn't care what they think," Bridie snapped. "It takes a rooster to grow our flock. Then, as well as selling the eggs, I'll be selling chickens at market, and I bet they'll bring in a pretty penny."

Now that Bridie didn't have to spend half her day running up and down stairs with meal trays or laundry or a lonely lady's whims, she had more time to herself. Well, not really. She had packed much of that time with gardening, but that was rewarding. Most mornings, after breakfast, she and Brendan took a walk. She combined it with errands, but along the way they explored different neighborhoods. Sometimes, they'd stop by the boarding house on Hayne Street, to chat with Shirley and Mrs. Millbury while Brendan played with Shirley's son.

Bridie and Brendan became a familiar sight, the lad happily waving at anyone who smiled at him. In addition to the parks, his favorite places were the empty lots with buildings crumbled to rubble. What had happened to them? It couldn't still be from the war, could it? Good Lord, that was over thirty-five years ago.

"Did the house fall down?" Brendan asked.

"Aye, lad. That's what an earthquake can do," a man's voice said, just behind them.

Bridie spun around in surprise.

"Beggin' your pardon, ma'am. I hope I'm not being too forward, but I overheard the boy's question."

"I didn't know about an earthquake," Bridie said, trying to hide how he had startled her.

"Oh yes, back in '86. One minute everything's standing fine and upright and the next… well, boom. All gone. Hard to believe it's been nearly seventeen years already. There's only a few of these sites left. Most of them have been cleaned up. Your boy sure looks interested in the goings on."

Bridie laughed. "My boy here would play in it all day if I let him. He really loves to watch when the men are clearing them up. All that activity."

"Maybe he'll be a builder when he grows up. You never know, right? Allow me to introduce myself. Name is Daniel Sweeney. I own Sweeney's Tavern down on East Bay Street and the corner of Exchange Street."

"Funny, my da ran a pub back home. Named Madden's, for the owner. He always wanted to have his own pub, and he would have named it Murphy's, for sure."

Chapter 12
1902–1903

Rory leapt out of bed, shot into the kitchen, put on the kettle, took out milk and butter from the ice box, and sliced some bread. He heard Devlin moving around in the other room.

"Hurry, Devlin," Rory yelled. "You're late."

"Slow down there, lad. There's no need to hurry," said Devlin as he ambled in, tucking in his shirt and buckling his belt. "Samel isn't going anywhere."

Devlin had told Rory he could help him in the colt's training today. "You're only eight, so mostly you'll just watch me."

Rory had been there when the chestnut colt, with a crooked white blaze down his face, was born. He watched him take his first wobbly steps to his mam to nurse. Rory immediately called the colt Samel.

"Samel?" asked Oliver. "I've never heard a name like that before."

"It's what I called my donkey. His real name was

Sam-u-el," said Rory, pronouncing each syllable slowly and with great patience. "But I was just a baby then, and I couldn't say the name right, but he liked it better, I could tell."

"Well, I think that's a grand name for this colt. His registered name will be 'Sir Samuel of the Bann.' All my Irish Hunters born at Campbell's Stables, are named 'Title… Name… of the Bann,' after the river that runs through Banbridge."

"I like that," said Rory.

The boy and colt became inseparable, chasing each other around the paddock, teasing each other, taking naps together. Sometimes they would stand facing each other, foreheads touching, the boy's red hair indistinguishable from the horse's coat. Devlin and Oliver never tired of watching them. Neither had ever seen such a connection between human and horse.

When Rory arrived at the farm four years earlier, he only knew he was four years old but could not remember the month or day of his birth. Devlin decided it would be January 1.

"Yay! Just like the horses!" Rory yelled out happily. Racehorse births were planned to occur in the beginning of the year, and all were given the first of January as their birth dates, thus allowing them to be raced against horses of the same age and maturity.

Sir Samuel and the other new colts were now seven months old and ready to begin their early training on this July morning. And Rory was to begin as a novice trainer, a newly created position and Rory's first official step on the ladder to becoming a trainer. Devlin would back him up, and Oliver would pay him a small salary. Rory fairly hummed with excitement. If Mammy could only see him now.

"You've helped in Samuel's early training," said Devlin. "Since the night he was born, every moment you've been with him. He's lucky. Most colts don't get their own little trainer to grow up with." He ruffled Rory's hair. "Thanks to you, he knows what it feels like to be touched, pushed, and pulled by us, and all with his mam right there. She's approved it all, including the halter training and the lead."

Rory soaked up everything Devlin told him and delighted in the compliments; the man's praise kept him warm when missing his mam chilled his bones.

Devlin went on. "Now, as a trainer, you need to be able to deal with every horse under your care. I know Sir Samuel is your favorite, but a trainer needs to know all his horses. Can you do that? You can still have a favorite, and you'll find that they will have their favorite humans."

Rory's head bobbed up and down. "I play with all of them. Princess Lily tries to butt Samel out of the way so she can snuffle her way into my pocket. She thinks she can bully him because she's a year older."

"All right then, let's get down to business. Now that Samel and the others are weaned, we can begin with their training. Right now, it's just groundwork— changing up their gaits, forward, backing, jumping, stopping, all of it on a halter and lead at our direction.

And they need to learn their manners, so to speak. Frisky is one thing. A bit of stomping and head tossing is alright, even good. But tantrums—kicking, biting, stubborn refusal? If we can't get to that part of his brain that allows him to trust us, that horse is useless, a goner. And, you'll see, lad, some will really fight you."

Devlin laughed. "I see that dazed look on you, lad. I know I go on, and it's a lot to take in. But you're a natural for the work. You'll see."

On Rory's off time, he continued drawing—everything. He learned to draw buildings, fields, trees, the sky… Horses were still his favorites, and he drew every horse in the stable. He also found the three fox hounds and the many barn cats had their own charms. One black kitten adopted Rory, following him everywhere, including up to the cozy apartment. Rory named him Bagheera after the black panther in *The Jungle Book*.

Under John's guidance, Rory had finally created acceptable drawings of his family. They were still imperfect to him, but it was comforting to have them hanging in his room.

One day Oliver came upon Rory as he was sketching Sir Samuel. "Good gracious, lad. You really are good. John was right."

Rory knew he was blushing. He wasn't used to anyone seeing his work. "Oh, they're nothing. Just scribblings."

"Well, I'd call them more than that. Have you done any painting? With colors and such?"

"No. John thinks I should keep on with pencil or charcoal, *the bones of art*, he keeps telling me. I like it, so I don't mind."

Oliver said, "Next time I go to Newry, maybe I'll pick some things up. For when you're ready to try new things like pastels, watercolors, oils."

A few weeks later, Oliver came back with a wooden suitcase full of art supplies, most of which Rory had never seen: oils, watercolors, pastels, pads of paper. Embarrassed, he thanked Oliver. The next time he was with John, he showed him the box. It looked huge in Rory's hands.

"Oh, Rory, this is a real artist's box," John said. "See how everything has its own place? Each tube of oil paint, the tray of watercolors. The pencils and pens and brushes are tucked in slots to protect them when you're holding the box by its handle. I have one, but this one is the nicest one I've ever seen. I'm envious."

"Then you can have it. I don't want it; it's too much," Rory said, almost in tears. "I know I should be grateful, but it makes me feel funny. Only rich people can buy this, and I'm not rich."

"No, but you're lucky to have someone in your life that cares enough to give you such a gift."

Now Rory felt guilty. "Do I have to learn how to use everything now? I just like drawing. What if he asks to see how I'm using it all?"

"It is a lot," said John. "But you're the artist, and

you can do what you want and when you want."

"I'm an artist?"

John laughed. "Yes, you are. A beginning one, but an artist, nonetheless. Maybe for our next session we'll try the pastels. You can get great shadows with them. You may never want to use those other things. But if you do, you already have them. Mr. Campbell is a very generous man."

Rory had finally drawn one sketch of Mammy that he liked; her mouth and eyes were close to how he remembered her. When he felt especially lonesome, times that had become less frequent, he gazed at the portrait. The look in Mam's eyes and her smile calmed him and gave him hope. Though America and the memory of his family were fading, he still dreamed that someday he might find them.

Rory's room was taken over completely by his art. Devlin brought it up to Oliver. "I've been wondering. What if we put in a window at the other end of the loft and made a room for Rory to work in? His own room is barely passable with all the supplies. As it is, all the walls are covered with pictures. But a separate room to paint in might be nice for him."

Oliver agreed. "A studio. That's a great idea. It's ironic, isn't it, considering the mistress, an art connoisseur, knows nothing about the young artist living in the barn. What a protégé he could be for her. As far as I know, she's totally forgotten about him."

In addition to John's lessons, after dinner, Devlin and Rory took turns reading aloud, the cat curled up on Rory's lap. Rory's reading had improved such that they traded off chapters with each other.

Oliver brought down the many books he had loved as a boy: *Treasure Island*, *The Swiss Family Robinson*, *The Merry Adventures of Robin Hood*. Some were new to Devlin also, meaning an evening's reading could sometimes go late into the night.

Presently, they were reading *Black Beauty*, which was proving to be emotionally difficult. It was sad enough that Beauty was sold so many times, but his last owner, Nicholas Skinner almost killed Beauty. Rory couldn't continue without crying, and Devlin had to finish reading the book, pausing often to take a deep breath.

Cruelty to horses—any animal—was bewildering to Rory. His horses, downstairs, were warm and dry, with plenty of food and attention. He knew that if anyone working in the stable ever showed even a hint of cruelty, that man would be dismissed instantly.

He asked Devlin the question that had been on his mind for months. "Will Samel be sold someday?" he asked, trying to sound normal. "How do we know he won't be sold to a mean person?"

"Oliver is careful who he sells his horses to. Most go to other stables for racing or equestrian showing. Sometimes, it's to a farmer or another landowner needing a good horse."

He took a puff on his pipe.

"Except for the brood mares and the two stallions, most all of our horses will be sold. You know that, right? This is a business, after all, and Sir Samuel is looking to be one of our best colts, so you should prepare yourself. I know how much you love him.

"You know Oliver auctions off one of his yearlings at the big benefit the mistress puts on every year in October. He never tells which yearling it's to be, but I'll tell you this time. You can't tell anyone, or else I'll make you muck out stalls for the rest of your life. It's Princess Lily."

"Lily? I love Lily," Rory sniffled.

Devlin patted Rory's shoulder. "If it makes you feel any better, I still feel sad every time one of them is sold. They're like my children."

October of 1903 found Campbell's Stables and the manor house in a flurry of activity with preparations for the Banbridge Annual Arts Council Benefit Gala and Auction. Always hosted by the Campbells, it was held in late October and was timed to occur a week before the two-day festival at the Down Royal Racetrack in Belfast, the start of their winter racing season. The auction included artwork and two big items. The first was a weekend in Belfast for that festival at the Down Royal Racecourse, and the second was one of Oliver's yearlings.

After living on the farm for five years, Rory had become used to the preparations for the event, which occupied everyone working on the estate. The mansion, the grounds, and the gardens were spruced up, the stables were spotless, the horses groomed to a high shine.

Oliver loved to give the guests tours of the stables and show off his horses, especially the yearlings. He played up the suspense by keeping his guests in the dark about which one would be auctioned off that night.

"Devlin," Rory said, concern in his voice. It was the night before the auction and they were in Lily's stall, giving her an extra brushing. Rory slipped her an apple. "Do you think they know that one of them is going to be auctioned off? Do they worry? Will they miss each other?"

"I don't know; they've never told me," Devlin said with a laugh. "Sorry, lad. I know you're serious. One of them might be off their feed for a bit, or whinny for his stable mate. But we keep them so busy, they don't have time to dwell on it. Maybe the one auctioned off might, especially if the stable isn't as good as ours."

"Can I watch the auction this year? I'm big enough now, aren't I?"

"I'm sorry, lad," Devlin said, shaking his head. "It's what Oliver wants. It's a grown-up party, and there won't be any children there."

Oliver had reminded Devlin to make sure the boy was out of sight. "My wife might take it into her head to come down."

Devlin did not want to repeat that to the boy, but the look on Rory's face touched him. In years past Rory had been too young to realize the auction meant a loss—the loss of one of the animals he loved. And he'd not been as close to the yearlings then as he was now.

"There may be a way you can hear the auction and see some of the party," Devlin said. "You're old enough now, but you have to promise to stay hidden. If Oliver, or God forbid the mistress, catches us, we'll both be fired. This is just between you and me."

Devlin and the other stable workers had fixed up the barn for its big moment. The building was shaped like a cross with stalls and storage rooms on the legs of the cross. In the middle was a large room, usually used for grooming, bathing, and vet and farrier visits. It was now cleared for the auction, with some chairs along the four sides for those who wanted to sit.

Devlin led Rory into the feed room. "You can stay in here during the auction," Devlin told Rory. "Stay ducked down behind the feed box. You won't be able to see anything, but you can hear it all. Just don't forget to stay low and out of sight. Many of the men like to walk around and see the other horses. Oliver's had more than one sale on auction nights."

Rory nodded. "I promise, I promise." The last thing he wanted was for anyone to see him. If no one could see him, no one would know if he cried when Princess Lily was no longer his.

"Afterwards," Devlin said, "I'll fetch you from here and we'll go up to the mansion. "You'll be able to peek in the window and sneak a look at the festivities."

"What if someone sees me?"

"Then we'll have to run like hell, won't we?" Devlin laughed.

Rory looked at him with surprise. Devlin rarely told

or played jokes. And now he'd cracked two jokes and was going to let Rory sneak a look into the mansion?

They heard voices coming toward the barn. It was Oliver and a man Rory had never seen before.

"Mr. Greenboro, it's nice to see you again," Devlin said.

"You too, Devlin. Someone told me a filly named Princess Lily is the yearling to be auctioned off. What a coincidence, seeing as I'm wanting to get a jumper for *my* Lily."

"Princess Lily will make a fine mount for your daughter," Devlin said.

Oliver looked askance at the man. "Paul, how did you know? It was Lucille told you, right?" Oliver asked.

Mr. Greenboro gave a guilty smile. "Yes, she couldn't resist tipping me off."

"When Lucille talked me into auctioning off Princess Lily, I knew she was up to something. In all these years she's never taken an interest in my horses. But Princess Lily for her god-daughter Lily? I guess that was something she couldn't pass up."

The night of the auction, Rory listened from his hiding spot. The event went on forever, the space was tiny, his legs and back cramped. When Devlin finally let him come out, his legs were numb, and he could hardly stand.

"Sometimes you regret getting what you wish for, eh?" Devlin said. "Do you still want to look in on the party?" At the mansion, Devlin told him where to go. "I don't think you have to worry," Devlin said. "That window is at the back of the room, and they'll be busy, eating and drinking and looking at each other's finery."

Rory crept through the hedges and edged close to the window. He realized his face was lit from the light shining out and he ducked down. Did someone see him? He dared to peek again and realized Devlin was right. No one was looking out the windows. The tables were draped in white, and between the candles, the gleaming plates and glasses, the room shimmered in his eyes.

The guests were eating and drinking, the talk and laughter a low hum through the glass. Servants began clearing plates. Others went around the table filling glasses with water or wine or tea. The door to the kitchen opened and other servants carried out trays laden with bowls filled with some kind of confection. His mouth watered imagining the sweetness on his tongue.

He crept back to Devlin, his eyes agog. "So that's what it's like to be rich."

Devlin chuckled. "It is. But remember, they're human too, with troubles and sickness and death. Their money doesn't make them any better than us. More fortunate, maybe, but not better. Never forget that."

The benefit went off without a hitch and Princess Lily would soon be living in Paul Greenboro's stable.

A week after the auction, Mr. Greenboro and his daughter came to pick up Princess Lily of the Bann. Oliver hugged his goddaughter hello. "Lily, I need to talk to your father a bit. This young man, Rory, is very knowledgeable. He'll tell you all about your namesake."

Rory could hardly breathe. He had never been around a girl his age. But his shyness faded when he began talking about the filly: what she liked, her little tricks and habits.

"Watch this," Rory said. "Lily, where's the sugar?"

Princess Lily tossed her head twice, snuffled, and went right for his pocket where the lump was hidden. "No matter where I put it, she finds it every time. Here, put one in your coat pocket. You're new to her, but I bet she finds it on her second try."

The girl laughed when the filly found the sugar on her first look. "Her lip is so soft. It tickles when she breathes on me."

"I know. Let me show you Sir Samuel. He and Lily are my favorites. I'm going to miss her, but I'm glad she's going home with you," he said and felt his face get hot. He was no longer worried; Lily Greenboro was used to being around horses. Princess Lily was going to be fine and was probably going to be spoiled rotten.

Devlin and Rory had prepared Princess Lily for her trip by horsebox to the Greenboro farm. It wasn't far, only about seven miles. If she was a mature horse, the trip could have been a nice day's ride, but as a yearling, she was too young for saddle training and needed to be transported.

Lily, her legs wrapped and dressed in her traveling outfit of blanket and halter with blinders, delicately walked up the ramp into her own special carriage like the princess she was.

As Rory and Devlin were locking up the horsebox, Rory had a sudden idea. Why hadn't he thought of it before?

"Miss Lily, before you leave, I want to give you something. Wait right there." Rory ran back to the stable and upstairs to his room. He picked up the painting he had done of the filly, then hesitated; it was his first oil painting and one of his favorites. But, no, it belonged with Princess Lily and her new owner.

When Rory ran back, the lady he knew to be Oliver's wife was just joining the group. Rory had never seen her at the stables before and he held back, suddenly nervous.

"Paul, good morning," Mrs. Campbell said. She looked pointedly at her husband. "Oliver, I thought you were going to tell me when Lily came to get her horse." She abruptly turned to Lily before he could answer. "Well, I'm glad I took the initiative and came down; I didn't want to miss you."

She gave Lily a hug. "It's been a while, hasn't it? At your brother's wedding, I think. You look quite the young lady now. I know your birthday isn't until next Thursday, but I wanted to give you your present now. It's just a little something, but you liked mine, so I bought one for you."

Lily tore the wrapping off the package and removed a thin, silver bracelet. "It is just like yours. I'll wear it to my birthday party, that's if I can wait," she said, giggling, as she gave Lucille a hug. "Thank you so much, Aunt Lucille."

"You're welcome, dear. And I'm so glad the two Lilys will be together."

As she turned to leave, her eyes landed on Rory. She stared at him, seemingly frozen in place. Oliver, Devlin, Mr. Greenboro, the groom who'd come with him, and Lily all looked at Rory. He could not run away, much as he wanted to.

"Here, Miss Lily. You can have this," Rory said, awkwardly handing the painting to her.

"Oh, Father, look. It's Princess Lily. It's like she's looking right at me. Look Aunt Lucille. I'm going to hang it in my room so I can look at it every day. Thank you, Rory," said Lily.

Paul Greenboro took the painting. "Rory, this is a most remarkable likeness." He turned. "Lucille, you should have auctioned this off the other night. I bet it would have gone for a pretty penny. How have you hidden this talent?"

The silence stretched as the mistress worked her face into a tight smile. "Oh. Yes, of course." She gave a strained laugh and glanced at the painting. "For a stableboy, he does have some talent." She picked up her skirt and turned to go. "Lily, dear, it was lovely to see you. I'm sure you'll be very happy with your new horse." With that, she nodded and left.

The muscles in Devlin's face twitched. "Come on, lad. Let's get back to work."

Rory puzzled over what had just happened. So that

was the mysterious Mrs. Campbell. She didn't seem to like him, but she didn't even know him, so how could she feel any way about him? Well, chances are he'd never see her again, so it didn't really matter.

Oliver took his time when he returned from the barn later that evening. Let her call for him. It was a convoluted game they played. They would argue; he'd leave for the barn; she would languish in her rooms and eventually send for him when he returned. They'd argue again, halfheartedly, and descend to the dining room for dinner.

This time he took his time after her summons and poured himself a sherry before trudging up the stairs to her chamber. She was lying on the chaise lounge.

"He's the boy you brought home, isn't he? The boy you promised you'd get rid of? You knew I would forget about him. And it worked, didn't it? In all that time, I never once saw him, and you never once mentioned him. You used me for your own selfish ends, Oliver. Just because you needed to fulfill your need to be a father. God, sometimes I just hate you." She rose, wrapped her dressing gown around herself, and tugged at the bell pull. In a few moments, a maid entered the room.

"Certainly took your time, didn't you?" Lucille snapped. "The master and I will have tea in the sitting room. And make sure there's a few shortbreads on the tray."

"Make it one tea and a bottle of sherry," said Oliver, smiling at the maid. "With two glasses, please."

All this time she had been pacing. After the maid returned with the tray, she finally sat down.

In a determinedly pleasant voice that ground on Oliver's nerves, she said, "Devlin must be taking good care of the boy. He's certainly grown up since then. He looks well fed and healthy, though dirty. And he paints. That picture of the horse was quite good."

"It was," Oliver said. The less he said the better. He poured a glass of sherry. No sense waiting; she was just getting started.

"But how does a stable boy find time to paint?" Her voice rose again. "And where did he get the paint? Paper? Canvases? Does Devlin buy them? On wages paid by… us? Are you buying them?" She glared over her teacup.

"Lucille…"

"Don't Lucille me. Now you can do what you should have done six years ago when you ignored my request to get rid of him. You will send him away." Her eyes gleamed with righteous indignation.

It was all he could do to not slap her face. "What is wrong with you, Lucille? Do you have no compassion at all? He's a good lad and turning into a fine trainer. He and Devlin are like father and son. It would be cruel to send the boy away."

"Your lying is cruel to me."

Oliver regarded his wife with bitterness. He had debased himself for so long with her. Why?

Whatever affection they had once had passed away with the death of their son. He sighed and ran his hands down his face. Silently, he took his time, sipping the sherry.

"Lucille. I will see that he is gone."

She looked at him in surprise. "That was quick."

In a harsh voice, he said, "But it won't be now. He's only nine, and Devlin is the only father he's had. When he's a bit older, in three or four years. When he can take care of himself."

"Oliver…"

Oliver stood up. "Don't Oliver me, Lucille. And don't bother arguing. As you well know, everything we have, everything we own is because of the stables. I can't risk losing Devlin because of the will of a vengeful woman. All that time you didn't even know he was here. Go back to being ignorant."

Chapter 13
1903–1905

Bridie woke in a panic. Was she going to have these dreams of Rory forever? Was he alive? Was he happy? Did he remember them? Why didn't she tie him to Finn? How could Finn have lost him?

How could Finn have lost him? It always came down to that. She knew Finn didn't *lose* Rory, but no matter how hard she tried, she took it out on him. Finn was only six then, for God's sake. It wasn't as if he did it on purpose. She knew he blamed himself; surely, he didn't need his mother's blame too. And it's not as if she was blameless. After all, she was the one who forgot to tie them together. How long was she going to keep torturing herself? And Finn?

Every month or so, she'd go back to the Custom House and ask the agents if they had found out anything about Rory. Always it was the same answer, delivered politely and kindly. She made herself return, knowing the probable answer would be no. But to not go was worse; it would be as if she had abandoned him completely.

It was after those visits to the Custom House that she'd have the dreams, and like clockwork, by the end of the next day she'd end up in a fight with Finn. He didn't help her enough, didn't do his schoolwork, sassed her, sassed his teacher, got in fights at school, fought with Brendan...

The outbursts were hard on them all. Finn was eleven and turning into an angry, nasty lad. And she was becoming a worn-out hag of twenty-seven. She worried about what he would become, fretted about how it was affecting Brendan. Then she felt guilty; it was a vicious circle.

Most Sundays, after Mass, she and the boys went to Hibernian Hall. Bridie could relax there and socialize with fellow country folk, most going through the same problems. The lot of them were poor and worked too hard. Their children lagged in school. If a crime occurred, the Irish were always blamed first, despite that fact that many of the police were Irish. It almost seemed as if they treated their own worst. Her boys had made friends, and for a while in the hall, they could play without being teased or beat up. Though lately, Finn was refusing to go. "It's just for old people and babies," he muttered to her and sulked in his room, refusing even to go to Mass.

In addition to the Sunday breakfasts, there were frequent events and dinners. Depending on the type of event, she and Shirley and some of the other women at their table pooled their money and slid it to the barman. In return, he would bring a ceramic pitcher of beer to the table, which they poured into their teacups.

"It's a pleasure ladies," he'd say. "You're always happy and generous. The men might drink more, but they get rowdy and hate partin' with the money."

Sometimes Ian came over to chat with the two women. The same easy warmth he had shown the Fleming sisters was evident in all his dealings, and he was well liked by everyone. After he left, Bridie talked him up to Shirley. Again.

"He's perfect for you, and you know it. And now that he's done with his apprenticeship, he's making good money. Think of the house he could build you," Bridie said, slurring her words a bit. She got tipsy after two or three cups, which luckily seemed to be her limit.

Shirley shook her head and laughed. "Yeah. He is a catch. No doubt about it. But, in case you hadn't noticed, he's only interested in one woman, and that's you."

"Oh no, not so. It's only because we became friends on the boat, and he helped me after Rory was lost. Besides, he's way too young for me."

"Only four years. That's not too young."

Mrs. Millbury had hired Shirley and was paying her room and board *and* five dollars a week. Shirley and her baby lived in the third-floor room Bridie and her boys had stayed in. Well, he wasn't a baby anymore. Five he was now, and a playmate of Brendan's.

Thanks to Shirley's nagging, Bridie finally got up the nerve to ask the ladies to pay her. "You need to speak up for yourself, Bridie; it's disgraceful how they treat you. I can't believe I'm saying this to you, of all people. If it was me, you sure would have told me to open my mouth. It's been too long, for God's sake. Those two witches will use you up," she said hotly.

Bridie finagled three dollars a week from the sisters. She knew they were poor and three dollars a week would be hard for them to pay, but she should be paid a wage. She could understand Shirley's feelings about the Flemings, but *disgraceful* was not the word she would use to describe how she was treated by the sisters.

After all this time together, they knew each other quite well, and a grudging respect and affection had grown between them. Miss Elizabeth continued to lord herself over Bridie and remind her of her place, but it was more from habit than animus. Bridie didn't take it personally and ignored most of it.

After a particularly bad storm, the outhouse Bridie and the boys used collapsed. Luckily no one was in it, but something had to be done. Ian was invited for tea.

"It's not worth it to repair the outhouse," Ian said. "What you need is a bathroom in the cottage. It would be a lot of money, but worth it in the end. No one has outhouses anymore. The only place for it is at the back of the cottage, and I'd have to knock out part of the back wall."

Bridie held her breath. What a dream that would be. The sisters looked at Ian with distress.

"If I have to do that, it's only a little more to get rid of the whole wall. That way I could also add another bedroom and some windows."

Bridie's heart soared. The sisters looked sick, especially Miss Elizabeth. "We can't possibly do that. What kind of money are you talking about?" she snapped.

"About $450."

All three women gasped.

"That would be tops for a regular customer." He smiled. "But you aren't regular. I can get it down a lot. It will take longer because I'll have to do it on my off hours and pay someone to help me, but maybe $250?"

"What if Finn helped?" asked Bridie. "You wouldn't have to pay him."

"That would help. Though I'll still have to use a plumber. That's not something I do. So, lets figure between $200 to $235."

"We have to do it, Elizabeth," said Miss Mary. "They need a bathroom. And the bedroom too. The three of them are squeezed into that one bedroom."

Bridie couldn't help but think how the former tenants had been squeezed in.

❦

Two months later, it was done. Ian rolled Miss Elizabeth to the cottage so she too could see the results. The addition was a bedroom for the boys and a bathroom—with a tub! Bridie now had the front bedroom to herself. He'd also lined the cottage for gas lights, though Bridie still used kerosene lamps, as did the sisters in the big house. None of them wanted to spend the money on the gas.

The sisters offered Bridie free rein in their attic. She took another bed and dresser for the boys' room and traded out the large table in the main room—it and the bench took up the whole room—for a smaller one. Sitting in a corner of the attic, as if they were waiting for her, were two small armchairs. Placed in front of the fireplace with her father's lantern between, it was just about the coziest place Bridie had ever seen.

She was happy in her cottage, and she had her privacy. Life with her boys could be noisy and messy even on a good day. Now with Finn and her fighting so often, it was especially so.

Bridie, pushing Miss Elizabeth, accompanied the ladies when they visited their bank, The South Carolina Bank of Charleston on Broad Street. It was a regal building, its exterior blindingly white with arched rectangular windows, all topped off with a soaring gold eagle on the front gable.

When the ladies came out of the office, Bridie knew immediately they were upset. They hardly said a word on the way home. On entering the house, Bridie said, "You both settle in the library while I prepare tea."

She served them their tea and scones, then sat down to join them. Miss Elizabeth was incensed. "First of all, we couldn't meet with the president, who always met with Father. A foolish man, a Mr. Nutting, was assigned to us.

You just wouldn't believe his arrogance, Bridie. Trying to insinuate he knew Father so well… I bet Father never even knew the man… Puffed up like a fat, lazy cat, wasn't he, Mary? Him and his perfect suit and vest, all pressed just so… but that hair! Ten strands combed over from one side of his head to the other… absurd, he was."

She was shaking her head in disgust. "He said we were frivolous! I still can't believe it."

"I know," Miss Mary said, jumping in. "Said it was a waste of money what we spent on redoing our rooms downstairs. Never mind what he said about fixing up your cottage."

"Slow down, ladies. You have all afternoon. Did you notice I used peaches in the scones this time?"

"Bridie, they're delicious as always. I don't know how you do it," Miss Mary said. "He was a pompous fool if ever there was one. I am sure the president was there, and I just don't understand why we didn't meet with him. I have half a mind to go back there and complain. Elizabeth, you tell her the good news."

"Mary, you know we don't talk to the help about financial matters."

"Oh, for goodness' sake, Elizabeth, just what do you think we're doing right now? And why not? She knows everything anyway. Plus, she's the only one bringing in money with what she sells at the market."

"Well, you do have a point. But Bridie, you can't let out a whisper. The good news is we own the house and land outright and we've kept up on the taxes. The bad news is we seem to be cash poor. That's what that miserable old coot told us."

"Well," Bridie said. "I guess that's what you already knew, right? He does sound like a right eegit, though, doesn't he? In the meantime, I'll keep on selling at the market. That pays for the food at least." And probably her salary.

Bridie had been making her own speculations. It was good news about the house, but that was real estate and tied up. They needed money for bills and food, and as a cushion against bad times. What they really needed were new ways of bringing in money. More money than what she was getting at market for her eggs and a few chicks.

What if they sold some items? Many things in the house were probably worth a lot of money, especially the paintings. How many portraits of dead old men did one house need? Pictures Miss Elizabeth insisted Bridie dust.

In Bridie's wanderings through the city, she had noted shops that sold artwork and furniture. There were also pawn shops and a variety of stalls in the City Market that bought and sold odd pieces. She'd do more research before she broached such a topic.

One day when the sisters were out at a bridge game, she took her notebook and went room to room in the house, making an inventory. There were seventeen rooms in total. Seventeen! Why, it was almost indecent. On the first floor there were ten rooms: the grand entry (maybe not a room, but it had furniture, so she counted it), the library with three walls of books, the parlor, the music room, the dining room, the kitchen, and the apartment. And there was still a bathroom and bedroom for a cook. She didn't even add in the mud room, assorted hallways, pantries, and closets. Upstairs there were five bedrooms and two bathrooms, plus Judge Fleming's study, with two walls of law books and Mrs. Fleming's sitting room.

Had all these rooms ever been used at once? Bridie wondered. All these things? Who needed all this space? Had anyone ever read the hundreds of books?

She posed that question to the sisters during tea that afternoon. They looked at each other.

"Not really, Bridie," Miss Mary said. "Most of the books were our grandparents' and our parents'. Well, Father's. Mother didn't read much. And of course, his law books. But one shelf over there has our books, and we still have many upstairs in our old bedrooms."

"I'm not being rude, and pardon me for asking, but why on earth does anyone need such a big house?"

The sisters looked at Bridie with pity. Miss Elizabeth answered with a dismissive wave of her hand. "Oh, my dear, it's just the way it is. This is nothing compared to some of the other houses in town. Why, the Williams house is twice as big. It has thirty main rooms, and the ballroom ceiling reaches to the second floor."

For now, Bridie could stop her worrying. It appeared the sisters were solvent. She knew the women would not be keen on selling a thing; they could never appear to be in need.

Chapter 14
1904–1906

On January 1, 1904, Rory turned ten and Sir Samuel and the other foals turned two. He loved his birthdays, especially because it was the same day as Samel's. Devlin let him spend half the day with the colt, doing whatever they wanted. Oliver and Devlin usually gave him a few pounds, and Mrs. McCollough always made him a cake.

The two-year-olds were being introduced to a bridle with a rubber bit. At the moment, Sir Samuel didn't look much like a sir. He was slobbering and drooling and tossing his head up and down while mouthing the rubber bit in his mouth.

"They're funny how they carry on, but in a few days, they won't even notice it," said Devlin. "Some of the other stables start out right away with metal bits, but that can ruin their mouths. Then you end up having a nasty, stubborn horse with a hard mouth. A waste of their potential and makes them good for nothing. A feckin' tragedy if you ask me. Those trainers should be banned."

Each year, the different stables in the area put on shows for the growing horses, exposing them to the excitement and chaos of crowds and noise. For the weanlings and yearlings, they had been simple "in hand" classes, using only a halter and line.

Now, as two-year-olds, the foals were expected to do much more. Having done those early shows, Rory already felt he was an old hand. "I bet Samel comes in first. He could do the whole thing with no line. We've been practicing."

"Don't go getting all cocky on me now, lad," Devlin said. "You might have advanced to Assistant Trainer, but you're still new at this. Those other shows were just practice for you and the foals. Not only will it be with the long lines again, but there will be more gait commands, including cantering. Add in the bridle and bit, which they're still getting used to, and the odds go up for havoc. The judges won't be as lenient as they were with the yearlings."

"I know, Devlin. I know." Sometimes it was boring how Devlin just went on and on. But Rory knew he was lucky to have one of the best trainers in Ireland teaching him.

"I know I go on," said Devlin, patting Rory on the shoulder.

Rory nodded, smiling inside. Devlin was also a mind reader.

"You know some. More than some, I'll grant you. But you add in the noises and excitement of the crowds, people and horses, and judges? You've got the makings of a right holy mess. You can't learn enough, and for sure, you don't want to be one of those eegits who muck it up just because they're not prepared. Or cocky. I hate cocky trainers."

"Like the one last year, from that Belfast stable who jerked at the bit so hard, the horse started bleeding?"

"Jaysus. That bastard isn't just cocky, he's downright cruel. But he got his. He's been banned indefinitely from entering horses in any show."

One night after dinner, Rory piped up with his favorite question. "When can I ride him? I wish I could ride him now. I'm not too heavy, am I?"

Devlin took a puff on his pipe and smiled at Rory patiently. Sir Samuel was adapting well to all his training, which now included an empty saddle.

"Soon enough, lad. Soon enough. In the meantime, you just keep riding Limerick. That devil will prepare you for anything those babies will show you. You need to be as good and patient a rider as you've proven to be with the early training.

When Sir Samuel turned three, he could finally be ridden—well, after even more training.

"All right lad." Devlin led Samuel over to the mounting block where Rory waited with a big grin on his face. "Lay yourself across the saddle, easy like, on your stomach. That way you can just slide off if he objects."

Samuel's only reaction to the weight was to shift his legs. "I'm doing it! I'm riding him," Rory said laughing hysterically, his face red from being face down.

Devlin laughed. "Well, maybe not riding. But you're certainly atop him."

Over the next weeks, Samuel and his stable mates became accustomed to having riders atop. First in the stall, then led around the shed row, then to a paddock, and finally out to a field. Soon, they were responding only to the cues from their riders. The horses were ready for track training—the whole reason for their existence.

Sometimes Rory daydreamed what it would be like to have Samel as his own. Just a regular horse on a regular farm, where the horses did plow work and grew old together out in the pastures. It would be a small farm but bigger than the one he was born on. He saw himself astride Samel, the best and handsomest horse in the county, riding into town or making calls to his neighbors.

"Rory!" Devlin's yell ended his daydreaming. "Jaysus, boy. Where the hell were you? I just wasted my breath."

"Sorry. I got lost in my own thoughts. What were you saying?" asked Rory with a guilty look on his face. That would never be his life. Nor Samel's.

"Today you'll be watching how your horses do against the others on the small track."

"I wish I could be the one riding Samel," said Rory. It came out almost a whine, embarrassing him.

Devlin gave him a sharp look. "Good God. What in the world is wrong with you today? Get your head on straight. Remember, Rory, you're not a jockey; you're a trainer of racehorses. Note I said horses. And Samuel is just one of them. Rory, you have a knack for this work, which makes you special. Not many have it. But it won't be worth a damned thing if you don't get your mind straight."

The words *knack* and *special* got through to Rory's brain. Devlin really thought that?

"Can I at least ride him on my off time? Just in the fields, at a slow canter? It's like we each have the same fun when we're riding."

"Of course, Rory," said Devlin, shaking his head. "Maybe it's the faerie dust, or some such, that blew over you two, but you two do have a rare something."

Devlin's approval was high praise indeed, and Rory took it to heart. It was as if a switch clicked on in Rory's brain. He took to his trade with a seriousness that belied his eleven years.

Using one of his sketch pads, he made charts on each of the four three-year-olds he had been assigned, one of whom was Samel. What they ate, their exercise schedule, their schooling, who rode them... He studiously avoided any favoritism.

"Rory, these charts are great," Devlin exclaimed. "I keep notes; you've seen them, but they're just scribblings for me. These are real training plans for each horse I assigned you. You've got their times, their distances, how they break out..."

He put his arm around Rory's shoulders. "You even included which trainer they prefer and which pony horse they like."

Rory basked in the praise.

He tried to treat each of his horses the same. They were expensive, coddled commodities, ready for sale and their first races. Some of them would be sold to other stables before they even ran a race. Rory told himself he was prepared for their sales but knew he would never be ready if it were Samel. He put that thought out of his mind.

In the racehorse business, working at a place like Campbell's Stables, automatically increased a person's reputation as a horseman of prominence. Rory settled in to learn everything there was to know, and there was none better to teach him than Devlin.

Chapter 15

1906–1907

Bridie was surprised how Mr. Nutting called on the sisters for no apparent reason. He had never come around the first few years she had been working for them. Why was he going out of his way now to talk with the Flemings about their affairs? She giggled. Good Lord, could he be wooing one of them? Or were things worse than he implied?

Bridie became convinced of that on his last visit. After escorting him into the library, she listened through the door she'd left ajar. He was an insincere man and seemed to take enjoyment in delivering his news, further cementing her mistrust. She couldn't help but feel he was there for his own selfish interests.

"Ladies, I do have some bad news. The president has asked us bankers to personally speak with each of our clients to reassure them that all is well with the South Carolina Bank of Charleston. I'm sure you know that the profitability of banks relies on the financial health of the economy of the whole country, not just locally." He cleared his throat.

"There have been rumors of a recession, though mostly in the northeast. It's those blasted New Yorkers, and it's trickled down here some. We seem to be going through a little hiccup." He paused. "You know, I always like to visit you both. You have such a lovely home.

"These ups and downs are not unusual in the banking world, you understand. You don't have to worry your little heads. Our bank is in no danger of insolvency. But in respect to your father, may he rest in peace, I wanted to allay your fears, in case you hear any rumors."

"We appreciate your concern, Mr. Nutting. I'm sure you'll keep us up to date," said Miss Elizabeth curtly. She called for Bridie and asked her to see Mr. Nutting out.

Bridie escorted him to the door, then returned to the library with tea and shortbreads, beginning to compete with the scones as the sisters' favorites. Sitting herself down, she joined them. They sat quietly, the only sounds, small sips and satisfied bites. The sisters looked remarkably calm, considering the news.

"Bridie," said Miss Elizabeth, "I'm sure you heard what he had to say. It is a bit worrying, but he reassured us it's only a passing event and we'll be fine. Though I do still wish it was the president who had given us the news."

Miss Mary chimed in. "You can bet it would have been him if Father was still alive. It's because we're just women; all the more reason for us to be careful with our money. You're in your seventies already, Eliza…"

"Mary! For mercy sake! My age is my business, no one else's." She gave Bridie a terse nod. "Even if it is you."

Miss Mary tried to keep a straight face. "I'm sorry Elizabeth. But look at how the time has gone by. If one of us gets sick, we'll need a nurse to take care of us. Bridie, you won't be able to do it all."

Bridie kept a respectful look on her face. Nice to know they had no intention of letting her go anytime soon. "Ladies, I am honored that you feel comfortable sharing such information with me. I will keep it as the confidence it is.

"But I can't help but think his sudden interest in your finances is selfish on Mr. Nutting's part. He does seem a bit sneaky, doesn't he? It's as if he's checking out your home for himself. If things do go bad, I bet he'll be the first person to make you an offer on your house."

She was convinced that her employers were woefully unprepared for any disruption in their precarious finances. It really was time to open their minds to the monetary possibilities in their own house. Well, there was no use in waiting, especially as she suspected that Mr. Nutting's news was far worse than what he'd led them to believe. She shifted uncomfortably in her chair.

"I hope you don't think I'm too forward. And I mean no disrespect to you and your family, particularly in relation to your home. I've come to love this house over these years." The two women preened, looking at her expectantly.

"Maybe you should think of ways to bring in extra money, just in case. You could sell some of your belongings…" The glowing looks turned to frowns.

"Wait, wait. Just hear me out. I know everything here is very special to you. But… well, just to start with, look at this room. There are hundreds of books in here. Do you need them all?"

She rushed on. "Obviously, you'd keep your favorites. And thanks to your encouragement, I've got some favorites now too. Those alone will take up a wall. But the rest of them? All those law books that can't fit in your father's study upstairs? You might get a good price for them. Maybe you could turn the room into something else."

"Bridie. This time you have really overstepped your bounds," Miss Elizabeth said, staring over her lorgnette at Bridie, never a good sign. "Really. We could never dishonor Father's memory so."

Bridie nodded. Well, she had planted the seed. She stood up, gathering the tea items onto the tray. "I am sorry. You know I mean no disrespect to either of you or to your father. It was just a thought, maybe a way to cushion your financial state."

To Bridie, the sisters seemed to live in a perpetual fog of memories. During her daily ministrations, the house had revealed its beauty to her. She understood that each item in their home held great value to the women, touchstones to their past, but that emotional investment was a problem. Bridie hoped she could make them look at their home as a place filled with items that they could sell to support themselves while still living in it.

A pawn shop could be a quick and easy way, and there were quite a few around the city. But there was the issue of sordidness. Just to test how it was done, Bridie brought in her father's watch to one shop that she passed frequently—Uncle Morris's Pawn Shop, right on Market Street. The kindly gentleman behind the desk was anything but sordid. He proudly told her he had been in business since 1892 and told her that Uncle Sam's Pawn Shop, around the corner, was run by his cousin. "We're both honest as the day is long."

Bridie left feeling comfortable that she could at least mention pawning to the Flemings. And she was tickled to find out that he would pay five dollars for the watch. "This is a handsome watch, ma'am. I can tell you've wound it each day because it still keeps perfect time. Your father would be proud."

She visited the Charleston Museum and the Charleston Library Society, neither of which she had been inside. The respectful silence was soothing and enticed her to make return visits, many with Brendan, who loved seeing what each museum had. They became regulars at the library, with Brendan doing much of his schoolwork there.

With the librarian's help, Bridie's readings were expanding beyond the Flemings' books. She began taking books home to the ladies, and they took turns reading them out loud during tea. They called themselves The

Fleming Literary Society. Presently, they were reading *Black Beauty*, which had the three of them in tears, Bridie in particular.

"Oh, that terrible Nicholas Skinner. How can people be so cruel to animals? We had a donkey back on the farm. His name was Samuel. Samel, Rory called him. The two of them were so connected it was eerie. They'd stand head-to-head, Rory's arms wrapped around the donkey's neck, joined together like one. Like they were talking to each other through their skins."

"That's such a sweet story, dear. I keep forgetting you had another boy," Miss Mary said, patting Bridie's hand.

Bridie sniffled and wiped the tears away. "Oh God, I hope poor Rory is alive and healthy and happy."

Going to the museums and seeing items presented in such reverent displays changed her perception of everything she had been routinely dusting and cleaning in the Flemings' house. And it gave her an inkling of how the sisters might feel about parting with objects that held such meaning for them. If they had to sell, maybe they'd feel encouraged to sell to these institutions that treated everything with such respect. Perhaps she would suggest an excursion for them all. They could go on a Saturday and take Brendan. They loved Brendan.

⚜

Mr. Nutting showed up early in the morning of October 18, banging at the front door. He was puffed up with importance, and his hair and suit were askew.

Practically panting, he said, "Now is the time, ladies. Go today, immediately, and take out your money.
There might not be anything left by this afternoon. As
it is, the bank is unable to pay me, or anyone else for
that matter. That's gratitude for you."

The three women stared at each other in shock. His
appearance, his words, his tone were that of a madman.
"That crisis I told you about? The one in New York?
Now, they're calling it a Bankers' Panic! It's reached
here, and I fear a run on the bank. I suggest you go
down there immediately. The end is nigh!"

He started for the door, then spun around. "If you
find yourselves penniless, I would be more than happy
to make an offer on your house. It's the least I can do
to help you and honor your father's memory." Bridie
escorted the agitated man to the door.

"Good gracious me," Miss Elizabeth gasped. "The
man's lost his mind. Bridie, you were right about him
wanting our house. I'd rather die than sell it to him."

Bridie nodded solemnly. "Well, I don't want to be
right about something like that. But we should believe
him about the bank. Let's get ourselves down there
right now."

By the time they got to the bank, with Miss Mary
leading the way and Bridie pushing Miss Elizabeth
in the unwieldy wheelchair, there were already about
a hundred people waiting outside the building, with
more arriving by the minute. The gold eagle shined
sternly down upon them. "I wonder if Mr. Nutting told
all these people too," Miss Elizabeth muttered.

After two hours, they were let in by a guard, the doors shut behind them. The president, and other bank officers, went up to each customer to apologize. Because of the runs on the banks in New York, all banks in the country were limited to how much cash a customer could withdraw. Arriving so early, the sisters were among the lucky ones, able to take out the maximum, $1,500 in cash. Who knew if they'd ever see their remaining money?

They were gently ushered out with whispered apologies. The three women turned around at the sound of the doors being locked and the blinds pulled down. Bridie shuddered. They were the last to leave.

That afternoon's tea was a dour affair. "I should have listened to you sooner, Bridie. And you too, Mary," Miss Elizabeth said, between her tears and hiccups. She laughed joylessly. "Well, we finally met with the president, Mary."

"Yes, we did," Miss Mary said. "So much for that. Well, we certainly aren't the only ones in this predicament."

"Ladies," Bridie said. "I think you should stop paying me. At least until this crisis is over. We need to conserve every cent we have." Good Lord. When did *she* and *they* become *we*?

Miss Mary went to the pantry and returned with a whiskey bottle and three glasses.

Elizabeth gasped. "Good Lord, Mary. In the afternoon? I thought we were saving that for a celebration."

"Elizabeth, at the rate things are going, we may

never celebrate anything again. Right now, I could use a drink, and it won't hurt you either. Bridie, dear, I know you're Irish, and I know how you all drink, but you should be prepared. This is Old Grand-Dad, 100 proof."

She filled each glass half full. "This was Father's pure sippin' bourbon. Sip carefully, ladies."

Bridie felt like the wind had been knocked out of her. "Lord!" she hissed. "I don't think I've ever had anything quite like that, even in Ireland."

Both sisters' eyes were teary. "Just like Father said. Not for the faint of heart," little Miss Mary wheezed, as she topped off their glasses with what was left in the bottle.

Chapter 16

1907–1909

When Rory was thirteen, his world changed. Devlin, who had hardly touched his dinner, told him to stay seated. "Leave the dishes for now. We have something to talk about."

Rory's first thought was Samel. Something's happened to him, or Oliver's gone and sold him.

Devlin read his mind. "It's not Samuel. He's fine. But it's time to talk about your future here at Campbell's. You're still young, but you need to think about it. It should be you who decides what that future is. Not me or Oliver."

Rory looked at him in surprise. "My future? Here, I hope."

Devlin nodded. "If I could, I'd have you live here forever and hand off all my work to you. And if that's what you choose, I'd be happy.

"But before you came here, you were headed to America with your family. A whole different future.

Have you forgotten that?"

Rory suddenly felt a guilty helplessness. He hadn't thought about America or his family in a long time. Even Mammy. It was like they were inside a locked china cabinet. He could sometimes see them but couldn't get close enough to touch them.

"I don't know. When I first got here, I missed them so much, especially Mammy. I dreamed about finding them, but then, with Samel and you... It's not that I never think of them, but they're blurry in the back of my mind.

"I love Samel and all the other horses, and I love training them. When I do think of Mammy and my brothers, they're like shadows. Are they even alive? Did they make it to Charleston? Are they in another city? Did they come back to Ireland? Could I even find them? What if I never find them?"

By now he was almost crying. "I wish I could do both."

Devlin reached out a hand to him. "Maybe we can make it work, so you sort of do both. Do you want to stay in the horse business?"

"I guess so," Rory said. "It's all I know." He gave Devlin a worried look. "But, yeah, sometimes I dream I'll get to Charleston and find them."

Devlin nodded. "I always thought you'd leave one day to find your family. It's only natural, and it's what I would do, if it were me. There is a lot of horse racing in America, so you'll have no trouble finding work. Especially with the letters of introduction Oliver and I will give you.

"No matter where you end up, stay with horses, lad. It's your destiny. You understand them, and you're really good, a natural horseman. Stay here for at least another year or so, and I'll teach you everything I know to help you to become the best trainer you can be. Then we'll talk about America."

After Rory went to bed, Devlin stayed up smoking his pipe and sipping on a whiskey. He felt miserable, but hopeful. He had done what he had to do, and Rory had accepted what he had suggested. Unsurprising, really. Since his first day with Devlin, Rory had surpassed every expectation Devlin had for him.

Oliver had come to Devlin the day before, a somber look on his face. "We need to talk about Rory. As you know, the mistress never wanted Rory to stay here, but I knew she'd forget about him if she didn't see him. I never told you, but after she saw him when we were loading Princess Lily, she had a bit of a nervous breakdown. That's what she called it. I call it a tantrum."

He gave a grim smile. "Call it what you want, but take it from me. She can be spiteful, and I don't want her to use that on him. She will if she sees him, and Rory doesn't deserve that. The lad's older now, taking on more responsibility and beginning to be known in our world and eventually it will reach her ears. You and I both want the best for him."

Somehow Devlin hid what he was thinking. In all his years working for Oliver, he had never seen him be mean. Angry, sometimes. But always fair and honest. How did Oliver stay with someone so awful? Devlin remembered the pain that crossed Oliver's face when he talked about his dead son. It was true, you never knew what went on behind closed doors. What a burden Oliver carried.

"I brought Rory to you, Devlin, hoping I could still play a small part in his life. Watching him grow up, seeing him become a young trainer has been one of the best things in my life. I'm grateful and proud of you and him."

"Thank you, Oliver. Those are very kind words. But don't belittle your part in his life too. Having Rory with me has been wonderful, and when he leaves, you and I will both be lost. Between us, we've raised a good lad."

Two years later, Rory was in Belfast, working at Down Royal Racecourse. It had been a shock, but Devlin had prepared him well, and the head trainer, Sean Cullen, was a friend of Devlin's. Rory was treated the same as the other trainers, but Rory knew Sean was watching out for him.

Down Royal was all business and a huge one at that; Campbell's was a small, cozy barn in comparison. He missed Devlin and Samel, but he was too busy to dwell on them. The work, the hustle, left him little time to be homesick.

Now that he had left Campbell's, and realized he could live on his own, he began rethinking about going to America. Devlin was right. There were thousands of racecourses in America, many more famous than Down Royal. And maybe one of them would take him to Charleston.

❧

In October 1909, Rory saw Samuel run at Down Royal. Not just run! He won the champion race during the National Hunt Festival, running for Campbell's Stables.

As an employee of Down Royal, he had his own jobs and nothing to do with the care or training of Samel while he was stabled at Down Royal. But on his off time, Rory could be found in his stall. Oliver and Devlin didn't mind. They hoped it would make Samel even faster. There was no proof to that idea, but he did break the record when he ran.

The three of them had plans for dinner, but before leaving, they made a stop at Samel's stall. The horse whinnied loudly when he saw them, and Rory went into the stall. Devlin and Oliver stepped back, watching as if bewitched.

"What a horse you are," Rory whispered into Samel's soft ears. "What a wonderful friend you are." The horse snuffled around Rory's face, then nickered his way to a pocket with a treat. Rory continued whispering, the horse nickering as they put their heads together. Rory felt he was inside Samel's brain, both of them remembering their times together. Then he remembered Samel, the donkey, his brothers, his mother, his da…

At dinner, after telling tales of horses and racing, Rory told Devlin and Oliver his plans.

"I've decided I will go to America. I've learned it's not that hard to move and take on new jobs. I was afraid to leave Campbell's and come here, but once I was here, it was just another barn with different horses. I've been saving my money, and soon I'll have enough to go to America. And if I can't find my family, or if I don't like the work, I can save and come back here.

"Sean gave me the name of a trainer who used to work for him and is now the manager of Belmont Park. He said it's one of the biggest tracks in New York. Have you ever heard of it?"

The two men grinned. Devlin slapped his hand on the table. "Belmont! Oh my, lad. That is one of the most famous tracks in the world."

"Good for you, Rory. You've earned it." The two men looked at each other, nodding, the pride in their faces evident to anyone passing by.

Chapter 17

1907–1908

"Finn, get back here right this minute," Bridie screamed. "What in God's name is going on with you?"

His mother's words rang in Finn's ears. He couldn't have answered her even if he had wanted to. What was happening to him? Where was the boy who helped Mam get through those early years? The one who took care of his little brother, helped her in the house, did errands, helped Ian fix up their little cabin?

When he turned thirteen it was as if the devil had taken him over. Now, two years later, it had only gotten worse. He got in fights at school on the days he didn't skip. He took to hanging around street corners with a gang of other boys, all rough, rowdy loafers. They called themselves the Red Boys.

"Red Boys? What kind of dumb name is that?" Bridie asked one night.

"It's because most of the other kids' das are Red Shirts."

"Oh Jaysus. I've heard of them. They go around in their red shirts, with guns and sabers, bullying people. Some of them are on horses and chase people down."

"Mammy, they don't. During the elections, they ride horses in the parades. Most of them are businessmen, and a lot are Irish. They're looking out for us, the little guys, who no one cares about. You should be happy, Mam. Our group of Red Boys is all Irish," he snapped at her.

"Stupid name for stupid boys. Nothing good comes from lads ganging up together. Drinking and fighting and who knows what else. It's like your da all over again, except you're just boys. He was part of a gang, too, and look what happened to him."

That's all she did now—yell at him. Finn skulked off to his room. His stomach was killing him; like a pool of bitter poison was in it. It was always there, eating at him, ever reminding him of what a low Irish mick he was. Look at where he lived, for God's sake. In a slave shack! Sure, Ian had fixed it up real nice—and with his help, thank you very much. But it was still just a shack. And those two old hags his mam worked for? Who didn't pay her for years while she worked herself to the bone for them? Them with their privileged Scots ways.

Even back in Ireland, his own country, Catholics were treated like shit. Look at what happened to Da. Defenseless, in a jail cell and murdered by the feckin' Brits. Mam had told him and Brendan about it. Not the details, but Finn could figure it out. He could still remember their home back in Newry, a dank, dark, smoky hovel, like all the rest of them. In Ireland and here, the Irish were always at the bottom of the heap. The only ones lower were the Negroes.

And Mam? What happened to her? When did she get so feckin' nasty, lording it over him? After everything he had done for her? He knew she blamed him for Rory, even though she didn't come out and say it. How could that be his fault? He was only six then. And what about Rory? He was the stupid brat who ran away, like he always did. Sometimes it seemed like she couldn't hardly stand being in the same room with him.

But she sure doted on Brendan. "This little man is going to go to college, you just wait and see." Well, Brendan wasn't so perfect either. If he did go, it's all because his big brother practically raised him.

Finn couldn't help it. The poison inside galled him and ate at him like acid.

The only place he found relief was with his gang, who all were going through the same things.

He knew many people thought that the Red Shirts were like the Ku Klux Klan, but they weren't. The Klan were just stupid men in costumes with white hoods, looting and murdering and trying to look scary beside their burning crosses. No wonder they were banned, even though that didn't stop them.

The Red Shirts weren't like that. They were a social club, a rifle and saber club where anyone interested in gun knowledge, law and order, and the Democratic

Party could meet. It was because of the Red Shirts and their motto, "Force Without Violence," that the Democrats were now in charge in South Carolina, looking out for the little guy. And whatever that little guy might have, the Red Shirts would help him to keep it. Sure, there had been some scuffles and such, but they were defending themselves against bad people.

It was his friend Jimmy Sweeney who got him interested in the boys' group. They had been classmates since first grade. Because Finn had started first grade so late, all the kids called him names—eegit, halfwit, mama's boy. All because Mam had made him stay home and take care of his baby brother. Jimmy was the only one who didn't pick on him.

They became friends. Neither of them liked school, and they started skipping out, then playing hooky regularly. Soon they were best mates, hanging out at Jimmy's place, usually empty during the day. It was big and took up the two floors above Sweeney's Tavern.

His da owned the whole building and worked at his pub till all hours. Jimmy's two older brothers were policemen and worked at the tavern on their time off. Jimmy's mam had died when he was five, and he had pretty much raised himself. He and Finn practiced rifle and saber tactics that Jimmy's brothers taught them. The two boys snuck beers and boasted of feats to come when they became Red Shirts.

Once Mam asked about his friend. "Why don't you bring that Jimmy Sweeney you're always talking about home? I think I met his father one time on one of my walks. He's got a tavern, right? Sweeney's? He's the one who told me about that earthquake that happened here."

⌒⌒⌒

Jimmy was dying to see the mansion, and Finn's house. "Didn't you tell me your cabin was once a slave shack? Ain't you scared of gettin' lice or something? You know, lice from niggers live forever. I bet you never went into the mansion, though, did you? Those old ladies wouldn't let a lowlife like you into their place."

"Did too. I been in there plenty of times. Look who's talking, Mista Bogtrotter himself. I'll even get you in there. Tomorrow."

Small as it was, Finn knew his home was nicer than Jimmy's place, thanks to Ian and himself. Though he'd never say so to Jimmy's face. The Sweeneys two floors were big, but no one kept it up. It was dirty and dark; near the docks; and stank of men, beer, and fish.

On Tuesdays, now that the bitchier one could get out in her wheelchair, the two old biddies went with Bridie to the market, leaving the big house empty for the morning. The two boys watched the three ladies leave, then snuck in the gate and around to the back, where they went into the kitchen.

Jimmy's mouth fell open. "Holy feckin' shit. Look at the size of this place." He didn't linger and headed for the door that led to the rest of the house.

"Wait," Finn yelled. But Jimmy didn't stop, and Finn had to follow.

Within minutes Finn wanted to leave the house. His stomach was aboil as he watched Jimmy open every door, race along the upstairs corridor, test the beds, and slide down the banister. Downstairs, he fondled knickknacks with his dirty hands, items Finn knew had been carefully dusted and shined by his mother.

In the library, Jimmy pulled open a drawer. "Holy shit. Look at these." Inside were guns, neatly laid out with written labels underneath. "A whole feckin' collection. Can you imagine what Da would say about one of these?"

"Jimmy, close the damn drawer. God, I knew I should never have let you in here."

"What're you scared of? Afraid the old ladies will come back?" But he shrugged and followed Finn.

Back in the kitchen, Jimmy pulled open drawers and cabinets, rifled through the ice box, slugged down milk from the bottle, grabbed some cookies from a plate. "Well, why not? They're just sittin' there waitin' to be eaten," he mumbled, a milk mustache working his upper lip, crumbs slipping from the lower.

"Jimmy, you're disgusting. Stop. We gotta go now. They usually get back around eleven, and it's quarter of now."

"You're worried about two old ladies?"

"Well, yeah, you eegit. My mam works here. If she gets fired, we're homeless."

"Okay. Don't be such a holy Joe. Anyway, you won't be homeless, cause you're practically livin' with us already."

They went out the back door and stopped at the shack. Jimmy just glanced inside from the porch. "It looks okay, considering what it was. I just don't need to see the inside of an old slave cabin. A little spooky, you know?"

Finn sneered. "Scared of ghosts, are you? I'd never thought that of you."

He jumped at the sound of the front gate opening. "Shite. They're back. Get in."

Jimmy held back, but Finn shoved him inside. "God, you're such a baby. Mam can see out to here from the kitchen window, and the only way out to the street is past that window to the front gate. So we'll just have to wait. In an hour, she'll be serving them their lunch in the dining room, and we can leave then. Come on, let's play a game of poker."

Ten minutes later, Bridie wrenched open the door to the cottage. Both boys jumped. "Oh, there's two of you? Sometimes Finn, I am dumbfounded by your brainlessness."

The boys stared at Bridie.

"Stand up, both of you. I don't know whose idea this was, but the next time you decide to break into someone's house, I'd hope you'd use more sense. The front gate was open, you moved stuff around inside, left crumbs and milk in the kitchen, and the back door was half open.

"And you? Jimmy Sweeney, I'm guessing. I think I met your father once. Does your father know what you do in your spare time?"

"Oh Mam. I was just showing him the place." Finn raised his chin. Couldn't let Jimmy see him scared.

"Oh, really. So, Jimmy! What's in your pocket there? Yeah, that one. The one that's bulging. Well, now, if it isn't one of Judge Fleming's guns. Hand it over, you eegit. I should use it on you, you little bugger." She turned to Finn. "I can't believe a son of mine would associate with a common thief. Get the hell out of here, both of you."

Jimmy took off running. Finn stayed behind long enough to yell, "You think you're so high and mighty, Mam. You're not. You're just common yourself."

More and more, Finn stayed over at Jimmy's place. Sometimes a few of the other Red Boys stayed too. They usually had to, after all the beer Mr. Sweeney let them drink.

The few times Finn went home, it always ended in a fight. Quitting school was the final insult. Mam went berserk.

"After everything we've gone through? And you're just going to throw it all away? You think your da would want you to quit school? He went to college. God, how did I raise such an eegit?"

"Yeah, and that sure got him far, didn't it, Mam? He was just another mick that got killed by the British. Me? I'm smart Irish. I'll lay low, work in a job, stay out of sight, and keep on training so I can become a Red Shirt." The words came out like vomit.

"You know what they call us Irish, Mam? You who's been working herself to the bone for those old bitches? 'Negroes turned inside out,' or worse, 'Smoked Irish.' You're nothing to those two. Just a nigger for them to boss around."

Bridie slapped him. They stood staring at each other in shocked silence.

Brendan stayed in the bedroom during their fights, but at the sound of the slap, he appeared beside Bridie. "Finn? What's happening to you? How can you talk to Mam this way?"

"Shite. Now I have to hear it from my feckin' baby brother too? I'm leaving."

"Good," Bridie yelled. "Get out. I never want to see you again. You have dishonored your family with your foul words."

Finn banged out the door and ran to the Sweeneys', where he was warmly welcomed.

"Glad to have you, lad," said Mr. Sweeney. "You can use the room you usually stay in, but I'll take a bit in rent when you start workin'. Four bucks a day. That's what you'd pay in a rooming house."

The next day Finn went back to the cottage to pack some clothes. One of the older Sweeney brothers, still in uniform, went with him. "Just in case there's a problem," he said.

Finn's stomach curdled. The man was talking about his mother and two old ladies! He just wanted to cry and curl up into a ball.

Jimmy had already quit school and was working at

the Charleston Consolidated Railway, the city's electric trolley system. Finn got a job there, too, in their car maintenance space, known as the Trolley Barn. The boys had to ride two trolleys to get there. Finn didn't mind. He was making money, no one was nagging him, and he enjoyed the ride, looking at the different neighborhoods of Charleston.

At night in bed, though, the image of Mam yelling, with the veins in her neck standing out below her red face, took months to go away.

Chapter 18

1908–1910

Bridie felt like a body of holes, hollows left by missing people: Mam, Da, Charles, Rory, and now Finn. Why did she have to yell at him? Bridie brooded, hating him and herself. Why could she not say, I love you and I want you safe? All the fear and love came out as angry words.

Since he had stormed out, she felt she was in mourning. She moved slowly, spoke only when necessary, ate and slept little. If she could have, she would have stayed abed all day. She would have worn all black, so the world could know what happened to her. She was thirty-two and felt fifty-two. The cottage and the big house both showed signs of her neglect. Her cooking was hit or miss; the kitchen counters were littered with crumbs and dirty dishes filled the sink.

The sisters cornered Brendan one afternoon on his return from school. They had been waiting on the piazza and called him over with waves and stage whispers.

"We have to be quiet. Bridie's inside, but she's in the kitchen. Doing what, I have no idea. We haven't had a decent meal in weeks," Miss Elizabeth hissed through pursed lips, though her face was worried.

"Elizabeth, there's no need for sarcasm. It's just that we are terribly worried about your mother, Brendan. She's not herself."

Brendan was worried too. But he knew his mother wouldn't want him telling tales to the ladies. They were her bosses, after all.

"She's going through a bad time, what with Finn gone. She just misses him. I'm sure she'll get over it soon."

But Brendan was terribly worried. He had never seen her like this. Maybe when Da died or Rory was lost, but he was just a baby then. He went to Hayne Street and asked Shirley for her help.

The next day in Bridie's cottage, Shirley was watching her friend shakily put the kettle on the stove.

"Good Lord, Bridie. Look at you," Shirley said. "Sit down, lovie, and let me do that. I knew you hadn't been to Mass lately or the Hibernian. I was worried, but I just figured you weren't feeling well. The monthlies or something. But when Brendan came to me, I knew it must be serious. Excuse me for saying it, but you look bloody awful. Whatever is going on?"

"Jaysus, Shirley. Can't a woman just be alone for a while?"

She had no intention of telling Shirley, or anyone else for that matter, what had happened between herself and Finn. But she betrayed herself by bursting into tears and blubbering out the whole story.

Shirley was shocked. "That ungrateful little brat."

"Oh, Shirley, don't say that. He is, but in a way, he's the one who's had it the worst. Lost his da, his home, his wee brother, and all when he was only six. I know he's blamed himself, and if I'm being honest, I did too. Oh, not openly, but he knew. I couldn't help it. That's why this is so awful for me. I caused this. And how is all this going to affect Brendan?"

Shirley wrapped her arms around Bridie. "Let me give you a big hug, you poor thing. You are not a bad mother. And you've had to do it all alone. I know, and I only have one child. Brendan will be just fine. Don't be so hard on yourself."

She moved over to the stove and poured the hot water into the teapot. "Do you have anything sweet down here, like your scones, or did those two old biddies eat them all?"

Bridie couldn't help but smile at Shirley's cheekiness. "I haven't baked in days, but there could be some shortbread cookies up in the cupboard there. They last forever, thank goodness."

Shirley took a bite of shortbread. "You're right, they're stale. But a dip in the tea will perk them up." They sipped their tea in companionable silence.

Shirley looked at Bridie. "Remember what you told me way back? When we became friends? I was so shy and worried about being pregnant without a husband. And you just said it was a new country, no one knew my story, and it was none of their damn business. Just make up my own history and stick to it. It was the best advice anyone ever gave me.

"Believe me when I say that you are a good mother and a good person. Finn's a young man now, and he will make his own way. And one day he'll come back."

After Shirley left, Bridie sat at the table mulling over what they had talked about. It was as if she had a committee of crazy people in her head, all telling her how bad she was. But, thanks to Shirley's words, her own voice began to come through, reminding her of who she really was and all she had done.

Ever since Charles had died, it was she, alone, who took on everything life had thrown at her. Finn's leaving was just one more hurdle that she could rise above. And he wasn't dead—just away.

Bridie felt a small glimmer of her old self returning. She took a bath, put on a clean dress, and went up to the big house, dreading what it must look like.

She found Miss Mary in the kitchen making tea for herself and her sister. "Oh, Bridie, dear. We've missed you so." She looked around the kitchen. "I tried to keep it as tidy as you do."

"I can see that, Miss Mary," Bridie said, holding back the tears that wanted to flow.

"By the way, there's a letter that arrived for you to-day. From Ireland."

"Oh, look at that." Bridie took the envelope, her hand trembling a bit. "It's from my friend Kathleen. Remember when you went with me to mail her a letter?

I'll read it later. For now, how about I fix us all tea and join you both in the library?"

Kathleen wrote back! Bridie was amazed. She never really thought her letter would be answered. She wondered if Aileen, her shipmate from Loughgilly, had received her letter too. It was shocking to realize ten years had passed since she'd arrived in Charleston. Wouldn't that be a small miracle if they could reconnect? She had become proudly self-reliant, but that shouldn't mean abandoning her few friends.

During tea, she gave the sisters a cleaned-up version of Finn's leaving and how hard it was on her. "I guess I just wasn't ready for him to leave yet." She swiped at the tears that suddenly sprang up. "Sorry. I still feel a bit lost, as you can tell."

Miss Mary patted Bridie's hand. "Dear, it's all right. We understand, don't we, Elizabeth?"

"It must be part of growing up," Miss Elizabeth said, looking a bit tearful herself. "You're a good mother, Bridie. In time he'll come back."

Bridie was touched, especially as the kind words came from Miss Elizabeth.

Kathleen's letter was just like her, chatty and gossipy. She still worked at the hotel, now in charge of the restaurant. She had married five years before.

"Oh, Bridie, he was a looker, just like your Charles. But gone all the time too, and NOT on noble work, which at least Charles thought he was doing. No, he was doing very little

work, in fact, all while carrying on with a few hussies. One had the nerve to come to the restaurant and yelled at me to 're-lease' him. Can you believe that? I had her tossed. Remember the doorman? The one who had a crush on you? (He says hello, by the way!) I brought him home with me and had him throw the bastard from the house. Now I just see men who are easily released! Ha, ha. It's just me and my two lassies. I'm teaching them well what to look for in a man..."

It occurred to Bridie to ask Kathleen about Rory. The last time she went to customs to ask about him, the man, a boy really, and a rude one at that, told her to stop asking. "Lady, it's been ten years. Give it up and move on." It was all Bridie could do not to slap him.

She wrote to Kathleen that very night and asked if she'd heard anything about Rory, even though she knew deep in her heart that the rude customs agent was probably right.

She met Ian for a coffee one day at the Kaffee Store, a new German bakery that served excellent coffee to go with their even better pastries. Ian was like an older brother to Finn.

"Aw, Bridie. I'm sorry for both of you. I remember what it was like at that age. Me and my parents got into it all the time. Then they both died, right after I'd had a big row with them."

Bridie was surprised. "You never told me that. At the same time?"

"Yes. It was just a horrible accident. After a row, over something stupid, as it always is with cocky young lads. I had stormed out and stayed the night with a mate in town. Somehow, during the night, while they slept, an explosion from the gas line blew them and the house apart. Of course, I blamed myself, though now I know the only thing that would have happened was my death too. After we buried them, I was at a loss. I was the last of six kids, and each one of them offered me a place to live. I was honored, and it was generous of them."

"Oh, Ian, I'm so sorry for you. Why didn't you stay if you had family there?"

"I don't know. I couldn't get beyond my guilt, I guess. At first, I thought I would stay, but then I just felt I had to get away and make a new start. I saw an advert in the paper for a carpentry apprenticeship with free passage on a ship leaving from Newry to Charleston, and… well, you know the rest."

Bridie gave his hand a squeeze. "And thank God you did. I don't know what I would have done without your help. You were then the same age as Finn is now. I can't imagine him making such a grownup decision." She gave a small laugh. "Well, maybe he just has, hasn't he? Though grownup might not be the right word to describe it."

Ian nodded. "I don't know, Bridie. I don't think I was acting maturely, and I do miss my family. I think I just wanted to run away from the guilt I felt. But I miss my brothers and sisters. I've written to them all, and they've accepted my apologies, but I still regret how I left."

He took another sip of coffee. "Finn will come round. It just takes a while. If you want me to, I can talk to him for you."

"No, you don't have to. Not for me anyway. If you want to see him on your own, go ahead. Maybe he'll listen to you. I guess he's living with the Sweeneys, over the tavern." A strange look passed over Ian's face. It happened so quickly, Bridie thought she had imagined it. "It will be good for him to see someone he likes, someone who's normal and not involved in those silly Red Boys."

The three of them, Bridie and the two sisters, sometimes four if Brendan was available, became frequent visitors at the museums and library. Miss Elizabeth was reluctant at first, but between Bridie and Miss Mary, she was persuaded to go on the outings. One day, they ventured to the Charleston Museum, promising her she'd enjoy seeing the elegant china, furniture, and art in the collection. Brendan went along to help with the wheelchair and carry Miss Elizabeth's umbrella. It was he who called attention to a special exhibit.

"Wait till you see this exhibit, Miss Mary. It's all guns, like the ones you have in the library, except way more."

Bridie had begun to suspect that Miss Mary was starting to come around to the idea of selling some of the family treasures, but Miss Elizabeth would not even discuss the subject. Now Bridie saw a light in Miss Mary's eyes and knew they both had the same thought: they would start with the guns. Miss Elizabeth didn't give a hoot for guns.

Miss Mary whipped the wheelchair around before her sister went further. "Elizabeth, come along now. I know you're not interested in guns and insist on storing Father's collection out of sight in that chest. But I find them quite fascinating."

"You were just trying to impress Father."

"Really, Elizabeth. Don't be so petty. It doesn't become you. You never showed an interest in guns, and I did. So, Father talked to me about them: who owned them, how he got them, what kind they were. He even let me help clean them. Some are quite beautiful, with decorative carvings and etchings on the silver inlays—one is even inlaid with gold. It won't hurt for us to at least look."

Afterwards, almost as a rebuke to her sister, Miss Elizabeth insisted they go back to the section displaying clothing and textiles. On the way home, Miss Mary chattered. "Maybe we should sell the guns. You certainly will never miss them, Elizabeth."

Bridie winked at Brendan as he rolled Miss Elizabeth home.

~~~

"It's tasteless—vulgar, Mother would say. No one does it, and I don't want people to know my business," Miss

Elizabeth clucked. "Mother and Father would roll over in their graves."

It was another day of listening to the sisters quibble about whether to sell or donate. Finally, Bridie couldn't stand it anymore.

"Good gracious, you two. You're driving me crazy. Just start with the guns. I'll go to the museum and ask for someone to come out and look at them."

A curator from the Charleston Museum came out three days later. After looking at the guns, he requested a tour of the house, especially the closets. Miss Elizabeth nearly had a case of the vapors.

"Sir, could you excuse me for a minute? I have something to discuss with my housekeeper." She rolled herself into the kitchen.

"Bridie," she whispered, "How can we let this man we hardly know upstairs to our private quarters? Well, not anymore, but still. Have you even been up there to clean since we moved downstairs?"

Bridie took a deep breath. "Miss Elizabeth," she said sweetly, "Of course I have. I do the upstairs every Tuesday. And this is Thursday, so it will still be looking tidy. And your sister will be with him."

Miss Mary took the gentleman upstairs while Bridie made tea, Miss Elizabeth sitting stonily in the wheelchair, her fingers tapping the armrests. When he and Miss Mary returned, Bridie served them tea in the parlor.

"Bridie, please pull up a chair for yourself," said Miss Elizabeth. Privately, she may have gotten used to routinely having tea with the maid, but it was still important to keep up proper etiquette in front of others.

Bridie nodded. "Thank you, ma'am."

The gentleman reminded the women that his museum had limited means. Guns and fine antique clothing, though, were items they specialized in, and after going through the elder Flemings' closets, he made a generous offer on their contents and the guns.

He was profusive in his thanks. "Your home is lovely, ladies. You can't know what a privilege it is for me to enter such a well-maintained house. You are to be commended. If we had the means, there would be many more items we'd be interested in."

The sisters preened. Bridie glowed inside.

After he left, rather than have dinner, the sisters retired to the music room, eager to discuss the day's events. "Bridie, just bring us some savory snacks and our sherries here," Miss Elizabeth said. "And bring a glass for yourself."

Miss Mary, the official gun expert, prattled on. "I think we did well. He gave us $200 for all of them: the four Civil War guns, the one from the Revolutionary War, the one from the Spanish American War, and the six newer ones."

"And $250 for the clothes," said Miss Elizabeth, her face looking wistful. "Those gowns of Mother's were so beautiful. But as you both said, they are surely out of style, and none of us will ever wear them. And I had no idea of the number of suits Father had. When I'm feeling wistful, I'll just go to the museum and gaze at them. Maybe on our next walk, we should go into the Gibbes Museum and see how it compares."

Miss Elizabeth now agreed that perhaps there were a few things she could part with. "I'll start with the linens," she said, rolling herself into the pantry. Bridie and Miss Mary smiled at each other.

Miss Mary took on her father's imposing collection of law books, made less so by finding in his files a detailed list of his library. In his study upstairs, the drawers in his massive, ornate desk held a treasure trove of notes, correspondence, and lists. She wrote letters to various libraries and colleges about the collection.

When Miss Elizabeth tired of the linens—she never was able to choose between the multitudes—Bridie rolled her into the library to begin on the books, with instructions to put the keepers in one pile. This proved to be even more daunting as Miss Elizabeth had emotional ties to many of them.

When Bridie returned a few hours later, with tea, Miss Elizabeth was asleep, *Little Women* opened on her lap. There was no pile, only opened books scattered on the table before her.

Miss Mary shook her sister awake. "Elizabeth, dear, I know these are all special to you. They are for me too. But at this rate, it will take you a year to get through one shelf. I'm almost done with Father's law books."

"Well, aren't you just the perfect one. But they're dusty, dry law books, plus Father kept an inventory.

These require care and time," Miss Elizabeth said huffily.

That afternoon, with the cooling hint of fall in the air, they had tea outside on the sisters' lawn, now edged with flowers and shrubs. Bridie and Brendan had planted them the previous fall with input from Miss Mary.

The sisters might be showing more interest in selling some items, but guiltily so. The ghosts of their parents haunted them, especially Miss Elizabeth. Not surprising, Bridie thought. After all, she was the elder, the more serious and responsible, the one most affected by their parents' failings.

"'Greed begets greed.' Don't you remember Father preaching that to us, Mary? I can't help but feel we're doing something sinful. Do you think we're being greedy?"

"Elizabeth, dear, you're being dramatic, although I know what you mean. Going through this house, our parents' house—our grandfather's house—with thoughts on how much money we could get for their belongings, is a bit ghoulish. And yes, greedy. But at the same time, I can't help but feel they would want us to do whatever was needed to help ourselves now.

"When I went to the library the other day, I sat down to read *The News and Courier*. I've been doing that lately. You'd be amazed at what's in the paper regarding local events, especially things for sale. It gives me a good idea of what we can ask.

"But also, ever since that panic and that weasel Mr. Nutting, I worry about the banks and the financial state of the country. It's still not totally stabilized, so all this talk of us being greedy might be something we should be doing more seriously. After all, we are two elderly women alone and we must take care of ourselves."

Miss Elizabeth looked at her sister with respect. "Mary, listen to you. My baby sister, the financial brain in the family. And no, I am not being sarcastic. I'm impressed, and our parents would be too." They looked at each other affectionately.

Bridie thought of the sisterly times she'd had with Kathleen and now with Shirley and gave a little cough around the lump in her throat. What if she had had a sister? Would they be close too, backing each other up?

In addition to corresponding with Kathleen, Bridie had finally heard back from Aileen. Her husband, Patrick, had died shortly after arriving in Charlotte.

"Numonia, the doctor said. Remember how he was ailing on the ship? He just got worse and worse. It was terrible, and he worried so about me. He knew he was dying. It was hard when he passed, but he was so sick. And I had to go on. I stay busy though, living here with my son and wife and the four children. Thank God for them. You can't sit around and cry with little ones around. You of all people know how that is."

Knowing she had friends, even if far away, made Bridie feel more complete. She wasn't just a housemaid in a city far away from her home. She had connections, people who knew her and cared about her.

Ever since moving downstairs, which meant that Miss Elizabeth could get about outside in her wheelchair, she became more willing to venture into the world. The two women were getting about town again, reconnecting with old friends and going to other's homes for tea and card games.

When the sisters hosted a bridge game, Bridie baked like a fiend, polished the silver, shined the crystal, pressed the linens, and finally got to use more of the fine china. She had to laugh. She was a far cry from that nervous woman twelve years ago when the word *entertain* almost made her faint. Now she loved it when the sisters had people in. She wondered what the other women's houses were like and eagerly eavesdropped on their conversations, trying to hear how others hosted events.

Usually they talked about mundane things: their husbands, children, grandchildren, their help. One woman, whose husband was an editor of *The News and Courier*, spoke about events in the rest of the country and how they might affect Charleston. Only Miss Mary joined her in those conversations, briefly. The other women always shushed them.

The University of South Carolina Law School bought the law books and Charleston Public Library accepted many of the other books as donations. Now, the books that remained were those dear to them, but they looked lost on the bookcases that covered three walls of the library. The three women looked around the room with critical eyes, the empty shelves glaring back at them.

"Well, what now?" said Miss Elizabeth. "All that talk of clearing out space and for what? It looks awful in here. I never noticed before, but there's only one window."

"I suppose we could just close it off for now," Miss Mary said. "Seems a pity though."

"What about keeping the library a library?" said Bridie. "There are still plenty of books to fill one wall of shelves. We could convert the music room into a bright room. What do you wealthy people call those rooms?"

"Solariums," said Miss Elizabeth, chuckling. "You're getting there, Bridie. You'll be speaking like a cultured woman soon." The lady actually laughed. "My idea of humor. Shocking, I know. But every now and then I like to loosen up a bit."

"That was the word I was looking for," Bridie said, leading them into the other room. "There are three windows in here. I'm not sure what's needed for a real solarium. But this is a clean, well-lighted room and more feminine than the library. I bet we can ask Ian to do the work in the library."

❦

It was going on two years since Finn had left home. Bridie never expected their row to last this long. She missed him; well, she missed the old Finn. Maybe he had changed. Brendan pestered her constantly about his missing brother.

"Mam, how long are you going to stay mad at him? You're the one who always told us to forgive each other. I miss him. It's lonely here without him." It was unusual for Brendan to whine about anything.

She knew Finn was working at the Trolley Barn. Ian had told her. He had just walked into Sweeney's and asked the barman, who turned out to be Jimmy.

She screwed up her courage and went there and asked to see Finn. How was it possible he hadn't contacted her once? Or worse, that she hadn't contacted him?

The boss man looked up from his logbook and confirmed he worked there.

"But he can't just leave the job in the middle of the workday. And what business do you have coming down here to disturb him anyway? His shift ends at five, and you can see him then."

It was four o'clock, so Bridie waited outside. She saw Finn right away when he walked out. He was walking with that Jimmy Sweeney and two other boys. Boys? They all looked like men now.

Finn saw her—perhaps the boss man had told him she'd been there—and walked over to her. They faced each other uncomfortably. It was Finn who broke the silence.

"How are you, Mam? You look good."

"I'm fine. You look good too. A lot more grown up."

"How's Brendan?"

"He's good too. He misses you."

"Yeah, I miss him too. But I'm real busy, Mam. They about work us to death here, but they pay good."

"Where are you living? I worry about you, you know."

"You don't need to worry. I can take care of myself. I'm staying with Jimmy at his place over Sweeney's Tavern. It's big, and I even have my own room, and I pay his da some rent."

Bridie nodded, wondering where her voice had gone. Finn looked down at the ground, scuffing his shoe. The silence grew.

Finn coughed. "I gotta go, Mam. There's a meeting tonight."

"Oh. Still doing those meetings, are you? Well, you go on then. I just wanted to see how you were doing. I'll tell Brendan you said hello."

"Thanks, Mam. You take care now."

She watched him walk away, forcing herself not to fall to her knees. She was his mother and he was her son and that was all they could say to each other? But at least now she knew he was alive and well. It was a start.

Ian, with Brendan as assistant, had the shelves in the library and the wallpaper torn out of the two rooms in a day. Miss Mary, who avidly read the "Ladies Section" in the paper, wanted the walls painted. Miss Elizabeth shook her head. "Only paint? It will look so bare."

"Oh, I think you'd be pleasantly surprised, Miss Fleming," Ian said. "You sure are up to date on things, Miss Mary. We've been doing it in a lot of our new houses, and people like it."

"Bridie, dear," said Miss Mary during tea that afternoon, "You know that Ian is such a sweet young man. I'm surprised you two haven't become a couple."

"Oh, Miss Mary, he's a lot younger than me. He's like my little brother."

"Well, I don't think he thinks that way. Maybe you should look at him differently. I think he'd be quite the catch for you. Who cares if he's younger? Our mother was five years older than our father."

Bridie took a sip of tea. And that worked out well, didn't it? The father stepped out on their mother, and she took to her room and died.

Yes, Ian was a good catch, but not for her. She'd had her one love. "Well, Miss Mary, one husband was enough for me. And I like my life here with you two." She smiled. Considering how she'd felt in the beginning, it seemed strange. But it was true.

The two rooms came out wonderfully, even impressing Miss Elizabeth. The library had one wall of crisp white shelves filled with the women's favorite books. The walls in both rooms were cream-colored, and the sparkling-clean windows were framed with new curtains.

"Well, will you look at this," Miss Elizabeth said, with no sarcasm. "Mary, you were right about the paint. And Bridie, did you make the curtains? I hope you didn't take them down from one of the bedrooms upstairs. Did you, Bridie? Mary?"

"No, Elizabeth," said Miss Mary. "There are a lot of things stored up in the attic, including even more fabrics. Bridie made them, just like she did in our rooms downstairs. Our Bridie, bless her soul, can sew. Just one of her many talents. I knew it when I found her."

"You did not, Miss Mary. I was pitiful and desperate, and you took advantage of me," Bridie said laughing. "You both keep forgetting I took classes in domestic science, and sewing was just another class. What do you think about me recovering some of the chairs in the entry hall and putting them in here? And the piano is lovely in this room. Maybe one of you will play it again."

The sisters were so pleased with the work that when they found out Ian and his friend would be eating with Bridie, they insisted that everyone have dinner together in the dining room. Bridie and Brendan kicked themselves under the table. How much had changed in the years she'd been working there.

Chapter 19

1910

Bridie continued to fret about the rift between herself and Finn. Maybe if she went to see Mr. Sweeney himself, he might help. Surprisingly, she had never seen him at the Hibernian, one of the few Irish who didn't make it a second home. She just assumed that all the Irish in Charleston went there, but apparently not. She'd stop at his tavern and leave a message.

Standing on the steps below the door of Sweeney's Tavern, a wave of nostalgia swept over her. When she had to see Da when he was working, she'd have to wait outside. Women, and especially girls, were not allowed inside.

A man was trying to get past her. "Excuse me, ma'am. The ladies' door is on the side there."

"Sorry. No, no, I don't want to go in. I just need to speak to Mr. Sweeney. I wonder if you could ask him to come outside for just a minute to see me."

"Certainly." He entered, and she heard him say

under his breath, "Not the first time either. Don't know what that man has that so attracts the ladies."

Mr. Sweeney was indeed the same man she had met previously, so long ago when she was walking with Brendan. He stood in the doorway, looking down on her.

"I'm sorry to bother you, Mr. Sweeney, but *my* son, Finn, is a friend of your son Jimmy, yes?"

"Aye, he is. And he rents a room from me. In fact, he's been stayin' with us for a while. I'd a thought you knew that, bein' his mam. That's not a problem, is it?"

"I'd prefer him home."

They looked at each other uncomfortably for a minute. Catch more flies with honey, Bridie thought. "Excuse my manners. My name is Bridie Murphy."

"I remember you. The mother of the little builder, right? How is the lad? Still playin' in the dirt?"

"Not so much anymore."

"Time flies, don't it? So, what is it you want from me?"

"Well, I guess I should thank you for taking in my Finn. We had a bit of a row, and he stormed out. I talked with him the other day, and that's when I found out where he was living. I'd like for him to come home, and I was hoping you might help."

"I don't know if I can," he said, in a curt voice.

Bridie was a little stunned. Well, that was pretty rude. Here she was, the boy's mother, and he didn't know if he could help her? "I'm sorry. What do you mean, exactly?"

"No offense, ma'am. But the boy left home a while ago. A coupla years, already, and you're just comin' around now? He seems happy where he is. We all, my older sons, me and Jimmy, get along with him. It ain't like he's been beggin' to go home neither. He's workin', gives me a bit of rent. Maybe it's just his time to move out and be a man."

The nerve. "Maybe. Maybe not. I was just hoping we could come to an agreement about my son." She turned to go.

"Hold on there, Mrs. Murphy. Hold on. I didna mean to insult you. It's just he seems fine where he is. Whatever spat you two had will blow over soon enough."

Spat? Soon enough? For God's sake, it had been two years, as he so nastily reminded her.

Sweeney half turned. "I have to get back inside. Maybe we can talk about this another time. I know what it's like to have a split with a child. Me and my sons have gotten into it every now and then, but we always get over it. How about we meet next Sunday at twelve? I assume you go to Mass, aye? We can meet at Washington Square. It's a nice little park behind City Hall on the corner of Meeting and Broad Streets. Sometimes there's a man sellin' ice cream there."

Bridie accepted the invitation, unusual as it was. Since when do women walk alone to meet a man? But she had to think of Finn. He had been gone long enough; she couldn't lose another son. Rory still came to her in her dreams, and the last time, he shook his

head at her. It was if he was blaming her for Finn running away. Like she didn't feel guilty enough?

That Sunday, after Mass, Bridie walked with Shirley back to Hayne Street. She was the only person who
knew about Finn and how torn up Bridie was. Over tea,
she told Shirley about her talk with Daniel Sweeney.

"Well, he sounds like a right eegit," Shirley said. "A
little full of himself, ain't he? You're not goin' to meet
him, are you?"

"I am, in a half hour. He's the only link I have to
Finn, so I may as well give him a chance. What have I
got to lose?"

"Sweeney, you say. Odd he doesn't come to the Hibernian, isn't it? Maybe I'll ask around. I'd guess that
most of the men there, especially the dockworkers,
know him and his bar. Wouldn't you think?"

She looked at Bridie with a devilish smile. "All these
years of clean livin', with nary one boyfriend, and
you meet a man who's actin' the father to your kid?
Wouldn't that be something?"

Bridie looked askance at Shirley. "Something?
What are you saying?"

"Oh, Bridie, don't be gettin' your bloomers in a
bunch. You do have to admit though, it will be the first
official date you've had in a long time."

"I wouldn't call it a date. Just a way to keep up with
my son. I just want to persuade the man to send Finn
home."

Shirley and she were close, but Shirley didn't know
everything about her, Bridie thought huffily. Then

she laughed. She surely didn't know all about Shirley, either.

Bridie had gone for casual walks and tea with a few men. There were many more who had tried to chat her up, to no avail. There was one man, an older carpenter friend of Ian's she'd become very fond of, awakening long lost feelings she might have given in to. But he moved away before the chance arose. Being with a man again was not in the stars, and that was fine.

But she was still a woman. Not vain, but she knew she was pretty and enjoyed, sometimes, the attention that brought her. And she did what she could to try and maintain her looks.

She kept her dark hair shiny with one hundred strokes of her brush every night and protected her fair skin from the Charleston heat and sun. She wore a straw hat and long sleeves when gardening and bonnets when out walking. Often, she used a parasol, which always reminded her of Kathleen and how they used to laugh about them. She didn't have to buy one; the sisters let her use any of the many they owned. In fact, they insisted she use them.

"You don't want to get sunspots," Miss Elizabeth said with concern. "You'll look common."

Miss Mary, despite her advancing age, still had good skin and knew a trick or two. "I use a bit of lard, paired with some oil of rose or lavender into my weekly bath. Try it. That's what I've always done, and it will keep your skin soft and your hair shiny. And use this, Pond's Vanishing Cream. It will keep your face young and help to prevent sunspots. Use it on your hands too." She gave Bridie a small white jar. "Here, you keep this one; I have another. You know, you really are quite a lovely woman, Bridie."

Bridie laughed. "Miss Mary, you sound just like an advertisement in the paper."

All that, Bridie remembered as she walked towards Washington Square. It was early September and cooling slightly, with some leaves just beginning to change, hinting at the colors to come. She'd been walking around Charleston since she'd arrived and knew well where she was going. But it still rankled. A real gentleman would not ask a woman to walk alone to meet him.

About a block from the park, she felt someone slip an arm into hers and turned in alarm.

"Just me, Mrs. Murphy. Just me." Mr. Sweeney was smiling at her. She was surprised to find that up close he was the same height as her. Then she remembered he had stayed in the doorway before, looking down at her. Was that his way of lording it over people?

"I'm not a complete cad, you know. I wasn't goin' to let you walk alone the whole way. But I didna want all those busy bodies at St. Mary's or the Hibernian to know what I'm doin'. None of their damn business. The less anyone knows about me, the better, I always say. Or who I choose to step out with. Don't you agree?"

Bridie removed her arm as politely as she could. "I certainly don't make it a practice of letting anyone know my business, but I don't boast about it."

"I wasn't boastin', ma'am. Just the way I am too. See? We already have something in common other than your son."

At the park, they sat on a bench enjoying their dishes of ice cream. Bridie was surprised to find herself chatting comfortably. Maybe it was because they were foreigners from the same country? It did give them common ground other than her son. When Bridie took out her father's pocket watch she was surprised to see that an hour had passed. She jumped up.

"My goodness, look at the time. My employers will be wondering where I am. Thank you for the ice cream. It was delicious."

"And thank you for your company, Mrs. Murphy." He smiled. "I hope you'll consider seeing me again. I'd like to see a lot more of you, Bridie Murphy."

Chapter 20

1910

Their next meeting ended the same way—agreeing to meet again. Bridie and Daniel progressed beyond the stiff conversation of their first meeting. Her frostiness melted, his cheekiness abated, and they dropped the formality of Mr. and Mrs. Soon they were meeting weekly, still meeting at parks, but it no longer irked her. She was a woman used to doing her errands alone, and Charleston was a city that encouraged strolling through its parks, each competing to be the most flowery, the shadiest, the most picturesque.

She remembered the first time they met, that time when Brendan was little, and how charming he had been then. He was that charming man now—attentive, amusing, and intelligent. What she had first thought was smugness was just self-confidence. Plus, he said he understood her longing to have Finn at home and promised he would help to make that happen.

She tried not to compare him to Charles, but how could she not? They were opposites in every way. Charles had been tall and slim and strong and with his shock of red hair and ruddy complexion, ruggedly handsome. Daniel was attractive also, but differently. He was stout, only an inch or two taller than her, balding and with a smooth, florid face. On closer look, there was a scattering of veins on his nose and cheeks. Bridie wondered if they were caused by drink. He was a barkeep after all. Though Da didn't drink much.

Daniel appeared a bit of a dandy, always in a suit, crisp shirt, and tie, sometimes with a vest and a bowler hat. All he needed was a gold-handled cane. She giggled at the image, embarrassed that she thought this about a possible suitor.

Charles had been well educated yet was a poor farmer and a renegade who cared nothing for appearance—and *never* would have been thought a dandy. Daniel was amusing, smart, successful, and insistent in his attention to her—and he was her link to Finn.

Bridie had lived so long in charge of her life, her children's lives, her employers' lives that she had forgotten how nice it was to have someone tending to her for a change. Daniel seemingly found her delightful. She found herself daydreaming about where their acquaintance might lead. Was it possible she could ever feel about Daniel as she had about Charles?

She knew her daydreams were interfering with her life. Her attention to Brendan and the sisters had become careless. Brendan didn't seem to notice. He was a young lad still, with friends and school, at which he excelled. His mother was the last thing on his mind, she told herself. Though one morning for breakfast, she gave him fried eggs instead of scrambled.

"Mammy? Are you getting me mixed up with Finn? He's the one who likes them fried."

"Will you look at that?" Bridie said. "I was thinking of him this morning, and I guess I just forgot."

"It's fine, Mam. They're good."

Because they were needier, the ladies noticed her lapses more than Finn did. Especially Miss Mary, who spent more time with her.

"Bridie. Did you hear me?" Miss Mary asked. "Really my dear, what is going on with you? It's as if you're living in another world or something."

Bridie jumped. Was she so transparent? "I'm sorry, Miss Mary. I know I've been a bit distracted these days, but I have been keeping up with our work. In fact, the curator from the Gibbes Museum is coming here tomorrow."

"Tomorrow! Bridie, when on earth were you planning on telling us this? We must prepare the house, a tea… goodness knows what else. Elizabeth and I haven't even discussed prices." She was wringing her handkerchief, a sign of imminent tears.

Bridie smiled reassuringly. "Did I forget to tell you? I'm sorry, but don't worry. I'll bake early tomorrow morning. I gave the house a good clean today, including upstairs in your parents' rooms. Just in case he might be interested in some of the other things in the house."

The Flemings had once been a large part of Charleston history, and some of the portraits were of well-known Charlestonians. The Gibbes was particularly interested in the family pictures and portraits. Being the newer and wealthier gallery, the museum paid handsomely for them, including at the last minute, much of the crystal, silver, and china.

❧

Bridie and Daniel's meetings were hit or miss, depending on Daniel's availability. It was he who determined the next meeting and where it would be. She couldn't put her finger on it, but she always felt just a bit uneasy when she was with him. It nagged at her. He was still the dandy, the attentive charmer. But underneath, there was a tenseness, a coarseness about him, hinting at something she didn't want to test.

He was very determined in his attentions, flattering her with small gifts: a scarf, hat pins, decorative hair combs, chocolate… She found herself relaxing her aloofness. Their accidental touches led to kisses. He pled for more, she resisted.

She was reminded of the early days with Charles. But now she had responsibilities, a child still at home, and a reputation to consider. Despite her reservations, when she was with Daniel, she surprised herself with how eagerly she responded. For years she had closed off that part of her mind and body, now reawakening.

In the months since they had been seeing each other, her social life, what little she had, diminished to nothing. She went to Mass sporadically, and the last time she had been to the Hibernian was a month ago. She wasn't sure why. Mostly, she didn't want anyone asking questions. She hadn't seen Shirley either, in all that time. So, she was surprised when her friend showed up at the cottage one Sunday afternoon.

"Shirley, please come in." Bridie embraced her. "I was just thinking how long it's been since I saw you. I've missed you. Come in and have some tea with me."

"I'm surprised you even recognize me," Shirley said. "Though, I think I know why you haven't been seen in a while." She laughed; she was not a holder of grudges. "It's that Mr. Sweeney, right?"

Bridie blushed. Just like Shirley to get straight to the point. "Maybe," Bridie said coyly.

"Oh, come now. You have been seen with him, you know. People talk. Tell me all."

"We have been seeing each other. And he's not at all what I thought earlier. He is a bit rough around the edges, but quite the suitor."

"Do tell."

"He likes my smile. Says I'm beautiful… he doesn't seem the type to be so flattering, but he is." Goodness, she was blushing like a schoolgirl.

"I wouldn't know. I've never met the man."

"Well, I'll just have to take care of that, won't I? Come with me tomorrow. We're meeting at Washington Square at two. That was where we had our first meeting, which he reminded me of. Sentimental, for a man, eh?"

"They all are in the beginning, aren't they?" said Shirley.

❦

"Sorry, Shirley," an embarrassed Bridie said. "He's not usually this late." They had been sitting on a bench in the park for fifteen minutes. She tried making small talk. *Tried?* She and Shirley never lacked for words together. When Daniel finally did show up, he sat stiffly on the bench looking down at the ground or up at the sky. It was like he was pouting, for God's sake—he barely said a word. And Shirley? She didn't talk either; just stared out across the park. Their only words were in response to her comments.

Jaysus, it was painful. Thankfully, Shirley stayed for just a few minutes, then excused herself.

"I'd never guess you were shy," Bridie teased Daniel. "I'm glad I only asked her to stop by for a few minutes."

He grabbed her arm tightly and glared at her. "Why the hell did you ask her at all, Bridie? Why in God's name would you invite someone else to our meetings? Especially such a feckin' eegit."

Feckin' eegit? Shirley? "Daniel! What do you mean? She's my best friend. And let go of my arm, you're hurting me."

"What we have together is too special, and I don't want anyone else to know about us. No one need be part of it." He pulled her to him, kissing her roughly.

He calmed down, though he kept one arm tightly around her. He kissed her gently, then more urgently, forcing her lips apart. Moving his other hand along her arm and sliding it over her breast, he whispered into her ear, "We don't need anyone else, do we darlin'?"

Jaysus, God. He was too close, too intense! And in public! She felt his hot breath in her ear and thought she might scream. It was all she could do not to shove him away as she squirmed out of his embrace.

"No, Daniel, we don't need anyone else. But I do have to go. I promised Miss Mary I'd be back early."

She tamped down her panic. Making herself move slowly, she stood up, worried he'd yell or forcibly hold her back. He did neither, just stared at her. Then with a small smile and in a perfectly normal voice, he said, "Next week, same time, same place?" She nodded, wondering how she could have such opposing feelings for one person.

Bridie stopped by the next day at the boarding house to apologize to Shirley. "I've never seen him like that. He told me to tell you he was sorry." She blushed. "He says it's because he loves what we have together. That he thought it was only going to be the two of us, so he was taken aback."

"If you say so. But talk about being taken aback. I don't know how you can say he is a nice man if that's how he treats your best friend. It makes me wonder how he treats you when no one's around."

"Jaysus, Shirley, you didn't help any. You're never quiet. Two of the chattiest people I know suddenly clam up, and I have to pretend there's nothing wrong."

Shirley looked uncomfortable. "You're right, Bridie.

I'm sorry. I should never have agreed to meet him." She looked down at the floor. "I already didn't like him."

"What does that mean? You said you never met him."

"I hadn't, but remember when you started seeing him and I said I'd ask around about him? Well, I did, and he has a reputation for being bad tempered, especially if he's been drinking. That's why he never comes to the Hibernian—he was thrown out years ago. Word is he's a big man in the Red Shirts too. You know, those guys who push everyone around during elections? They should be taken down a notch or two."

"Shirley! And who did you ask? Does everyone know I am seeing him? How could you do that behind my back?"

"Aww, don't be that way, Bridie. I wish someone had told me about a few of the men I've been with."

The next time Bridie met Daniel, they walked to White Point Garden on the Battery, the southernmost tip of Charleston. On the other side of the park was South Battery Street, famous for its elegant antebellum mansions lining the side of the road, forming a stately procession.

They sat in the gazebo, snacking on pastries and sarsaparillas. He was conciliatory to her, apologizing profusely for his behavior to Shirley. "It won't happen again. It's just that I wanted to tell you that day how much I care for you. When she showed up, I was surprised. I certainly wasn't ready for company. Please don't stay angry at me."

"Daniel, it's all right. I wasn't angry. A little disappointed maybe, but I don't hold grudges."

He leaned over, kissing her very slowly, his hand caressing her thigh. "Ah, Bridie. I dream of what we could do to each other."

Bridie moved his hand. "Daniel, there are people over there."

"Just ignore them. They're not lookin'. I can move my hand even higher. Like this. Do you like…"

Bridie stood up. "We can't be doing this in public. Let's go."

He smiled a crooked smile. "Always prim and proper, ain't you? I know deep down you want it as much as I do."

Again, she was reminded of Charles, always pushing her to let him do more. She knew it was foolish to compare them. Everyone has their good and bad sides. But Charles had been sweet and fun and, admittedly, she was young and easily led. Daniel was not sweet. There was always that tenseness about him, that hint of anger. And she was certainly not that young girl anymore.

They walked along South Battery. Daniel put his arm around her waist and gave her a squeeze. "I bet if I lived in one of those houses you wouldn't hold back, would you?"

"Well, it would certainly offer us a place to be alone, that's for sure."

"Ha! I knew you wanted it. Alas, I'm naught but a lowly tavern keeper. And between the taxes and having to pay off the feckin' police who are always sniffin' around the place, it's all I can do to keep my head above water." He slid his arm out of hers and patted her behind. "A man can dream though, can't he?"

A month, later a man knocked at the kitchen door of the Fleming house with a note for Bridie. It was from Daniel, telling her to meet him the next day at noon in front of the Hibernian. There? He hates the Hibernian. Said they're all downtrodden Irish who only talked about the old country. If they liked it so damned much, why didn't they just go back to the old sod?

When she got to the Hibernian he was already there. Surprising, as he was usually late. He smiled and took her arm. "I know. I still hate this place, but it was an easy landmark. Come with me, my dear. It's not a long walk."

He walked her down the street about five hundred feet, to the St. John Hotel. "Here we are, madam. I hope it wasn't too long a walk."

Bridie stared in surprise at the imposing building, pink, with an iron balcony across the front façade and terra-cotta cornices above the windows. Anyone of any note visiting Charleston always stayed at the St. John. President Teddy Roosevelt had stayed there in 1902 for the South Carolina Inter-State and West Indian Exposition. She'd walked by it hundreds of times on her way to the Hibernian. She certainly never once imagined herself entering it. It was far too grand for the likes of her. Or Daniel.

"Daniel, I can't go into a hotel with you. I am not that kind of a woman."

He took her arm. "Oh yes you are, Bridie. Deep down you are. So, let's go in and enjoy our room. We only have it until three." He walked her around to the back of the hotel, where a young man waited. Bridie balked.

"Daniel, I can't do this," she said in a strident whisper.

Pulling her towards him, he whispered into her ear, "Let's not do this here, darlin'. We can discuss it in the room. He's one of the desk clerks and a frequent cus-tomer at the pub, so I bribed him to give me a room for three hours."

He winked at the man. "She's a bit shy."

Once in the room and after a sip or two from the flask Daniel always carried in his back pocket, Bridie relaxed and allowed herself to be pulled over to the bed where he was seated. She still was resistant, but Daniel was patient, whispering sweet words as he kissed her. She felt herself responding.

She was already in the room for goodness' sake, and it wasn't like she was a virgin anymore. "Maybe I'm not as shy as you thought," she said, feeling the desire to lie naked beside him. She began to unbutton her dress.

Later, still entwined, lying in the now rumpled bed, he slept, and she daydreamed. She had to pinch herself.

She was in the same hotel that the president had stayed in! She had just made love in this room. She would never forget this day.

❦

The last two years, most banks and businesses had returned to profitability. The Fleming women were certainly not wealthy, but thanks to the sales to the museums, they now had a small cushion of savings.

At tea one afternoon, Miss Elizabeth looked at Bridie. "It's high time we started paying you your wages again. It was overly generous of you to deprive yourself during the panic, but we are doing all right now."

Bridie wanted to give the old lady a hug but held back. She was touched, but hugging her would be overstepping her bounds.

Then the sisters opened a bottle of champagne. "Bridie, come have a glass with us." They toasted each other happily, retelling the highs and lows of the past months.

"Bridie, dear, we wouldn't find ourselves in this position of solvency without you, you know that, right?" Miss Mary said.

"Well, I don't know if that's true. I'd say we all played a part," said Bridie.

Miss Elizabeth coughed and gave a little ping on her glass with a spoon. "Bridie, Mary is right, and you know it. So, dear, in addition to paying you again, we wanted to give you a little gift. We opened an account at the bank in your name."

Miss Mary was fairly dancing beside her. "Elizabeth, get on with it, for pity's sake. Never mind, I'll tell her. We put in two hundred dollars. All for you!"

Bridie sat down with a thump, slurped down the rest of her champagne, and held out her glass for more. She giggled. My, what a long way they had come.

The next day she ran to Hayne Street to see Shirley. "Can you believe it? I told you they weren't so bad."

"I take back everything evil I ever said about those two old biddies. Good for them."

Bridie waited for Daniel in the park two blocks away from the St. John Hotel. She couldn't wait to tell him the good news. After twenty minutes, she was getting ready to leave. Damn him. Why is he always late? She had things to do too.

She looked out and saw him stomping towards her, anger seemingly propelling him forward. She'd seen him angry more than once, usually about business and all the meetings he had to attend. A few times, though, it was directed at her. He hadn't hit her, but he yelled and threatened. She hoped she wasn't the target now.

"Don't start in on me, girl." He pulled her up roughly by the arm. "I don't need your grief right now. Those feckin' bastards in City Hall are increasing the property tax starting next month. Like I don't already pay through the teeth? Shite! It never ends." She knew better than to disagree with him. When he got into one of his moods, it was better to leave him alone.

"You know what, Daniel? I think I'll just go home. Miss Elizabeth has been ailing, and I should go back to her. Plus, you obviously have other things to attend to."

He usually snapped out of these moods when he was with her. He'd always say, "You're good for me, Bridie. I can never stay mad when I'm with you."

But this time a look passed over his face that froze her in place. He grabbed her tightly by the arm and dragged her to the back entrance of the hotel and into the room. After locking the door behind him, he turned back and began tearing at her blouse while pushing her back towards the bed.

Afterwards, she lay there while he snored, and remembered how she felt the first time with him and how she dreamed of... what? A possible future with him? This angry, cruel man? Foolish, foolish woman.

She left quickly, rushing home to wash herself.

In the next few weeks, he sent her notes asking to meet. Only the link to Finn made her agree to see him again.

He was profusely apologetic. "I'm sorry, Bridie. I just get into these funks every now and then and take it out on anyone nearby. Give me another chance?"

He had a package under his arm, which he dramatically opened in the hotel room. It was a bottle of whiskey. "There is a story behind this particular bourbon, my dear. Its founder was smitten, just as I am with you, by a beautiful young lady and sent her a note requesting her hand in marriage. She wrote back that if her answer was yes, she would wear a corsage of four red roses on her gown to the upcoming ball. When she arrived, she indeed was wearing the corsage, and he named his bourbon 'Four Roses' as a symbol of his devotion. So, you see, in a small way this is a symbol of my affection for you."

She couldn't help but laugh at his gift of the gab.

Later, before she left, she asked him about Finn. Daniel sat up angrily. "There you go again. Always ruinin' the moment. He's good. Just a stupid sod slavin' away at the trolley barn. I don't know how he can work there—they're all niggers. Jimmy got out, and he's workin' for me now in the pub. He's a natural; got a talent with the pours and in the kitchen too."

He fell back on the bed. "You know what? Just go and leave like you always do. I'm tired of all your feckin' questions about your precious son. If he's so dear to you, why's he livin' with me, eh?"

She had no answer.

Chapter 21
1910–1911

Between work and the Red Shirts, Finn had little free time, which was good. He didn't want time to think about his life. He missed his family, but he felt locked into the choice he had made when he stormed away from home two years before. Sometimes on his walks, he'd find himself outside the gate of the Fleming house, but he never got up the nerve to see his mother and Brendan.

When he first moved in with the Sweeneys, his relief at being away from his mother's nagging sustained him. And living in a house full of men was a lark. Daniel Sweeney's only rule was that no women were allowed. "You can feck 'em, but not here." There was booze, mostly beer, sometimes whiskey. Meals were scattershot, usually leftovers brought up from the tavern downstairs. Sometimes, they sat down for a real dinner prepared by Jimmy, who had become an able cook.

Jimmy had been fired from the Trolley, though he told his father he quit. "Too many niggers," was all he said. That was reason enough for Daniel, and he hired him full-time as the bartender, where he flourished.

Last year, when Finn turned seventeen, and with Daniel vouching for him, he joined the Red Shirts. Daniel reminded him often of his allegiance. "We take care of our own, lad, but woe to anyone who doesn't toe the line. If you feck up… well, let's just say it won't be pretty." He laughed and tousled Finn's curly black hair. "You'll do fine boy. We're all on the same side here."

The Red Boys had been fun. Playing games with boys, had given him a sense of belonging when everything fell apart between him and Mam. But the Red Shirts were another story. They acted as the military arm of the Democratic Party, and they were deadly serious. Their goal was to keep the Democrats in power. Using intimidation and force, they kept the Republicans out of office and repressed any civil and voting rights of freedmen.

On his own, he probably wouldn't have joined. But the Sweeneys had invited him into their family and his membership just happened. The Red Shirts did not look kindly on members having outside interests or loyalties—once a member, always a member. Those that walked away or were expelled spent their days fearful of retaliation.

Democratic presidential candidates in the South relied on the Red Shirts for security as they toured their states. Their slogan was "Force Without Violence," and there was nothing more impressive than a group of Red Shirts, in their red jackets, armed and mounted on horses. The upcoming election for governor was a time for the Red Shirts to shine again.

Some in the group openly pushed for more violence. Their anger and pettiness made Finn nervous. Using organization and scare tactics, they disrupted challengers' rallies and proudly marched in the open to support their beliefs and their candidates who they knew would turn a blind eye to any lawlessness. Thankfully, this year there was no opposing candidate, and Finn allowed himself to relax.

"I guess that means we don't have to do anything, right?" he said one day to Jimmy.

Jimmy stared at him like he was crazy. "What the feck are you talking about? Of course we're doin' stuff."

"But we don't have to. None of this will make any difference in this election. The Republicans don't even have a candidate, and the Negroes can't vote. Why do we have to do anything at all?"

"Jaysus, Finn. Because we can," Jimmy retorted. He lowered his voice. "Don't you get it? Sometimes I think you're really stupid. How many times have you heard Da say it's not just the election. It's keepin' the opposition down."

"Yeah, but who's the opposition? No one's even running."

Jimmy stared at Finn and shook his head. "Boy, you'd best not let Da or my brothers hear you talkin' this way. The opposition is anyone who's not a Democrat; they need to be reminded often about who's in power. And it's because we can, you eejit.

"Haven't you heard anything we say? There's no place for niggers and other lowlifes here in this city. Hell, in the country. Anyone who's not a Democrat wants to change our way of life. And we need to protect it. Don't you get it?"

Finn did not get it, but he did keep his mouth shut. He had seen how others had been rousted out of the group: publicly shamed, their businesses boycotted, sometimes looted, and their houses ransacked. He felt like a prisoner, and he started thinking like one, pondering escape.

Daniel, along with four or five other Charleston businessmen, all members of the Red Shirts, chose and approved the targets of comeuppance. Because the outcome of this election was known, nothing serious was planned. It would be a good time to let the younger members choose their targets, get some experience planning and executing events. They could harass and intimidate through lesser means—vandalizing, blacklisting, taunting, bullying. Maybe a few broken windows, some looting. There were many options for them to choose from.

Jimmy's two older brothers, the policemen, liked to do their agitating at the docks. Most of the longshoremen in Charleston were Negroes. Hell, they had their own union. Not even the police were unionized, for God's sake! That particularly galled the Sweeneys. In Ireland, and in most of the northern US ports, the majority of dock workers were Irish. "Why should niggers have those jobs?" the two Sweeney brothers griped. "Those jobs belong to the Irish."

Jimmy, who had been participating in these activities since before Finn had moved in, was the leader of the small group Finn belonged to. Jimmy targeted the Trolley and the Trolley Barn, for the same reason his brothers chose the docks: they hired mostly coloreds. Plus, getting fired from there still rankled. Finn working there was a bonus.

"Finn, you're the one who works in the Barn, so you figure out what to do inside. I'll take care of outside the building, breakin' windows and such. You can be the hero inside," Jimmy said.

Finn felt anything but a hero. The Sweeneys had been good to him, and he owed them his loyalty. But the Trolley Barn had also been good to him, and he didn't want to lose his job. Yes, it was hard work, but being white, Finn had more opportunities than the other workers. He got along well with everyone, both the workers and management. He had been promoted three times and was next in line for head mechanic, a plum job.

"Sure, Jimmy," Finn said, hoping he sounded enthusiastic. "I'll come up with something. Slowdowns, broken equipment, worker agitation. There's a lot I can arrange, but if you want to keep stirring things up in other elections, it can't be known it's coming from someone on the inside."

He had rehearsed this speech over and over and was very thankful it was Jimmy he had to convince and not Daniel. "I'll be that man. But we'll never get another chance if I become known as the agitator. I'll be out on my arse and of no more use to you."

It was going to be like walking a tightrope if he did what the Red Shirts wanted. That telltale sign, his upset stomach, was again making itself known.

He ruled out any actions that involved worker unrest; it would be too easy to connect it to him. But there were things he could do to the streetcars while they were in the Barn for repairs. At the end of the day, when workers were distracted, he could "accidentally" dent a wheel, fray an overhead wire, break a door, dilute or omit oil… any one of them could cause major disruptions when in service. He didn't do them all, but he made sure Jimmy knew when he did something.

The Democrats won handily, and the Red Shirts happily patted themselves on their backs until the next election or other civic event worth getting worked up over. Finn went back to being a person uneasy with his life.

The Red Shirts were boastful, bitter men dedicated to the past, the Confederacy, and slavery—things foreign to Finn. They were only happy when they were agitating or talking about old conflicts. The Sweeneys were particularly vocal in their allegiance. It was exhausting to listen to them every night. He was tired of it and wanted out. But he felt guilty. After all, they had taken him in, fed and cared for him, and admitted him into the Red Shirts.

There was one meeting recently that convinced him he had to rethink his life. It was held downstairs in the pub, which Daniel had closed to the public. Someone complained that recent protests had been weak in comparison to previous years. Others joined in agreement, their voices rising, anger palpable in the room. Everyone had their own private grievance and aired it. One of Daniel's more unlikable cronies started in on Finn.

"Hey, boyo. How come you didn't do more to feck up the streetcars? I guess it don't matter none since we won. But you didn't do nothin' but break a wheel or two. Makes me think you like working with those niggers. Do you boy?" He started jabbing Finn in the chest. At first everyone laughed. "Is that it boy? You owe something to them?"

"Hey, feck off, you big lout," Jimmy called from behind the bar. Daniel came over and took the man over to a corner and calmed him down.

Finn left the bar and took a long walk. He had to find the courage to leave the Sweeney's. He would talk to Mam. He'd just have to apologize and beg her to let him come home. He wasn't too worried. She was the one who always preached it wasn't worth it to carry grudges.

Working at the Trolley Barn made him aware of the struggles of others. It was true that most of his fellow workers were Negroes. But they worked hard, earned their money, and raised their families. Why did they earn so much less than he did? Many of them were more able and experienced than he. Why were they ignored? Why was he given the title head mechanic back when he hardly knew what he was doing?

A sudden thought made him stop walking. The Negroes are like the Irish. And the whites are like the Brits. Wasn't that what his father had fought for? Equality? What he was murdered for?

His confusion at how to end his exile came in an unexpected way. Brendan showed up at the Trolley Barn at closing time.

"Jaysus! Will you look at you!" Finn said, trying not to hug the breath out of his brother.

"Yeah, and the same to you." Brendan laughed. "It's all right to be here, isn't it?"

"Sure. Once we're done with our shift." A worried look passed over his face. "Everything's all right at home?"

"Yes. But Mam misses you something terrible. She doesn't say anything, but I know she does. And you both are stubborn fools. So, I figured I'd just start the ball rolling. I told her I was coming to see you. She said for you to come for dinner tomorrow night."

Finn was having trouble getting a breath. "Funny, I had already decided to talk to her, but I didn't know how or when. Tell her yes. And thank you, Brendan, for taking the step."

Chapter 22

1911–1912

"I cleaned my room and the bathroom, Mammy. Anything else?" said Brendan. "Here, I'll set the table."

"Thanks, dearie. I am a little nervous, I have to say." Finn was coming for dinner! "You said he looks the working man now. I hope he likes the job. And I hope he's not so angry all the time."

Oh, such a long time, over three years. How she missed her boy. He's nineteen and she'd missed most of his growing up. Just like she'd missed all of Rory's life. Brendan looked happy too. How he must have missed his brother. An unbidden thought scrabbled through her head. Could that mean she'd been seeing Daniel for more than two years? Jaysus.

Finn arrived at the cottage, right on time. After an awkward hug for Bridie and a punch on the arm for Brendan, they settled into their seats at the table. Bridie could hardly eat, with the effort to hold back her tears. The boys did most of the talking, catching each other up on their lives. She so enjoyed listening to them, she didn't participate much in the conversation. When Finn left home, Brendan was only eleven. Now he was fourteen and chattering away about the courses he would be taking in high school: Latin, Greek, English, algebra, biology... It was mind-boggling.

Finn looked at his little brother with respect. "Listen to you go on. You really like school, don't you? I wish I had. I fecked that up, didn't I? But I do like my job. There's always something new to learn."

Bridie remembered how she had begged her father to let her go to school and take those classes at the Domestic Science Centre. And thank God she did, seeing what she'd been doing for these past years. Now her youngest boy had all this available for free. Wouldn't Charles be proud?

Finn hugged Bridie when he left. "This was nice, Mam. I'm sorry about how I acted to you when I left. I felt such a failure and I was in such a fury, I had to get away." He smiled. "I've missed you."

The next day, after breakfast, Bridie rushed over to Shirley's before she went to the market. "You'll never guess! Finn came for dinner last night!

"Oh, get on, Bridie, that's great news," said Shirley.

"He's grown up, that's for sure. It went well and he promised to come by again."

༄

The guilt Bridie felt about Daniel was overwhelming and going to Mass made her feel worse. She wasn't married, so she wasn't really committing adultery, but she was sure what she was doing with Daniel was a sin. She no longer had the courage to confess. The last time she entered the confessional, she ran out when she heard the shutter open. Father James *knew* her. How could she ever face him again?

Sometimes she found solace in Charles's Bible. She still had it, kept on a shelf in her room. Sometimes she read from it, but just holding it and knowing that Charles had grown up with it gave her a sense of calm. Seeing the names of his family and their boys reminded her she was part of something. And always, seeing the name *Samel Murphy*, as one of their children, made her smile.

She had also stopped going to the Hibernian. She told herself it was because she was too busy. But the real reason was embarrassment. Shirley said people knew about her and Daniel, and she did not want to see people looking at her strangely or whispering as she went by. What if Ian knew?

Bridie saw Daniel less often, coming up with excuses when she could. She had tried to break it off completely, but he became angry—frighteningly so. He even slapped her a few times, only to apologize profusely as he made love to her.

Afterwards, he taunted her about Finn living with him, and not home with her. He bragged about how Finn had come through for the Red Shirts during the past election. Often, he'd take a swig from his flask, look her in the eye and say, "I wonder how Finn would feel if I told him his mother was feckin' me. Like a whore."

And that was the crux of her problem. He would tell her son.

Shirley had just been left by her latest beau. "I knew he wasn't good material. Kind of like Daniel. But, still, he was better than nothing. You know what I mean?" She laughed. "I don't know, Bridie. Seems unfair, don't it? Here we are, workin' ourselves to the bone, you'd think the good Lord would see fit to reward us with two good men, don't you think?"

"I do, Shirley. And now it's a chore to pretend I like it. In fact, I'm always on edge waiting for the next shoe to drop. God, I just have to end it. But if I break it off with him, I know the first thing he'll do is tell Finn what he's been doing with me. His mother! That's after he beats the daylights out of me."

A week later, on her way to market, Daniel came up behind her and slid his arm under hers. "Remind you of anything, dearie? Remember that first walk when I took your arm? I've missed you so. You know you miss me too, don't you?" The smell of stale whiskey seeped from him.

"I've not missed you," she said, trying to pull away.

He sneered at her, gripped her arm more roughly, and tugged her along.

"What's wrong, Bridie? I've been worried about you. I thought you must have been sick because you missed our last date. But here you are lookin' just fine."

"Daniel don't be angry, but it's over between us. I don't love you, and I don't think you love me either."

"Love? Darlin,' love has nothing to do with us. Never did, luv. But I do love it when you're under me." He dragged her to his tavern.

"What are you doing? Why are we here?" She tried to pull away.

"Well, my friend got himself fired, and I'm sure as hell not goin' to pay for a hotel room you don't even appreciate. I've got a whole empty house upstairs for us to enjoy." He pulled her around to the back of the tavern and shoved her up the stairs. An hour later, he threw her out the door. "Don't forget, darlin.' Next week, right here, same time."

He had roughed her up more than usual before slamming her to the bed where he had forced himself on her. She walked slowly, feeling her way on the cobblestones, afraid she could fall at any moment. What in God's name was she to do now?

She couldn't go to the market; she'd make something from the pantry for supper. Luckily, Brendan was still in school, so she didn't have to face him right away.

As soon as she got home, she tore off her clothes. There was blood on her knickers. She prayed he hadn't injured something inside her. Stepping into the bath gingerly, she groaned from the heat and sting on the chaffed areas. There were marks on her breasts and thighs from where he had pinched and grabbed her.

Penance. She deserved this pain. Another voice said no. No one deserved this.

She laid in the water. Always, after being with Daniel, she douched with water and vinegar. Not just to prevent pregnancy, but for disease also; she was sure he laid with other women.

She dressed in warm clothes, had a cup of hot tea, and for the hundredth time asked herself why the hell she was with this nasty man. It was obvious he didn't love her. Maybe he didn't even like her.

Like she didn't like him. The thought jolted her. How can she be with someone she didn't even like? What did that say about her? God, what a mess, and for what? A few bits of news about Finn?

The next morning, after chores, Bridie went to Shirley's. They took their tea in Shirley's room, leaving behind a curious Mrs. Millbury. Bridie told her everything.

Shirley was outraged. "What a feckin' maggot he is. Oh, dearie, I feel so bad for you."

"Maggot. I knew you'd make me feel better," said Bridie, with a weak laugh. "What am I to do? I can't bear going through that again. But, if I don't go with him, I know he'll tell Finn about us, for spite. I can't imagine the words he'd use."

"Bridie, luv, you know what to do. Tell Finn. It's better if he hears it from you. Once he knows, then Daniel can't hurt either of you with the information, and you can leave the bastard. Just do it and get it over with. While you're at it, you'd best tell Brendan too."

Shirley gave her a hug. "It's what you'd tell me to do, right?"

But Bridie couldn't tell Finn. Not yet. She went meekly back to the trysts with Daniel, though she quickly found out *meek* was not what he wanted. She played the wanton, made him happy, then rushed home to cleanse herself. She wondered how long she could continue this way.

Chapter 23

1912

Bridie stopped her sniffling and put a smile on her face. "I'm so proud of you, Ian. That's wonderful news, but I am going to miss you. You're my oldest and dearest friend. Goodness, it's been thirteen years." Her throat ached from holding back her tears and the despair she felt. Jaysus, Bridie, get ahold of yourself. He's your friend and you want the best for him.

"I know. We've seen each other through a lot, haven't we?" His voice was thick, too, and his face showed mixed emotions.

Usually when they got together, it was at the Kaffee Store. But when he told her he wanted to discuss something private, she suggested he come to the cottage.

"What about that girl you were seeing?" Bridie asked. "I thought it was serious this time."

Ian's face reddened, and he looked away. "I thought so too. But, when I told her I was thinking of moving, she wasn't too keen on it. Her family is here, and Newry is far away."

"What? Newry!" Bridie sputtered. "You're going back to Newry?"

He laughed. "I know, some coincidence, eh? No, it's here in South Carolina. It's a small town built around a cotton mill. The owner of the mill named it after our Newry, which is where his family came from. The town is self-sufficient, and they rarely go outside to look for help. I would never have heard about the job if it wasn't for my friend Sam. He has a cousin that works there.

"He knew I was thinking of moving from Charleston and talked me up. My boss here gave them a good report, so off I go. I'll be the head carpenter there. Besides, how could I resist working in a town called Newry?"

"It's destiny, and of course you must take it," said Bridie. "I am truly happy for you, even though there's a part of me that wants you to stay. You've done well for yourself, and you should go out on your own. If you ever need it, you know the sisters would always give you a good recommendation."

Ian nodded. "Even Miss Elizabeth?" They laughed.

"The clincher is they have a baseball team. Mill baseball is a big deal, and Newry's team is one of the best. They said that was one of the reasons they went outside the mill to hire me. That's why I'm starting now so I can start spring training with them. Who knew playing ball would get me a job?"

He stopped talking and stirred his tea. Bridie too was quiet, and soon the silence became uncomfortable.

They both started to speak at once, but Ian forged ahead.

"There's one more thing I need to say. Daniel Sweeney…"

He knew about Daniel? Her face burned. "Oh, Ian. We've never gotten into each other's private lives. Let's not start now."

"I know, Bridie. But I can't leave without saying something. He's not a nice man. Or honest or legitimate. He runs a lousy bar, is a big man in the Red Shirts, and he's a bully."

Bridie couldn't look at him; it was awful to hear him tell her everything she already knew.

"Ian, you don't understand. Finn lives with him and…"

"I know. Shirley told me."

"Jaysus! You two are talking about me?" She started to get out of her chair.

Ian took both her hands and looked pleadingly into her eyes. "Bridie, we're your friends. You know that both of us care about you. I know him. Sit down and hear me out.

"I've met him, and more than once. As an apprentice, I was on crews that did work at Sweeney's Tavern. It's an old building and often needed repairs— work that should have been attended to earlier. By the time we carpenters were called in, the jobs were emergencies, demanding instant attention. Sweeney always complained about the results, bickered about the bills, was late in paying, and when he did, he usually shorted them. Eventually, the company told him that he was required to pay half up front before work began.

"My first personal run-in with him was right after I'd become a master carpenter. When I asked for the payment upfront, he got right up into my face. 'What kind of eegit do you take me for, you stupid mick? No one pays up front.'"

Ian took a shaky breath. "His outburst was frightening, and I was new and young. But my boss had warned me and said he'd back me up. I stared right back and said, 'Charleston Lumber has already notified you of the payment conditions. Take it up with them.' I backed away, took my workers, and left. Sweeney eventually accepted the terms. Later as I rose in the ranks, and with a bit of finagling, I was usually able to get out of any more jobs at Sweeney's."

He looked at her pleadingly. "Bridie, you can leave him now that Finn is talking to you again. You don't need anything from him."

She was mortified that Ian knew, and even more so, that he was right. She knew Ian only wanted what was best for her. When she stood up, he hugged her. "You know you're my best friend and you deserve to be with better than him." All she wanted to do was cry.

When Bridie told the sisters that Ian was moving, they insisted he come for tea.

"Make it special, Bridie, like you do when we host bridge. And bake your scones with cinnamon on top. You know how he loves them."

During the tea, Miss Mary surprised them all by saying she knew about Newry. "There was an article in the paper last month. I had forgotten that was the name of the town you both came from, otherwise I would have mentioned it to you both."

❧

The News and Courier now offered subscriptions for home delivery, and Miss Mary signed up right away for the service. She read many of the articles out loud to her sister and Bridie during tea.

One evening, Miss Mary popped her head over the paper. "Wait till you hear this, Elizabeth. There's another piece in the paper about Newry."

"Goodness. I wonder why they would write about such a small town?"

"Well, partly because, and this will interest you, it's about William Ashmead Courtenay."

Miss Elizabeth sat up in her chair and turned to her sister with an interested look on her face.

"In case you didn't know, Bridie, Mr. Courtenay was a past mayor of Charleston, the same man who was in office during the earthquake. But way before that, he was also a young man that our young Elizabeth had set her eyes on. We were all in the same social circle and went to the same parties."

Elizabeth actually blushed. Bridie had to turn away so Elizabeth couldn't see her smile.

Miss Mary made a big production of shaking out the paper and adjusting her glasses. Then she read the article to them. It described how Mr. Courtenay went from politics to owning and running a cotton mill in the Upstate. His ancestors had come from Newry, Ireland, and he named his new town the same. He said this new town in the Little River Valley reminded him of that city by the sea, also tucked down into its own valley.

Miss Mary looked coyly at her sister. "Just think, Elizabeth. If you two had married, you'd be queen of your own little town right now."

"Mary, don't be silly. Sometimes you're still like a simpering girl."

Miss Mary gave a smug smile and a wink to Bridie and continued reading.

"'A year later, in the summer of 1894, with fifty-one houses built, they tried a first run with the mill and by the end of the year, the mill was in full operation. One of the old timers told this reporter the mill was immediately profitable, and the investors made a 15-percent return that first year.'"

"Perhaps I should have been more obvious in making my feelings known to William," Miss Elizabeth muttered.

The Flemings were in their seventies now and Miss Elizabeth especially, was becoming frailer, though she liked to sit in the music room and receive visitors—those friends still alive and able to get around. They held their bridge games, but only Miss Mary went to the games at the other women's homes. And she still played lady-in-waiting to her big sister.

Sometimes, Bridie wondered what her life would be like when they died. She'd probably just work in someone else's house. She had saved a goodly amount of money, enough to tide her over for a bit. She had a good reputation. Well, she hoped so, despite that rotter Daniel.

∽

Finn asked her if he could move back home. It was all Bridie could do to not jump up and kiss him. If she had, he'd be so embarrassed, he'd run away forever.

"I'm grateful to Daniel for giving me a place to stay, but I think I'd rather be home again.

"I've outgrown the Red Shirts and their games. When I was younger it was fun, but not so much anymore. They're very serious, and it's all they talk about. I'll pay rent, so I can help you out."

As happy as she was at the news, Bridie was filled with unease. Daniel would mess this up somehow. She didn't know how, but she knew he would make life miserable for her and Finn. Without giving away her own secrets, she tried to warn him about Daniel.

"Oh, Finn luv, how I've wanted to hear you say that. But you might want to think about it before you say anything to him. You told me how angry he gets when someone stands up to him. I don't want you being the object of his wrath. He really does have a bad reputation."

"Mam, he doesn't care about me. I'm just one little cog in his rotten machinery."

They were in the Kaffee Store. Bridie had introduced Finn to the place, and now they usually met on Tuesday afternoons, his short days, when he got off at one. It was a fun routine they'd started, though a little bittersweet for Bridie, as it always reminded her of when she and Ian went there.

Finn loved the pastries and the strong coffee. The waitress was nearby and asked him if he wanted seconds, to which he nodded yes. The girl turned to Bridie with a shy smile. "And you, Mrs. Murphy? Anything else I can get for you?"

Today, Bridie finally took note. Good Lord, Emily! Emily Becker, the owner's daughter. Finn liked her! Goodness, what kind of a mother was she? How could she have missed it? And it was no wonder! She was lovely; like Kathleen with that light brown hair and those green eyes. She didn't look sassy like Kathleen, though, which was probably a good thing.

"No thanks, Emily. I'm fine." Dread suddenly flooded through Bridie. How would Daniel react when Finn left? He'd take it out on her son, for sure. And if he found out Finn liked Emily, he'd taint that too. He'd tell Finn about their shameful affair, that she was his lover. Oh God. He'd use disgusting words and boast about it. It was all she could do to not vomit.

"Finn, luv. I have to go," she said. She shoved her chair back, stood up, and ran out the door without looking back.

Finn was surprised. Emily came over and asked, "Is your mother all right, Finn?"

"I don't know. I'm sure she is, but I'll find out later."

Before Bridie could break it off with Daniel, Miss Elizabeth died, suddenly, in her sleep. Bridie was surprised at her own sorrow. The crusty old lady had wormed her way into Bridie's heart. Who would have thought? Bridie was relieved that she passed so quietly and said a prayer of thanks, but little Miss Mary was inconsolable.

"What will I do now? We've been together all our lives," Miss Mary said, twisting the ever-present handkerchief and trailing Bridie around the house. It was a sad reminder of their early days, when she had bustled after Bridie, telling her what to do, or not do.

Bridie made the funeral arrangements for Miss Mary, who felt unable to make decisions. The service and burial were at the First (Scots) Presbyterian Church, where the sisters had attended services since they were children.

It really should be called a cathedral, it's so enormous, Bridie thought. Four giant pillars stood before the front entrance and two bell towers rose high over the roofline. Inside, the minister's eulogy echoed in the massive space.

Miss Mary sat between Bridie and Brendan. Even Finn came, and he sat on Bridie's other side. Shirley was there, and the few remaining friends of the sisters still able to get around. Miss Elizabeth was buried next to her parents in the family plot behind the church.

The small reception, an afternoon tea with all the trappings, was held back at the house. Bridie went all out with the best china, linens, and silver. That morning making the scones she found herself crying. It took her back to the first time she had made the sisters tea and served them her scones. She remembered how Miss Elizabeth fought to hide the smile on her lips.

The small group of sad little ladies perked up when Bridie poured them each a sherry to toast their lost friend.

Bridie and Brendan had sometimes eaten with the sisters in their dining room. Now, with Miss Elizabeth gone, the three ate dinner together every night. For variety, Bridie changed the locations: sometimes in the dining room; sometimes in the kitchen; sometimes in Bridie's cottage, which is where they were when Brendan made his announcement.

"Guess what! My math teacher, Mr. Thorpe, says I can get into college!"

Bridie leapt up and kissed him. "Oh, my sweet lad. Didn't I always say you'd go?"

"You did, Mammy. You always had faith in me. He's going to help me with the applications for admission, and there are scholarships and loans I can apply for."

༄

With Brendan's college news, Bridie could no longer put off dealing with Daniel. She was terrified that if he heard about Brendan's good news, he would blow everything all up. She could just hear him.

"How do you think your precious college boy will look at you when he finds out you've been feckin' me for the last few years? And Finn? The son you threw out. The son I've been raisin' these past years. He likes it where he is. He's one of us, and we take care of our own." Oh, yes, he would delight in ruining her life.

She had to break the hold he had on her. She left a note at his bar for him to meet her at Washington Park. By the time he showed up, late, she could tell by the way he walked that he was angry and drunk.

"So, now you're missing me, are you?" Daniel said, leering at her. "Well, let's not stand here." He grabbed her arm.

She wrenched her arm free. "No, Daniel. No more. I don't want to see you anymore. We're really not good for each other…" Right there, in the park, he slapped her, leaving her speechless and frightened.

"You ungrateful bitch. Didn't we go through this before? Is it another man? It can't be that fairy man, Ian, who used to hang around you, who left you? Oh yes, I know all about him. I know everything about you.

"If your friends find out about us, they'll drop you like a bag of shit. Word will get out that you're nothin' but a whore, who came on to me. Who will they believe? Me, who owns my own business and who's involved in the politics of this city. Or you, just a maid to old spinsters? No one's goin' to believe you. So, get it through your dumb head, you can't leave." Then he stumbled off.

She looked around, relieved to see there was no one else in the park and ran home. At least she had finally told him it was over and good riddance to him.

Chapter 24

1912

On March 27, 1912, eighteen-year-old Rory boarded the ship SS *Mobile*, set to sail from Belfast to New
York City. Finally! He had a job lined up at Belmont.
He didn't know how, where, or when, but he could
finally begin his search for his family.

He let the crowd move him along and stepped onto
the gangplank. Each step forward reminded him of
things he had forgotten. The crowds. Mammy trying
to keep them all together; and Finn, who, even though
they were tied together, wouldn't let go his hand. Tears
suddenly came to Rory's eyes. Finn had always been
the big brother, watching out for him.

He remembered the crowd funneling through a
door, the passengers jostling each other to go below ...
the crewmen barking orders to each other and the passengers ... the strange accents ... yelling, complaining,
crying ... the odors of bacon and sausages stuffed in
pockets ... the dark passageways leading to the echoing

room filled with bunks … the scratchy, wool blankets … the hot milk and bread …

Without warning, the vision of Mammy leaning against their bunk on the *Newry* came to him. It may have been fourteen years ago, but it was as if she were right in front of him. She had that almost smile on her face while she sipped a cup of tea. It was so sharp, he wanted to stop right there and draw it. The vision filled him with joy. That's the first picture he will draw on his trip, a redo of the picture he had drawn so long ago.

When he found his cabin, he was surprised. It was not at all like the huge room of bunks that he remembered. This was an actual cabin with a sink and six bunks, each neatly made up, two on each side and two at the other end of the room opposite where he was standing in the doorway.

Two young men were inside already. They welcomed him and pointed to the top bunk at the end, the only one without belongings on it. "That's it mate. The rest are taken."

"Looks good to me." Rory threw his bag and the paint box on top of the made-up bunk. There was a loud whistle, and a voice over a loudspeaker ordered all visitors to go ashore. He needed to get out. He needed air. After quickly checking his pockets for his papers and wallet, he bolted from the cabin.

Once on deck his panic lessened. It was too crowded to walk around, but he didn't want to wander. He wanted a spot at the rail within sight of the gangway. Once situated, he stared at it. How could no one have seen him getting pushed along? Who would believe a little boy could fall and get lost in the ruckus. But it was busy and dark, and he had been just a lump, kicked down the ramp. Jaysus! It seemed impossible. But it had happened, and he was living proof. He could be standing in the exact same place he was when he saw the flowers. The ones he just had to get for Mammy...

He shook his head to clear it and breathed slowly, calming himself. When boarding the ship, he was given a pamphlet, with The SS Mobile printed on the cover. Now, as the ship pulled away from the harbor, he opened it to the map and ran his finger along the route.

It all came back to him. The nights in the dark cottage, how Mammy gathered them around the table and, using the same kind of map, pointed his and Finn's fingers along the route. How she sang out the place names to them and how they yelled out *Charleston*, stressing the *Charles*.

Now he did the same, though not alone. An announcer was calling out the points of interest. In a whisper, he chanted along: "Now you see Helen's Bay on your right, and Crawfordsburn... Bangor... around Orlock... now we're passing into the Irish Sea... past the Isle of Man on the left... and Carlingford Lough on the right, where the Newry River empties into..."

My God! Newry! He stopped his recitations and stared at the lough. Way up at the other end was Newry. He felt bewitched. He was now on the same route his family had taken.

He looked at the map again and traced the route. Like them, he would pass into the Celtic Sea and on into the Atlantic. Though he would go to New York … But he would get to *Charles*ton one day. He smiled. It felt good to remember, freed of his ghosts and eager for what came next.

He went below to the cabin. The two men he'd already met had been joined by the three other cabin mates, brothers from Ballycastle on the northeastern coastal tip of Ireland.

"There you are. We were beginning to worry about you, you left here in such a hurry. Are you all right?"

"I'm fine," said Rory. "I just felt a bit cramped for a minute. The fresh air felt good, and I got to see Belfast fade away in the distance." He wanted to change the subject from himself. Maybe he'd tell them his story, but not yet. "So where are you headed once you get to New York City?"

The three brothers piped up. "We're goin' to Boston. Our uncle went there last year. He's a fisherman. Said there's lots of work on the ships and the docks." They spoke almost as one, finishing each other's sentences. Rory wondered if he and his two brothers would have been the same way.

The other two, friends from Belfast, were headed to California. "The land of milk and honey," said one, laughing. The other one was more serious. "And oil. We're going to work at the Los Angeles City Oil Field. They're paying our way."

The six of them walked around the third-class deck,

watching Ireland fade in the distance. Except for his fragmented memories, Rory knew nothing about ship travel. His bunkmates had had more time to read the pamphlet and shared what little they knew.

Much had changed, especially in third class, previously called steerage. Now there were cabins of varying sizes and actual bathrooms with toilets and showers scattered throughout the passageways.

For the third-class passengers' pleasure, there were an assortment of rooms: Reading, Smoking (men only), Sitting (ladies), and a General Room for games and gatherings. Outside on the third-class decks, there were chairs and shuffleboard courts. If this is third class, what do second and first look like?

The General Room was full of passengers drinking and socializing. Rory and his friends happily spent their time there until their dinner seating was announced.

When they entered the dining room, Rory stopped short. He was in awe. Never had he seen something so grand. Once, maybe, when he sneaked that look through the window into the Campbells' dining room. But this was a hundred times bigger. He looked at his friends, who were as impressed as him. They started laughing.

"We're going to eat here? They're going to let us in? I wish my mam could see me now..." They were all talking at once, laughing and jabbing each other with their elbows and staring at the elegance before them.

Between the glaring lights above and the multitude of long tables draped in white, the room was dazzling bright. They tried making a quick count of the seats. Each table sat sixteen; there were twenty tables in each of the four rows... around thirteen hundred total? And if the pamphlet was right and third-class had two thousand passengers? Well, no wonder it required two seatings to feed them all. And they even had an orchestra serenading them.

After dinner, which they all agreed was quite grand, especially the beer and wine, they went back to the open space, by now very raucous. Many of the passengers had their own musical instruments and had formed pick-up bands, taking turns playing to the room, the crowd singing and dancing along with them.

Rory wasn't used to being with people who were not in the horse business. Nor with lads his age, which his bunkmates were. Even though he enjoyed the night, socializing with others was new to him, and uncomfortable. He left early, begging off with a headache.

During the days, he spent most of his time outside, walking circuits around the deck—like a horse on a lead line. That made him smile. His thoughts jumped everywhere. Was Samel still tearing up the racing world? What about Devlin? Was he happy? Was Oliver all right?

On the second morning, he took the artist box that Oliver had given him and found a quiet corner out of the wind. He made himself draw. He had been so busy these last years, drawing was something he'd had no time for. It had been a long time, and he was out of practice.

His first attempts with the pencil were pitiful, but in no time at all, he was back to normal. He drew that picture of Mam that had come to him, and it was a fine picture.

For the rest of the crossing, when he wasn't walking, he drew. In the lee of his corner, he drew the people walking by. Some stood and watched him, then one or two offered to pay him to do their portraits. He couldn't wait until he got to New York to write Devlin and tell him he was getting paid for drawing.

During the crossing, he wondered what Belmont would be like. It was one of the greatest racecourses in America, a once-in-a-lifetime opportunity. And, if all went well, it should almost guarantee him a job at any track in the country.

❧

All the time he was at Down Royal he had worked hard at learning the trade. Always in the back of his mind was America. But it was always someday. Now, six days after departing Belfast, the ship was docked in New York.

After clearing customs at Ellis Island, Rory said farewell to his travel mates. He was the only one with an address, of sorts. "Belmont Racecourse, New York. That's all I know," said Rory. He got a ferry ticket from the railway ticket office, then stood at one of the spots designated by the rail agencies and waited for one of the many ferries taking passengers across the harbor to the various railway stations.

He felt quite chuffed with himself. He was in America! It wasn't Charleston, but it was a lot closer than Ireland. He had navigated the confusion of ship travel and made some friends. He was drawing again, and hopefully he'd get a job at Belmont. Not bad for a Mick orphan in a new country.

Once at Pennsylvania Station, he was directed to take the Long Island Railroad to Queens Village, the closest stop to Belmont. When the train came to the stop, he paused at the top of the stairs, the famous racetrack shining in the distance.

The station master gave him directions; it was only a half-mile walk to the track. At the four stone pillars marking the grand entrance, he paused and took a deep breath. Then he stepped onto the famous grounds. They're just horses and it's just a racetrack.

Rory found the man he wanted to see, Tim O'Brian, and gave him Sean's letter of recommendation. After reading the letter, he looked at Rory and shook his head.

"Man, that's a great letter, but I have bad news. Back in 1911, our revered politicians in Albany deemed that wagering on horse races was illegal, and just like that, they banned betting throughout the state. Half the tracks in New York shut down.

"We still have races, but none of any note. Who the hell wants to watch a race without betting? What owner of any decent horse is going to risk him on a piddling race with no purse? All the big farms here are shipping their horses over to Ireland, England and France to race. Sure as hell, I never saw such a time coming. You shoulda stayed back in Ireland, lad."

Rory was dumbfounded. He'd come all this way and there was no horseracing? At one of the greatest tracks in America?

Mr. O'Brian saw Rory's face and smiled. "I can still use you, though. My head trainer left last week for Kentucky. Can't say as I blame him; I'd a done the same. You can have his job."

"That's great," Rory said. "I'd settle for mucking out stalls."

The man looked at Rory. "Down Royal, eh? I read about a horse that won the National Hunt Festival there. Two years in a row—1909 and 1910. His name was Sir Samuel. Did you ever hear of him?"

Rory about fell over. "Hear of him? I saw him born. I trained him. I grew up at Campbell's Stables."

Mr. O'Brian looked at Rory with new respect. "Well, if you can stand the boredom, you're hired. We still have some races, and we do have a lot of horses training here. If you need housing, we have plenty and it's free. But you know what it's like. Basic and not much different from what you had on the ship. Or I can recommend a few boarding houses."

"No, I don't mind staying here. It'll feel like home."

Mr. O'Brian gave Rory an odd look. "I gotta warn you. Because of the loss of income, the owners rent out the racetrack for things other than horse racing. It kills me to say it, but they've arranged for an air show in October." He looked almost embarrassed.

"An air show," Rory said. "Sounds like fun."

Rory quickly got back into the routine of the stables. Except for the accents, it was pretty much the same as life back home. It was bittersweet being with horses again—each time he entered the barns, he expected to see Samel's head sticking out his stall door, tossing his head and nickering a hello. But the smells and sounds of horses soothed him.

Because of the lack of racing business, there was a lot of down time, and Rory began drawing the horses. Mr. O'Brian was all right with it. "Call me Tim, by the way. I get the idea you don't plan on staying here forever, right?"

Rory nodded. "I'm headed to South Carolina to try and find my family. We were going to Charleston, but we got separated when I was four."

"Don't worry, lad. People come and go in horseracing all the time; you know that. How did you come to be separated as such a wee one?"

For the first time, Rory told someone about how he got lost off the gang plank, about the chaos, about finding himself hiding behind a shed on the wharf in the dark and alone. "But I was lucky. The owner of Campbell's Stables found me, and I lived with his head trainer, Devlin Kelly. Everything I know about horses I learned from them."

Tim was sympathetic. "How terrible for you. You were a lucky one to wind up at a place like Campbell's. We've heard of them, even over here.

"You said you're going to Charleston? You know

those big pillars out front? They came from Charleston. Mr. Belmont was down there for some big expo held on the grounds of Charleston's old Washington Race Course, and he commented on them. Later, in 1901, when they closed the track, the city of Charleston gifted the pillars to the park.

"I have to warn you. You might be disappointed when you get there, I don't think they do a lot of racing down there anymore, so it might be slim pickings for you."

Rory sketched the horses, and just as Oliver had done, Tim hung each sketch above the stall door of each horse. "Gives the place an artistic look." Some of the owners paid for them.

The practice pushed Rory to try drawing Sir Samuel and Princess Lily again, along with his other favorites, from memory. He used the picture Oliver had given him of Sir Samuel in the winners' circle as his model. The horse he knew began to appear under the charcoal.

When Tim saw the finished product, he was amazed. "My, God, that's that horse! Sir Samuel, right? It's like he's alive and looking straight at me. What an animal he must be."

Rory was embarrassed but elated. "Yes, he is. Here, you can have this one. I can do many more."

Chapter 25

1912

"How can I help you, sir?" said the waitress, smiling at Finn.

He smiled back. "Why don't you surprise me."

He still couldn't believe he was flirting with a girl and not just any girl, but Emily. He'd never felt at ease with girls until he met her, but she made him feel comfortable. He would always remember the first time he saw her. It was the first time he had met Mam in the Kaffee Store, and Emily waited on them. It was all he could do to swallow his coffee.

He had shown up the next week by himself, hoping his shyness wouldn't embarrass him. Mrs. Becker served him, but Emily came over to say hello. After that, it was always Emily who waited on him. Any extra cash he had, he spent at the store.

It took all the courage he had to ask her to go walking when she got off work. "Would your parents mind?" God, that was so stupid. *Go walking.* What was he thinking?

Emily smiled. "Oh, I don't think that will be a problem. My mother already said they like you. A *netter junger Mann.* It means you're a nice young man," she said, blushing.

They walked and they talked on their off times. Emily listened to him, understood him, cared for him, though she didn't know about his being a Red Shirt. He knew she would not like that about him; like Mam. If he told her he was a Red Shirt, would she even speak to him again? Ever smile at him again? He began to dream of a different future, one with Emily in his life. But he had to leave the Sweeneys. All those ugly tales of what happened to those who dared to leave the Red Shirts flew through his head.

The Sweeneys were getting curious about where he spent his spare time. He didn't want them to find out about her. He fretted about how to tell them he wanted to leave and move back to his mother's.

In the end, he chose the coward's way out, and on a Friday morning, after all the Sweeneys had gone off to their jobs, he packed up and left a note of thanks. When his shift at the Trolley Barn was over, he got off at the closest stop to the Flemings' house and walked into the cottage with his bag.

෴

"Oh my God. You're really home! Brendan come here. Your brother's home." Bridie was laughing and crying at the same time. She plopped down hard in a chair. "I think I'm going to faint."

Brendan gave Finn a big hug. Her two boys, together at last. And look at them; they were almost the same height now. The ghost of Rory was smiling in the corner.

Bridie recovered, though she couldn't stop looking at Finn and touching his arm. "Come up with me to the big house. We take our meals there now, and I have to finish cooking. Wait until Miss Mary sees you. It'll do her a world of good."

"You two go on up," Brendan said. "I'll be up in a few minutes. I have to clear off Finn's bed. It's covered with books and stuff."

Finn was shocked when he saw Miss Mary, she looked so small and frail. But she still had a gleam in her eye. "Finn. I do declare you might be the tallest lad I've ever stood beside. And handsome too," she said winking at him and Bridie.

During dinner he noticed that Mam was getting quieter. Maybe she was tired. He *had* just dumped himself on the doorstep. Well, it would probably take a while to get used to each other again.

When Mam came back to the cottage after seeing Miss Mary off to her room, Finn knew something was wrong.

"Boys, sit down. I have something to tell you." She looked like she was going to be sick. Finn glanced at Brendan. Did he know what was coming? But he was looking to Finn for answers.

Bridie gripped the arms of her rocking chair and took a deep breath. "I have a terrible confession to make to you both. Remember that time I came to see you at your work, Finn, and you told me you were staying with the Sweeneys? Well, I introduced myself to Mr. Sweeney. Daniel.

"I should never have gone to see him. But I wanted to know how you were doing. I wanted him to convince you to come home. He said he would be glad to help."

She looked down at the floor. "He was very charming at first. Then he started badgering me to go out with him. I was worried about you, so I started seeing him. One thing led to another... and... um... we had an affair."

Shamefaced, she finally looked at them. Finn looked sick and turned his head away. Brendan looked shocked but politely waited for her to continue.

"I didn't start out wanting that, Finn. I only wanted to know how you were doing. Daniel said he'd help convince you to go home. But he didn't. Instead, he doled out information like it was gold. I was so stupid, I know. When I told him I didn't want to see him anymore, he threatened to tell you about us. Said he'd tell the world what we did together. Then he said he'd hurt you."

"Shite, Mammy! Daniel? You laid with him? How could you do that? Jaysus." Finn jumped up, paced the room, sat again, paced again. Bridie thought the room would explode with his anger.

"God, Finn, don't ask me that. Why do you think? I missed you. I'm human, and even mothers get lonely and do stupid things. I've never claimed to be a saint," she said through her tears.

"I never said you had to be one. But Jaysus. You had to do it with him? Did you do it in his house? What if I had come in? Or the others? How could you, Mam?"

"When you told me you wanted to come home, I knew I would have to tell you. I wanted it to be me who told you, not him. I didn't want him to tell you in his words, which wouldn't have been pretty."

"No, instead you tell me using your own ugly words," Finn shouted.

"Finn. Come on," Brendan said. "This is as hard on her as it is on us."

She stood in front of her boys and abjectly apologized again. "I have made a clean break with him. Whatever you do, Finn, please don't try to talk to him about it. Confronting him will only make things worse. I know how he can get."

She went into her room. She could hear the boys talking. Not the words, thank goodness. Finn's angry voice eventually lowered, as Brendan's more level voice prevailed.

Even though he had lowered his voice, Finn couldn't stop. "I don't know if I can ever get the image of Mam and that bastard Daniel out of my head. How could she have been with him? Maybe I should leave again. But where can I go?"

"I don't know," Brendan said. "Yeah, it's ugly, but all she wanted was to find out if you were safe. Is that so bad? I guess it's something we have to forgive her for."

"I honestly don't know if I can," said Finn. He made himself get into bed and lay there looking up at the ceiling, trying to calm down. A sudden image of their cottage in Ireland came to mind. Where did that come from?

"Funny. Here I am in a fury, and I just remembered our old house in Ireland. Maybe it popped into my head to settle me. This cottage reminds me of it. You were too little, but..." Finn talked about the home they were born in, until he heard his brother's snore. He'd forgotten about how Brendan could fall asleep at the drop of a hat. He laid awake for a while, comforted by the sounds coming from his brother. His blood, his kin.

Bridie calmed when she heard Finn's voice change from anger to normal. Then it became almost like he was reading a story aloud to Brendan. The low hum put her to sleep.

❧

The next day after work, Finn went to see Emily. Just being with her was soothing. They went for a long walk, and he told her about his mother and Daniel. He didn't dare tell her the details, but she got the gist. Emily had a forgiving nature, and she had friends in school who hinted at nightmare scenarios with their parents. He didn't tell her about being in the Red Shirts. One bad story at a time.

"I don't know, Finn. Your mother lost her husband, then your brother, and then you left. She had to work hard and in a new country. I'm not a mother, but I would imagine a mother would do almost anything to get back a child who ran away."

Finn shook his head. "But with a man like Daniel Sweeney? When you first meet him, he comes across as the charmer, the welcoming pub owner shaking hands and all that good cheer. But up close, he's mean, dishonest, and cruel."

"Well, your mother wasn't the only one taken in, was she?" Emily said. "Even you were, right?"

Finn nodded ruefully. "I guess so. But what she did is so shameful."

Emily was right, and it embarrassed him. Not only had he been charmed by Daniel, but he had also joined the Red Shirts. How could he be so easily swayed? Would she still care for him when he confessed his involvement with them?

That evening when he came home, he hugged Bridie. "I'm sorry, Mam. I'll get over what happened. It might take a while, but I understand you did what you did to help me. I guess we all do stupid things, don't we?"

A week after moving back, he realized his stomach no longer bothered him. When he brought it up to Mam, she laughed.

"Oh, my. I'd forgotten about that. You were such a colicky babe, always crying. I was at my wit's end with you. You were my first, and I thought I was a failure as a mam."

"Not you," Finn said. "You've always known best. Maybe that's one of the reasons I was so upset about you and Daniel. It's the first time you ever did something wrong; at least in my eyes." He stirred his tea and realized he was relaxed for the first time in years. He had forgotten what that was like, it had been so long ago. He looked at his mother. She did go through a lot, like Emily said.

"Mammy. Come make a cup and sit with me. How ever did you handle everything after Da died? And Rory too. I think of them, you know." It felt good to say his baby brother's name.

Finn got off at nine on Thursdays, his late night. Recently, he had noticed two men he recognized as Red Shirts hanging around when he got out on those late nights. Curious, he thought. He nodded at them and waved hello, which they returned. The next time, he went up to them.

"What's up, fellas? Did you want to speak to me?"

"Nah," they said smirking. "The bosses said to keep an eye on you. Thought you might need help. Word is some people might want to hurt you, you bein' one of us and all. You know how we are, protectin' our own."

They began following him home, breaking off a block away. Finn changed his routine. Sometimes he wouldn't see the men for days, then one morning they were outside the Fleming house and followed him to work. He'd see them in different parts of town; they even followed him and Emily coming home from a walk.

Bridie looked alarmed when he told her. "I've seen two men lurking around here too. Sometimes they follow me to market. That damned Daniel. I knew he was going to do something, and he won't be satisfied with just following us. He's up to something for sure."

"They followed me too," said Brendan. Bridie looked at him in horror. "Only once, Mam."

Chapter 26

1912

"Those two cops, the ones you said were Daniel's sons? They came up to me again at the market," Bridie told her boys. "Rushed up, grabbed me by the arms, and yelled they saw me stealing. Caused quite the stir. Tossed my basket—full, mind you—then said innocently, 'Sorry, ma'am, we were mistaken.' Stupid eegits."

"I know," Finn said. "Call themselves coppers, but they're just bullies, plain and simple. They came to the Barn again, and made the boss bring me outside, while they searched me. Then they told the boss I was a known thief and vandal and that he should fire me. Said he better keep his money locked up. The boss likes me, but he's getting fed up. All that ruckus interrupts work."

Other than the one time someone followed him, Brendan had not been directly bothered. But he certainly was affected by what was happening to his mother and brother.

"What if we left town?" he said one night in the cottage.

Bridie stared at him. "And take you out of school? No. Who do they think they are anyway? We have as much right to be here as they do. More, really. We're hardworking and honest. They're criminals."

"We can't let them get the best of us." Finn scoffed. "We'll just wait them out." He looked at them with a sneaky smile. "I asked Emily to marry me."

Bridie was thrilled, but anxious. What if the Beckers found out about her and Daniel? Maybe they already knew? They were always polite to her in the store, but then again, they had to be, didn't they? If they found out she'd had an affair with someone like Daniel, for sure they wouldn't want their daughter to have anything to do with her son. Even scarier, what if Daniel found out?

A week later on her way to the market, someone grabbed her arm. Only one person grabbed her that way. She wrenched free and spun around and faced Daniel smirking at her.

"Still looking high and mighty, ain't you now? Word is your useless boy got himself involved with that German bakery girl. Emily? That's her name, ain't it? You don't want her family to find out about her future mother-in-law, do you? Best you tell him to leave her alone, luv." He reached out his hand and lightly ran his fingers down her cheek, then walked away. She shuddered and rubbed her face, trying to erase his touch.

Even though she was shaking like a leaf, Bridie made it home. It wasn't until after a cup of hot tea, in her bed under the covers with the bed warmer, that the tremors finally stopped. She knew she had to tell the Beckers, but she'd wait until after she talked with Finn.

"Don't do it, Mam. I already told Emily and them I had been in the Red Shirts. That was bad enough. Don't you understand how embarrassed I'll be if they know what you did with that man? It's mortifying, Mam," he said. In a voice that dropped to a whisper, he added, "You're too old."

She almost laughed. That's what he was worried about?

"Jaysus, Finn. I'm not that old. But I am old enough to know that secrets always get out and make things worse. Daniel is a vengeful man, and he won't hesitate to publicly try and ruin you or me or anyone around us, including the Beckers. I'll tell them myself. You don't have to do it."

"God, Mam, why are you so difficult? Well, if you're so set on telling them, I'm coming with you." He shook his head sadly.

The next evening, just before the Kaffee Store closed, Bridie and Finn stopped by. Mrs. Becker was in the shop, closing up.

"Karl, look who's here. Come in, come in. Emily said you might stop by. The kaffee is still hot, and there's a few pastries left too. Sit down." She ran to the back door and yelled up the stairs. "Emily, come down. Finn is here, with his mother."

"Please don't go to any bother. I'm sorry we're here so late," said Bridie, feeling ill. "It's not a social visit, I'm afraid. I have something I have to tell you all."

After putting the closed sign up and drawing the shades, they all sat down with coffee and pastries. The three Beckers smiled at Bridie. Finn looked as ill as she felt.

"This is good for us all to be together. We're so happy Finn is going to be part of our family. Soon we'll start making plans, yes?" Mrs. Becker said.

Jaysus, they're treating her like a queen. How can she tell them? She didn't even try to lift the cup; she was shaking so. She kept her eyes downcast.

"This is not a nice story I have to tell you. You know that Finn left home a few years ago after an argument with me. I found out where he was living and asked the owner of the house, a man, to send Finn home. He said he would help, but he just gave me little bits of information. One thing led to another, and to my everlasting shame, we began an intimate affair."

She paused, trying to find the right words. She never looked up.

"It is over now, but he is not a good man. He has hurt me before, and now I'm afraid he'll hurt Finn and maybe even Brendan. He's also hinted at confronting you two. And Emily," she said in a whisper. "Oh God, I'm so sorry to have brought this upon you all." She stopped suddenly, almost panting. It was as if she had said all those words with one big breath.

Now that the words were out, she was able to pick

up her cup with both hands and take a sip of coffee. She looked up to see only concern on their faces, which brought tears to her eyes.

"I'm so sorry, but I had to tell you. I didn't want you to hear about it through talk. And I worry he may spread rumors to try and ruin your business when he finds out about Finn and Emily." The concerned faces began to look astonished, but not furious. Finn still looked ill.

Mrs. Becker was the first to speak. "Mrs. Murphy, thank you for being so honest. I'm sure it was very difficult for you to come here and tell us something so private. It is hard making our way in a new country. We all barely get by, and we may do something that others disapprove of. I certainly can't hold what you did against you. You're a woman, a widow, and alone. Finn's your son, and you wanted him back."

Mr. Becker patted his wife's hand. "None of it matters," he said and looked at Finn. "You raised a good boy."

At that, Bridie's tears flowed.

Emily, who had been clutching Finn's hand throughout Bridie's story, had tears in her own eyes. "Finn already told me, and I hope that Daniel Sweeney drops dead."

Bridie laughed sniffly. She may have been a basket of conflicting emotions, but at that moment, she knew she really liked Emily.

The malicious acts continued, and even though Bridie had rejected the idea of moving when Brendan brought it up, the idea played at the back of her mind.

"Maybe it is something we should at least think about, especially for you, Finn. Those rotten Sweeney boys—police, my arse—are going to push you too far. You'll get angry and hit one of them, and then you'll end up in prison or worse. Like your da."

"Oh, Mammy, hold on there. Have faith in me. I am not the boy I was. You know that."

"But now you're getting married, and when you have children, they could be targets too. I don't put anything past those Sweeneys. Especially Daniel."

Brendan spoke up. "Maybe Finn's right and they'll get over it soon. No one holds a grudge that long."

"Daniel does." She looked at them both. "What about Newry?"

The boys looked at her in shock. "Newry?" they said in unison. "Ireland?"

Bridie laughed. "No, luvs. Newry, South Carolina. I told you about it, don't you remember? That's where Ian moved. It's a mill town about 250 miles north; the Piedmont, they call it. Far enough that those Sweeneys can't get to you. It could be the answer to our prayers."

"Are you saying we should move to Newry?" Finn asked.

"It's Ian, isn't it?" Brendan laughed. "You miss him, don't you? I always wished you'd marry him, you know. Now he lives too far away."

"Brendan. What are you talking about? He's like

my brother for pity's sake," Bridie said, a flush rising up her neck. She waved her hands in front of her face. The boys elbowed each other and smiled devilishly. "You don't know what you're talking about. You're the one who said maybe we should move, so get your mind back on that. And quit trying to make up a romance where there isn't one. You're too old to believe in fairytales.

"But Newry might be the answer. It's far away, and we know someone who lives there. I'm going to write to Ian tomorrow and ask him what it's like up there."

When Ian's letter arrived, she saved it to read later when she was alone. She didn't want any unsolicited comments from the boys about their nonexistent romance. Nor from Miss Mary, who, Bridie knew, felt the same way.

February 22, 1912

Dearest Bridie,

What a nice surprise to hear from you. I miss you. And Brendan and Miss Mary too, of course. And it's great news about Finn and Emily.

This Newry is not at all like our Irish Newry. It's a mill town, very small, and different from a regular town because everything centers around the mill. Most every adult, and a lot of the children, even the wee ones, work in the mill or in a store or another business owned by the mill. Finn, with his experience at the Trolley

Barn, should have no problem getting a job here. If he can't get one, I'll hire him, and he can help me build houses.

It was a rough trip getting here. It took us three days, but we left last winter, when it was cold and wet, and the wagon had axle problems. It's best if they travel after the spring rains and before it gets too hot.

Sincerely, Ian

God, it was totally business like, despite the *Dearest*, which did send a little shiver through her heart.

In February, Finn and Emily were married in the Kaffee Store. It was closed to the public for the first time ever, and passersby stood outside looking in at the guests enjoying all the good food and pastries.

"Oh, for sure this is absolutely the happiest day of my life," a slightly drunk Bridie said to Shirley and Miss Mary. "I was so afraid for him when he was gone. What was he going to do with all that anger? Now look at him."

Miss Mary patted Bridie's hand. She too was a little drunk, though maybe it was just the excitement of getting dressed up and being at a party where she was enjoying playing the family elder.

Finn and Emily moved in with her parents in their apartment above the store.

Brendan had applied to the College of Charleston. Mr. Thorpe felt he had a good chance of a decent scholarship. It had a good math department, which he'd need if he decided to go into engineering.

"All that digging and tunneling you did as a boy will be put to good use." Bridie laughed.

Her boys were on their own paths, which filled her with pride. Not just for them, but for herself too. It had been a rough road, sometimes.

∽

Bridie relaxed by working in the garden. Her first pitiful attempt many years ago had produced onions and garlic aplenty, while the turnips gave that Thanksgiving dinner a peppery punch. With Miss Mary's advice, each year produced a wealth of wonderful vegetables. Later in the summer, the tomatoes, pole beans, summer squash, and cucumbers would be ready for picking.

Miss Mary usually joined her outside, sitting nearby. She always brought a magazine or the paper to read, often reading certain interesting articles out loud to Bridie.

"Good Lord, Bridie. Listen to this. 'The RMS *Titanic* sank in the North Atlantic Ocean on April 15, 1912. It was the largest ocean liner in the world. *Titanic* was four days into her maiden voyage from Southampton, England, to New York City with an estimated 2,224 people on board when she struck an iceberg at 23:40.'"

Bridie was stunned. Her mind snapped back to their voyage some fourteen years before. God, those poor people. She shuddered.

One Thursday night, after his usual late shift, Finn was jumped by two men in the alley near the Trolley Barn. It was a quick and ruthless beating, done by the two thugs who had been following him. They didn't even try to disguise themselves. They ran away when the night watchman ran out. He helped Finn, bloody and moaning, to sit up.

"Don't call the police," Finn groaned. "I know those bastards, and I'll take care of them myself. I just need to get home. Can you manage a ride for me? Tell the boss in the morning, but nobody else. Just tell him I'll be back at work on Monday."

The Beckers were appalled at Finn's condition.

"I'll be all right," he said. "I can move everything, though I think they might have busted a few ribs."

In the morning, Emily ran to Bridie's and brought her back to see Finn.

"God, it's all my fault. No, Finn, it is. If I hadn't been with Daniel, none of this would have happened."

"Mammy, I would have left the Sweeneys anyway, and they probably would have reacted the same way, even if you two had never met. No one leaves them or the Red Shirts. You and Daniel being together just made it more personal, I guess."

Mrs. Becker sat with them while her husband minded the store. Bridie dipped a donut in her coffee. "I wonder if Emily and Finn should get out of town."

"Karl and I think you're right, Bridie. Finn told us there is this place called Newry. It is so far away." Her voice cracked, but she was a woman made strong by the trials she and her family had been through. "Maybe they should go now."

"Ian can take care of them when they get there," Bridie said. She was strengthened by the other mother's pain and courage.

Emily looked at Finn, who nodded. Looking at the two women, Emily took Finn's hand. "As long as we're making plans, I guess we should tell you now... I'm with child."

"Oh, my goodness," the two mothers said, laughing and crying. After they calmed down, Mrs. Becker nodded, her mouth set in a line. "Well, that settles it. Now you must move. There's no knowing when they will stop." Leaning over, she squeezed Emily's other hand. "Your pa and I are prepared. We want you to be in a place where you can have your baby and live safely.

"Pa will talk to Mr. Hanks today—you know, the livery we use—and explain the urgency. He should be able to get his truck here tomorrow or the next day to take you up there. It will not be suspicious. He's often here at different times of the day.

"When the police chief comes in today for his morning coffee, I'll bring him upstairs. He needs to see Finn and what those hoodlums have done."

Bridie looked uneasy. "Finn, aren't a lot of the police in the Red Shirts? Daniel's sons are. Is that wise to get him involved?"

"Not all the police, Mam. Daniel and his cronies don't trust the chief. From what I heard, he's pretty straight-minded and honest, and he's made life difficult for some of the members."

"He's German, not Irish," said Mrs. Becker with a sneaky smile. "That's why he comes here every morning. He will be most interested in finding out who is hurting a member of our family."

She leaned over to kiss Emily. "Now, it is unusual that I'm not in the shop. Pa is probably going crazy down there. You can tell him your news later. I promise I'll not breathe a word about the baby."

She gave Bridie a hug. "Do not keep blaming yourself, dear. Sometimes there is no explanation for evil. And our children will be fine, my friend— *Schatzi*, we say in Germany. And I think we can start calling each other by our first names, yes?" She turned again to her daughter.

"And you, my sweet Emily, can be the pioneer for another Kaffee Store. Later, when things have quieted down, Pa will go up there and help you open another one."

She stood up, gave a little hop, and a happy little scream. "A baby! We're going to have a baby!"

Chapter 27
1912

May 20, 1912

Dear Mammy,

 It's nice here, and we feel safe, but it's so far away from home. I miss you and Brendan. It was uphill the whole way, and the roads twisted and turned bad, but we had a good driver, and we made it in one piece. It was cold when we got here, much colder than Charleston, but now it's warmer.

 Working in the mill isn't much different from what I was doing before. Just different kinds of machinery, and noisy. Very noisy. I got a job real quick in the mill, in the weaving room. Usually there aren't many openings, especially in that room, and when there are, they go to one of their children or the next person in line. Thank goodness for Ian. He didn't say so, but I think he pulled some strings. For Emily too. She's working in the company store.

Right now, we're still living in the rooming house. Thanks for the money you gave us, or we'd be sleeping outside. When you're a new worker in the mill, you have to do a 5-week training period, without pay. After that, if they like you, you're hired, and then you can live in one of the houses. Seems like highway robbery to me, but I'm not complaining. My training time is almost over, so we should be up for a house soon.

That's all for now, Finn

Bridie sniffled and handed the letter to Ingrid—Mrs. Becker. They traded off reading their children's letters. They met either at the shop or at the Fleming house, where Miss Mary could join them. Ingrid announced that Bridie's scones and shortbread were equal to or better than her pastries. All the baked goodies were making Bridie's skirts a bit tight around the waist.

May 29, 1912

Dear Mrs. Murphy,

I got a job in the company store. It was dumb luck and for sure, I'd much rather work here than in the mill. It's all right, but I miss the Kaffee Store. Thank you for the scone and shortbread recipes. I'm going to try making some things on my own. They said I could sell them in the store.

We moved into our own house! I'll tell you about it in another letter.

By the way, your friend Ian came into the store. He told me you were his best friend.

Have to run, Emily

Bridie finished reading the letter to Miss Mary and gently folded it and put it in her apron pocket.

"Bridie, you're so sweet to read me their letters and include me in your family," Miss Mary said.

Bridie smiled. "Well, you are family."

Four days later, Ingrid came for tea bearing a letter from Emily. "Guess what! The baby moved!" The letter was passed around, the three women chatting busily about things to knit, crochet or sew.

July 24, 1912

Dear Bridie and Brendan,

You asked what Newry looks like. The mill and the bigger buildings are all brick, but the houses are wood and painted white, all lined up, side by side, on each side of the streets. Broadway, the main street, has elm trees for shade. Or they will give shade when they've grown some. They're still just saplings. It's a pretty town. They say it's like the mill towns up north, and they copied the houses, which they call salt boxes. They do kind of look like giant wooden salt boxes, like the one in the Kaffee Store by the stove.

Some of the houses are really crowded with lots of people in them—aunts and uncles and grandpas and grandmas and lots of little ones. Almost all the people are from around here, mostly farmers who got tired of nearly starving, fighting droughts or floods or just bad luck. There's a few mountain folk too. But they seem to have trouble taking to all the rules and the noise. Many of them go back to the peace of the hills.

Love, Emily

Bridie was walking home from the market, daydreaming, and didn't notice the two men who jumped out in front of her. She was only a few blocks from home and made to move around them, but they stayed with her, blocking her way.

"Whatcha doin', Miz Murphy? We heard you might need some help now that yer son is gone," one said, leering at her.

A man and a woman tried to go around them, and Bridie attached herself to the woman. "These men are bothering me. Do you mind if I walk with you a bit?"

"The nerve of some people these days. Ruffians everywhere," tsked the lady. The man glared at the two men as they slunk away.

"Lately it seems so, doesn't it?" Bridie said. "Oh, look, we're here already. I can't thank you enough for letting me walk with you."

She opened the gate and ran toward her cottage. Bridie berated herself for not seeing the men. She had become acutely aware of everyone and everything around her, which still usually included one or two of those awful men following her. Now she decided, in future she would carry an umbrella. Not one of those prissy parasols, but the big umbrella with a point at the end that had belonged to Mr. Fleming. She'd wield it like a spear; she'd show those men.

August 25, 1912

Dear Bridie and Brendan,

We have everything we need here. Which is a good thing, because the nearest town is Seneca, around 5 miles away on a very hilly road. We've never been there. Don't know how we'd get there anyhow.

All of us are paid every Friday, in cash, in an envelope that lists our deductions like rent and whatever we buy in the store. You don't really need money—there's no place to spend it. Even in the store it is charged to your account. I'm sure glad I finished school, or I never would have gotten this job.

People leave me their market orders in the mornings, and I keep a tally, which the bookkeeper will take out from their pay. We put their orders into pasteboard boxes and load them onto the dray wagon. Then the driver and Lightening, the old, blind mule, deliver them to the houses in the afternoons.

The store really does have everything. Listen to this! Coffee, sugar, lard, beans, clothing, patent medicine, wood and coal, writing paper, pencils and pens, blankets, bolts of cloth, linens, feed, nails, horseshoes, horse collars, bridles, plows, hardware, beans, potatoes, flour, pickles in a wooden barrel, fat back meat, chewing tobacco, snuff, smoking tobacco, pipes, clothes, shoes, tools, toys…EVERYTHING!!

If we don't have what you want in the store, we get it from one of the company's storage barns, where they keep the big things like furniture, wagons, and even caskets. That's where they keep the coal and firewood too. We haul it out to you and take it out from your pay. We can also order things from factories. The store motto is "Everything from Soup to Nuts." I say it's everything from coffee to casket!! Ha, ha.

Have to go. Love, Emily

Emily's letters were so good, Bridie could visualize the store. And *her* daughter-in-law was in charge of it. She ran to the Kaffee Store to show the Beckers the letter.

September 4, 1912

Dear Bridie and Brendan,

I'm as big as a house! The midwife says I'm doing fine, and I feel good. We go to church most Sundays. Back when the town was just starting out, the church services were held in a meeting room above the store, but then the Union Church was built and the Baptists and the Methodists share it, taking turns every other Sunday. Now that's Christian for you, isn't it? We go

*to the Methodist service. It seems more like the Luther-
an church I used to go to in Charleston. It's a pretty
church, small, white wood with a white steeple and
stained-glass windows with points at the top.*

*There's always something going on upstairs in the
community hall. Meetings, gatherings, weddings and
dances. The Masons meet there and other clubs like
the quilters. There are quite a few men who play in
a band: banjos, fiddles, and guitars mostly. And they
play baseball against teams from the other mills. Those
are always big days. Ian's on the team, and Finn says
he's as good as a professional player. He's teaching
Finn now so he can get on the team too.*

Emily

The harassment of Bridie had not ceased, and she
stopped Miss Mary from accompanying her to the
market. It wasn't just because of her age. The last time
they went, the little old lady, still very sharp, noticed
the men following them. "I don't think you've been totally honest with me, Bridie. Those men look quite evil.
You shouldn't be walking alone."

That afternoon over tea, Bridie told her a cleaned-
up version of the trouble the Sweeneys were causing her.

"So that's why Finn and Emily moved so far away.
Goodness, dearie, you should get away from here too.
It's too dangerous for you. What if they do something
to Brendan?"

"They just want to irritate me. This is Brendan's last year in high school. He graduates next year, and then he'll be going to college. No, they'll get tired of it soon enough. And I can't leave you, now, can I?" She really couldn't leave Miss Mary—she was family now.

September 10, 1912

Dear Mam and Brendan,

The mill is so noisy that when all the looms are working, Emily can hear the clatter up in the store. The shuttles are way bigger and stronger than what you use on a regular loom. Everything is motorized, so they just need one man at each loom. Twice the output with half the labor. And those shuttles fly back and forth like crazy. They're heavy and sometimes they'll fly right out and can really hurt someone. There are about 400 workers on 650 looms. That's a lot of machinery, I can tell you! And when the mill shuts down for the night, the silence almost hurts, it's so quiet.

Cotton fluff is everywhere! It floats around and gets in your hair, your ears, nose and mouth and all over your clothes. It even floats around outside. All us workers wear caps of some sort to keep it out of our hair. If you want to make someone mad, just call him a lint head.

Sometimes I think about how bad my life got. I'm sorry still for the hurt I caused you. I was so angry about everything, and I know that was why I ended up in all that trouble with those Red Shirts. Thankfully there's none of them here. Though people say there's KKK around these parts.

Love, Finn

P.S. Ian taught me how to play baseball, and now I'm on the team! Well, I'm mostly on the bench, sitting. When I do play, it's usually at the end of a game, mop up time. He plays shortstop and he's really good. He's always asking about you, Mammy. Brendan was right. He's the man you should be with.

Bridie read the letters from Newry avidly. Emily was a dear, writing her chatty letters, allowing Bridie to become fond of her in her own right, not just as Finn's wife.

Finn's comment about Ian made her laugh. Her boys were still playing matchmaker. Well, it was going to be a long time before she ever saw him again, she thought wistfully.

In December, Emily gave birth to a healthy baby boy they named Charles. Bridie wondered, if there really was a heaven and if Charles was there, did he know he had a namesake? And if he knew that, did he also know she had forgiven him years ago?

If Rory had died, was he with Charles? How would they find each other? Did families get together? Or was it just spirits floating around bumping off each other? What a strange notion heaven is.

Chapter 28

1913

In May of 1913, the College of Charleston offered Brendan a fully paid scholarship. It was cause for celebration, and Miss Mary offered to host it. Bridie invited Shirley, the Beckers, the Thorpes, and some of Brendan's friends for dinner. Bridie cooked, and Miss Mary set the table, the two of them gabbing and laughing. If Miss Mary could have, she would have used every piece of china and crystal.

It seemed to Bridie that the harassment had dwindled. She still carried the umbrella, but she hadn't seen any more men following her. So, she was surprised when, one day in May, on her way to the market, a hand gripped her arm, forcing her to stop. She didn't even have to turn around to know who it was. Her heart sank.

"Hello, Bridie. I've missed you, and I know you've missed me too. What have you been up to, luv?"

Bridie tried to pull free, but Daniel had a good hold of her.

"Get away from me," she shouted. People turned to look.

He laughed and tugged her along, winking at bystanders. "She really loves me. This is just her little game she plays with me, ain't it, luv?" he slurred, his breath wafting alcohol. Jaysus, it was still morning.

At the back door of the tavern, she slammed the umbrella over his head. It did nothing but enrage him. He dragged her into the entry, tearing her skirt and dislodging her bonnet. She made herself fall in a heap at his feet. Her dead weight was too heavy to get her upstairs, so he settled for a few kicks aimed at her curled up body. Panting, he sat down on the stairs looking at her through his bloodshot eyes.

"You've been busy, haven't you, missy? Managed to get that useless rat son of yours out of town. Maybe, I'll see what I can do to the young one. Brendan, right? The little engineer?"

Bridie sat up. "No, Daniel. I'll do anything you want, but not him."

He leered at her, bleary-eyed. "As if I would want to do anything with you. You're going to fat, and you were never any good anyway. Just a cheap whore. And it's too late for that little mama's boy. My men are tailin' him already. He'll never know what hit him."

"You bastard! Why are you doing this? What did I ever do to you to deserve this?" She grabbed the banister and though in pain rose until she was standing above him.

He still sat on the stairs, eyeing her malevolently. Looking down on his balding head, his mussed hair sticking out in greasy strands, she was filled with disgust. A sudden rage overwhelmed her. Without even thinking, she raked her hands down both sides of his face, her nails leaving red welts, some beginning to bleed.

"Shite!" he bellowed. He leapt up, grabbed her by her hair and punched her in the face, then in the chest and stomach and back to her face—again and again—while yelling obscenities. Someone banged on the door, yelling. "Boss, is that you? What the hell is goin' on?" The door crashed open, and two men barged in.

Bridie slid to the floor praying they weren't there to egg him on. She would die. She didn't have the strength to fight three of them. She opened her eyes and stared at each of them. At least they'd never forget her eyes.

"Jaysus, boss, stop. You wanna kill her?"

She watched Daniel. He looked surprised to see them. It was as if he had just woken up. Their faces looked back at him in shock. Their normally natty boss was untucked, his hair was disheveled, and he had deep scratches on his face dripping blood onto his shirt.

"Christ, boss. She did that to you? You should see yourself."

Daniel took a step back, ran his fingers through his hair, and took a deep breath.

"She's just a bitch beggin' for it, and I gave her what she deserved. Get the hell out of here, you nosy bastards. You too, you whore," he spat out, giving her one last kick.

Somehow, she staggered home, once more in pain and humiliation and thankful she had worn her big bonnet and had the big umbrella to shield her. She kept her eyes down, forcing one shoe toe, then the other to appear under her skirt. If she focused only on her toes, she might make it home. This time, though, a small feeling of victory ran through her misery. She'd scratched his face badly, and it would be hard for him to hide those marks.

In her cottage, she drew a bath, sank slowly into the water, and scrubbed at herself, especially under her fingernails, trying to remove any trace of him. He could have raped her right there in the stairway if he hadn't been so drunk. She shuddered at the thought. She must have some ribs broken, but hopefully her innards were safe. She dried herself off gently, dressed in her nightgown, and kept herself under control until she looked in the mirror. Her face was another story, and there was no way of hiding it.

Brendan found her lying on her bed, under the covers, staring at the ceiling and shivering. Seeing him made her cry again

"Mam. Mammy. Whatever is the matter? It's all right now, I'm here, you're safe now." He was holding her, maybe too tight. Bridie groaned, and he loosened his hold. "I'm sorry, Mammy. I didn't mean to squeeze you so hard. Was it that Mr. Sweeney?"

She nodded mutely.

"It's all right, Mammy. You don't have to talk right now. Here, I'm going to cover you up again before you freeze. I'll fix us some tea."

Bridie reached for his hand when he stood. "Stay with me."

"I'm not going anywhere, Mammy. But you need to get warm. I'll be right back."

She knew Brendan had never seen her not in control. He was too little to remember how she was when Rory was lost or when his da died. Now here he was, grown up, taking care of her. It made her weep more.

"I put a little whiskey in your tea, like you used to with us. It can't hurt. And I'm heating up the bed warmer in the fire. It will be ready in a few minutes."

"Oh, thank you, luv."

It was all she could do to not cry out from the pain as he helped raise her up. He held the cup to her lips while she took small sips, then she laid back, exhausted, holding the quilt pulled up to her chin. "That tastes so good, dearie. I'm sorry, but I can't stop crying." Brendan crawled under the quilt with her, and they sipped their teas. She even took a nibble of shortbread.

"We should call the police, Mam," Brendan said.

"God no. Daniel's two older boys are policemen. They can't be trusted. No, dearie. Right now, I just want to sleep. You're my rock, Brendan, and after I've rested, we'll figure out something."

Brendan got up, re-tucking the blankets. "I'll get the warmer, then I'll go up to Miss Mary. Between the two of us we should be able to find something for supper.

I'll just tell her you aren't feeling well. You can tell her what you want tomorrow."

That night, Bridie dreamt about Rory. It had been a long time since he had appeared in her dreams. In those dreams he was always still a child, alone and crying. But in this dream, he was a man, like Finn. There were spires behind him. Were they churches? Masts? Was it the old Newry? America? Charleston? He seemed healthy but searching. For what? For them? It wasn't a scary dream; in a way, it was oddly comforting.

The next morning, she asked Brendan to help Miss Mary get breakfast. "Just tell her I'm still a bit poorly, but I'll be up there later in the afternoon."

"I'll tell her, Mammy. But later we're going to the Beckers so they can bring up that police chief. Like they did for Brendan. Those Sweeneys need to be punished."

When Bridie finally did go to the big house, Miss Mary took one look and started twisting the handkerchief. Then, as if a switch had gone on in her head, she called up the nursing skills she had used with her mother and sister. She dabbed on astringent and salves, wrapped Bridie's ribs, and made her lie down on the chaise in the music room. Bridie didn't resist and spilled out the story.

Miss Mary shook her head. "Poor Brendan. He didn't let on at all what really happened."

"Yes, he's a good lad, isn't he? Daniel said he was going to hurt Brendan next," Bridie said, her lip quivering.

Miss Mary shushed her and took her hand. "We'll get through this, dearie, and that terrible man will get his. I just know it."

When Brendan came home from school, Mr. Thorpe was with him. "He knows what happened, Mammy. I told him. Someone else needs to witness this."

The teacher gaped at Bridie, then quickly recovered. "I'm sorry I've interrupted you in your troubles, Mrs. Murphy. I'm sure you want to keep all this private, and I'll respect that. But if called upon, I will be a witness for you. And I hope the police do something. What happened to you is an outrage."

Early the next morning, Brendan walked Bridie, limping and wearing the big bonnet, to the Beckers' apartment. Ingrid clucked and fussed over Bridie, offering coffee and pastries.

Karl Becker looked sick. "This is what you were afraid of, isn't it? And to think it could have been Emily or Finn. Thanks to God, and to you, they're not here. The police chief is downstairs having his daily coffee. He saw Finn. I think I should bring him up here to see you too. This has to stop."

Bridie tried to control her panic. "I don't want to see anyone, but I know you trust him. Two of Daniel's sons are policemen, and they've been harassing me. But he saw Finn, and now he can see me. He should know what's going on."

"You're right," Karl said. "He should know. He and I have known each other for years. We all came over on the same boat, and you find out a lot about people crammed together in a small space. You know that. You can trust him."

Bridie nodded hesitantly. "I hope so. I can't keep living in fear."

Karl brought the chief upstairs to see Bridie. They told him the whole sordid story, and that Emily and Finn had left town in the middle of the night.

"I am so sorry, Mrs. Murphy. I warned Mr. Sweeney myself, after what happened to your son. Looks like he needs something more serious to happen to him. No one should undergo what happened to you. Or to your son. Those Sweeneys have always been trouble. And those Red Shirts too. They don't know, but their time is coming to an end," said the chief. "I can arrange to put some uncomfortable pressure on Mr. Sweeney and his tavern. He's always on the edge of breaking the law, and if we look, we'll find something wrong, for sure. Something requiring hefty fines. Or better yet maybe even close the place down for a while. And those two shifty sons who call themselves policemen? Maybe a year of night duty down at the docks will help them to think more clearly."

Brendan took Bridie home and tucked her in with the bed warmer. Then he ran over to Hayne Street and brought Shirley back with him. For a few minutes, Bridie allowed herself to bask in Shirley's wrath against Daniel. It was good to hear someone else express her own feelings. For a bit.

"All right, Shirley. No more about Daniel. *Ever!* We

know he's a complete bastard, but he's in the past now."

Bridie recovered slowly. Her mirror showed a plethora of facial bruises that changed colors daily: purple to green to light brown and finally to yellow. Miss Mary reminded her daily to use the Ponds Vanishing Cream. "It's more important than ever to keep your face moisturized, dear. You don't want any lasting scars." Bridie wondered if there was a miracle cream for the scars in her brain. Brendan did the marketing on his way home from school and escorted Miss Mary on her errands.

Bridie thought it curious that Miss Mary suddenly had her own errands, but Brendan just shrugged when she asked him what she was doing.

"She likes me to take her into the museums, and sometimes we stop for tea afterwards at the Kaffee Store. I enjoy it too, and it's the least I can do for her."

⌒﹏⌒

One evening, a few weeks after the beating, Miss Mary got up from the table after dinner, headed to the liquor cabinet, and took out the Old Grand-Dad. A new bottle, Bridie noticed. After pouring three glasses, she looked at Brendan slyly and they raised their glasses.

"To you, Bridie dear, for everything you've done for me, and for Elizabeth, God rest her soul. And to our move to Newry." She took a sip. "Go on Bridie. Toast to our good fortunes."

"*Our* move to Newry? What do you mean, Miss Mary?"

"Well, I wasn't going to make you wait until I died.

And at the rate that oaf Sweeney is beating up on you, you'd die before me. So, I sold the house."

"You did what?"

"Bridie, sit down, close your mouth, and stop asking stupid questions. A few months ago, when Brendan and I went to the Gibbes Museum, I overheard two of the guides saying they needed more space. Can you imagine? That big new building and they've run out of room already? I asked them how that could be possible. They said it wasn't that the museum was too small. But that their collection had become quite renowned, and they needed buildings to house visitors, like professors, historians, students, American and foreign… In short, they needed a house."

She took a sip of her drink, savoring it—and the look on Bridie's face.

"Then, after Finn and Emily had to leave town, and when I found out what that revolting man had done to you, I went to Brendan with my idea."

Brendan was grinning from ear to ear. "It's brilliant, Mam. Last week, they bought the house. The whole property."

"What exactly are you saying?" Even though she'd almost stopped breathing after the liquor, she held out her glass for another shot. "Miss Mary, Charleston is your home. You were born here, in this house, and you've lived in it all your life. Are you telling me that we are all going to Newry?"

Miss Mary smiled benignly. "That's exactly what I'm saying, Bridie. We're rattling away here by ourselves. You're in danger and so might be Brendan, and I hardly have any friends left. Elizabeth and I had always planned on willing the house to you when we died." She smiled at Bridie, who was looking totally dazed with that piece of news.

"Yes, dear, to you. Who else could we leave it to? You're the one who did all the work and saved us from bankruptcy. You're my family. But now your family is in Newry, and you should be with them. I know you would never leave me to be with them. Now I won't have to watch you wish I would hurry up and die so you could go live with Finn." By now both women were crying.

"Who knows?" Miss Mary said. "Maybe now you'll start paying attention to Ian. He's such a sweet man."

"You too?" Bridie laughed through her tears. "But enough foolishness. We've a lot to do if we're to move out."

"I've already made arrangements with Hanks Livery, the same driver who took Finn and Emily. He'll be here in five days, so yes, we have to get cracking."

"What about school, Brendan? You still have a month to go," said Bridie.

"I'm staying behind… Hold on, Mammy; hear me out. Mr. and Mrs. Thorpe have offered to let me live with them while I finish this year, and I've already accepted. When I graduate, I'll get a ride up to Newry and join you there for the summer."

"I'll be able to hold Charlie," Bridie said in a choked voice. Her grandson was growing by the day and Bridie had wondered if she'd ever see him. And Miss Mary was right—she'd see Ian again. She tried and failed to ignore the quickening of her pulse. Her mind needed to focus on moving.

"Remember, Brendan, when I told you we only have one or two chances to grab our lives? Well, this is one of them. For all three of us."

Her chin quivered. "I am so lucky; I feel guilty wanting more. But… it would be so perfect if Rory was here too."

"I know, Mammy. I miss him, too, even if I was too young to know him."

That night in bed Bridie let herself weep, mostly for joy, at Miss Mary's generosity, at Brendan's maturity, at Finn's new life, safe, with a family.

But some of those tears were sad. She still held out hope that Rory was alive and that someday he would get to Charleston to find them. But they'd be gone. Would he stop looking? If he heard the name Newry, might he put it all together and go there? To another town named Newry?

Chapter 29

1913

Bridie bolted up in bed. Jaysus, what the hell was that? Was that what the landlady was talking about last night? That would mean it was four thirty in the morning. Didn't she say there were more bells? Good Lord.

She was in shock. One day she was the maid in the Fleming house, a job she had held for sixteen years, and five days later she was in a boarding house, sleeping in a bed with her former employer, in a town named Newry, of all places.

Miss Mary let out a snore. Bridie laughed out loud. Mother of God, how her life had changed, and so quickly. She thought back to other instances: Charles flirting with her, their marriage, his death, the ship to America, Rory—Oh God, Rory—Miss Mary coming up to her at the employment agency, Daniel. (She would work to erase him.) Well, no one could say she hadn't led an interesting life, that's for sure.

The trip to Newry had been a frightening uphill trip just as Finn and Ian had described. They left Charleston early in the morning while it was still dark, with the same driver who had spirited away Finn and Emily. "I ain't askin', but there must be somethin' terrible back there for you all to be sneakin' out of town before it's mornin'."

Bridie wondered how they didn't drive off the edge of the road. But other than her crushed fingers from Miss Mary's grip, there were no mishaps. They'd stopped three times for the driver to put in gas. In addition to their luggage, there were five gasoline cans in the back of the truck.

"Never know what'll happen on these long trips. There's hardly any filling stations along the way. You two walk around a bit and stretch your legs."

He shuffled uncomfortably. "Um, you ladies might want to relieve yourselves behind those trees over there. I'll stay here near the truck."

Before they got back into the truck, Bridie asked him if they were in the mountains, it was so steep.

"No, ma'am. These are just hills, foothills. Here, look over there. That's north. You're lucky it's such a clear day. See out there, those dark bluish-grey points? Those are the Blue Ridge Mountains, and now you know why they call them blue."

It took them over ten hours to get to Newry. "Thank you, ma'am," the driver said to Miss Mary after he had unloaded all their luggage. He had been paid before they left, but she had just given him a tip of five dollars. "It was a pleasure."

Mrs. Queen, the landlady, was gruffly affable, like Mrs. Millbury. Guess it's a requirement for the job, Bridie thought, as the woman showed them to their room.

"I'm sure you're tired, so just take your overnight bags for now," she said to Miss Mary. "We can tend to your luggage tomorrow."

Looking at Miss Mary, she said, "Emily told me one of you was gettin' on, so I gave you my biggest room on the ground floor. The bathroom is right next door. The two other rooms are empty right now, so you've got the floor to yourselves." She offered Miss Mary her arm and led the way down a well-lit hallway to their room.

"I have to warn you about the town bell. The first bell goes off at four thirty in the mornin', and I start servin' breakfast at five." She smiled gruffly and left the room.

Bridie was glad that Mrs. Queen was so respectful of Miss Mary. The little lady deserved it, especially seeing as how she'd given up her house and life to come live in this far away, little town.

The room was fine, and within a half hour Bridie and Miss Mary were lying side by side in the bed, whispering to each other.

"It's like when Elizabeth and I were little girls. We had our own rooms, but we always snuck into each other's beds after we were tucked in."

Bridie, never having had a sister, was envious listening to Miss Mary tell that story.

The bell had thoroughly awoken Bridie and she slipped out of bed. She was used to being the first up, though usually it was around six. Miss Mary looked her age and more, snoring softly with the blankets pulled up to her chin. Bridie dressed quietly and shut the door behind her, eager to check out her new surroundings.

She had no trouble finding the dining room. She only had to follow the smell of fresh coffee and fresh baked bread. She passed the parlor, where their luggage was stacked. When it was packed into the truck, it had seemed so much. Now the pile looked a paltry amount to be starting a new life with. But maybe not. Compared to what she had with her when she left Ireland, it was enormous.

"Good morning, Mrs. Queen," Bridie said, thinking it the perfect name for a landlady.

"Mornin', ma'am. You heard the bell, then? Pretty hard to miss, ain't it?" she laughed. "There's more to come. This is a mill town, and the mill runs on a strict schedule. The next bell is at 5:15. The call bell goes off at 5:45, and at 5:55 it's rung once every minute until six, when they start work."

She pointed to the sideboard. "There's coffee and tea over there and some muffins and biscuits. Some of our guests need to be at the mill at six, openin' time, and I make sure they have time to eat."

"I'm an early bird anyway," Bridie said. "And if you need any help, just let me know. I know my way around a kitchen."

"Yes, Emily said you worked as a housekeeper. And you were from Ireland before that?"

308 ALIX CRAWFORD CARNEY

"Aye. I came from a town named Newry, in Ireland, so coming here seems like it was meant to be, if you know what I mean. I think I'll try coffee for a change." She poured herself a cup and took a biscuit off the platter.

"Yes indeed, meant to be." Mrs. Queen got herself a cup and joined Bridie at the table. "I can sit for a minute. Everything's most ready; I only have to scramble up some eggs."

She looked at Bridie. "It's different how you say our town. You say NEW-ry, and we say NUR-ey. To think you'd end up here in a town with the same name as where you grew up. In Ireland, no less. What are the chances, eh?" she said with a laugh. "You know, Mr. Courtenay, who owned the mill … well, his family was from a town in Ireland named Newry. He passed five years ago, and his sons run the mill now."

"I hadn't heard about his death, but I knew his family was from my Newry. Course I never knew them. But Miss Mary knew Mr. Courtenay. They grew up together in Charleston and went to all the same social events. Her sister, Elizabeth, had a crush on him, but they went their separate ways." Bridie felt embarrassed; she sounded like a foolish society lady gossiping behind her friend's back.

The coffee was delicious, especially after she added more cream and sugar; she felt quite awake.

"So, you know Emily. Do you know my son too? Finn?"

"Oh, yes. We all know each other in this tiny place. You've got a grandson too, now, don't you? Will you see him today?"

"Charlie. I can't wait to help Emily with him and get to be a real granny."

There was a knock on the front door, which Mrs. Queen went to answer. When she came back, she said, "I guess you know someone else in town," she said.

"Oh, Ian! How did you know I'd be here?" She gave him a hug. "You look just the same."

Jaysus, what must she look like? It had only been two years since she last saw him, but she knew she looked older. Of course she did. She was thirty-eight; almost forty, for God's sake. She had only done a quick brush of her hair; her dress was the same as yesterday's. Thanks to Ingrid's pastries, she had put on weight. And he looked just the same.

"I just wanted to stop by and say hello. Mrs. Queen, Bridie is my best friend. We met on the ship *Newry* that sailed from the city of Newry to Charleston, back in 1898. And now we're back in Newry. Funny how the name *Newry* keeps popping up, right?"

"You always tell a good story," Mrs. Queen said, smiling broadly at Ian.

"I have to run, Bridie, but we'll get together soon, when you've moved in with Finn and Emily. Tell Miss Mary hello for me."

Other boarders began to drift in. Bridie introduced herself and chatted some, then went to tend to Miss Mary. Despite the three bells that had gone off, she hadn't moved. Bridie wondered if she herself would ever be able to sleep through the ruckus. She laughed.

After everything else that had happened to her, a little bell ringing was nothing.

She didn't want Miss Mary to miss breakfast, so she gently woke her up and helped her dress. It was daylight now, and more people were in the dining room. Bridie was anxious to be about her own business, and Mrs. Queen promised to see to Miss Mary.

"She'll be fine. It might be June, but it's still chilly in the mornin, so bring a sweater," she said as she gave directions to Finn and Emily's house.

It was cool, far cooler than in Charleston in June, but refreshing. Once outside, it became obvious that she would have no difficulty getting around this town. Right beside the boarding house was a sweet-looking church, white with a tall, skinny steeple. Were there Catholics here, she wondered? Maybe yet another change in her life.

Small, neat houses were lined up like sentries on both sides of the road. Each house had a front porch and a chimney right in the middle of the roof. They were all white, and except for the sizes—small, medium, and large—looked the same. All were two story with front porches the width of the house. There was one front door on the small ones and two doors on the larger ones, house numbers in black, over each door. Depending on the house size, there were four or more windows down and up.

She easily found Finn and Emily's house. Before she could knock, the door flew open, and there was Emily...with Charlie!

"I knew he was the first one you wanted to see," Emily said. "Here he is clean and fed and happy to see his granny." She was crying as she handed off the baby. "I'm sorry. I'll be all right in a minute. But it's such a relief to see you here, safe and sound."

She gave Bridie, crying her own tears, an awkward hug around the baby. "Look at us both."

"I know. I can't tell if I'm crying for the joy of holding this one or for the relief of being here safe and with you both," Bridie was finally able to say.

Emily led her into the house. She started to reach for Charlie, then dropped her hands. "In the beginning, I couldn't share him. I just wanted him all to myself. Finally, Finn told me, 'he's part mine too.' And he's part yours too."

Bridie laughed. "I remember, I felt the same way with Finn. By the time the other two came along, I couldn't care less who held them." She twinged when she said it, thinking of Rory. Little Charlie wiggled in her arms.

There was something different about holding her own grandchild. He was a part of her and Charles too. He was proof of their love. She snuggled the baby, and he nestled his head under her chin.

"I hope you'll let me take care of him when you're working. From the minute he was born, that's what I've been dreaming of. And let me help with the cleaning and cooking."

"Finn said that's what you'd say. Of course, you can take care of him." Emily looked uncomfortable. "I've got to get this off my chest. I think you're the bravest person I know, after everything that happened to you with that animal Mr. Sweeney."

"Oh, I don't know. You and Finn had to flee, and you were pregnant," Bridie said. "But being free of him is like a stone lifted from my body. Let's agree to never mention him again."

They fell into easy conversation as Emily showed Bridie around the house and to the privy out back. "Sorry about that, but we only have running water at the kitchen sink. We get our drinking water from one of the wells scattered around town."

She looked uncertainly at Bridie. "I hope Miss Mary won't be insulted by our lack of niceties. I know she comes from money."

"She'll be fine," said Bridie. "This has all been a grand adventure for her. So far, anyway. She knows I'll take care of her, and she's never been a snob."

"She won't be the only old person living here, and they get by all right. Maybe she'll make some friends," Emily said. They were standing in the empty room outside the kitchen.

"It's lucky you'll be living with us," Emily said. "They call this house a four-room, for one family of four—or more. That's the least you can have, and believe me, they can pack in more. When we found out you were coming, it was perfect timing. Otherwise, we'd have had to share the house with another family."

Bridie, who was totally captivated by Charlie, suddenly looked up. "How did you find out we were coming? I just found out five days ago."

"Ahh," Emily grinned. "No one told you yet. When Brendan found out Miss Mary was going to sell the house, he wrote to us. Miss Mary included money to buy whatever we needed. We ordered two beds, two tables, a dresser, and two more armchairs, but they're coming from the warehouse in Anderson. It won't be here for another few days, so you'll have to stay in the boarding house a little longer. We'll sleep upstairs, and you and Miss Mary can have this room for your bedroom.

"I know. I can see you thinking it's a dining room. But here, a room is just a room, and people sleep wherever they can."

"You forget I come from Ireland. We know how to crowd people into tiny spaces."

Emily continued. "You'll always know what the time is because that bell rules the town. You'll get used to it, just like the rest of us did. If a worker is not in the mill by that last bell at six, they're not allowed in at all. And then there's the curfew bell at nine p.m., when we're all supposed to be off the street. Have to get our sleep so we can get up early and start all over again."

She looked embarrassed. "I sound like Finn. You know how he can get. I'm not complaining, mind you, but sometimes it gets a bit much. Everything for the company. The mill closes at 6:15, but they keep the store open till seven, in case someone needs something, so I don't get home till then. When I was still nursing him, they did let me run out to feed him at noon and again around five. Now he stays at Mrs. Burns's with the other little ones. Finn picks up Charlie on his way home. Well, picked him up. We won't be needing that now that you're here."

"At least you had a safe place for him."

"Yes, we did, and I suppose I should be grateful. But it's hard for one lady to look after a lot of babies, and I worried he wasn't getting enough attention. It will be so much better for him to be with you.

"Now, it's time for me to get to the store. It opens at seven, after the mill has started up. They don't want people hanging around the store before work. You'll come along and see it?" Emily took Charlie and put a sweater on him.

"Of course. And then I'll begin my new job as granny." They set off to the store, Bridie carrying Charlie.

"It'll warm up by late morning," Emily said. "I like the weather up here. None of the mugginess of Charleston and the air is cleaner here, in the hills. The mill puts out its own smell, but it's not that bad. Kind of a sweet, damp smell, like a wet dog. Finn says it's worse inside, and in the summer, the heat and humidity really get to the workers."

"I smell animals too," Bridie said. "Reminds me of the farm."

"The company built a central barn for equipment and the mules and then three other smaller barns for the cows, goats, and pigs that some people have. Most of us keep chickens in our yards, and we all have gardens for vegetables. The cattle that belong to the workers graze on Pasture Hill, that big hill over there, and when the wind blows the wrong way, you'll smell it. Like today.

"As you can see, the daffodils and irises are out everywhere, willy-nilly. We didn't have a garden last year. What, between moving, being pregnant, and then having Charlie, it was too much. But this year we put in a small vegetable garden in our yard. Finn's a pretty good farmer. He said he learned it from you."

Bridie was touched. When all the bad stuff happened between them, everything became dark and angry. She had forgotten Finn helping her. Funny how the mind works. And forgives.

"It was so dark in here before. It still is, but not as bad." Emily said as she unlocked the door to her workplace. The sign on it read, The Newry Store. "Those front windows don't let in much light because of the awning, and neither do the windows up high. The old man who worked here before wasn't much for keeping things neat, so I had my work cut out for me when I started. I have to say that the Courtenays never gave me any grief when I told them what I wanted to do with the store.

"The first thing I did was clean the windows. What a difference that made. I painted the inside walls white and put in more lights and had new shelves made. After that it was just a matter of organizing it."

Bridie was impressed. Every shelf was stacked neatly with supplies, the aisles clear, the floors swept. "You're quite the organizer, Emily."

"I got it from my parents. In the baking business you better know where everything is or your *krapfen* will be crap. Sorry about the language, but that's straight from my father."

"Don't apologize to me. I've been known to curse more than once," said Bridie, laughing.

After leaving Emily at the store, Bridie ran straight back to the house, Charlie happily jouncing in her arms. What a luxury to care for just one baby and not have to also run a farm. She puttered in the kitchen, cleaning up the few breakfast things, happy to do so.

Bridie cooked supper and insisted on cleaning up as well, though Finn helped by drying the dishes. Then they settled into chairs around the table to talk.

"I want you to have these," Bridie said. She gave the candlesticks to Emily. "Consider them a late wedding gift. They were a wedding gift to Finn's grandparents, his father's parents."

"Thank you, Bridie. To think you carried them all the way from Ireland. It means a lot to us." Emily put the candlesticks above the fireplace.

"Now we have a family heirloom for this one," Finn said, his voice uncharacteristically thick.

When the bedroom furniture was delivered a few days later, Bridie and Miss Mary set about making the room theirs.

"Look at us, Bridie. We're roommates. Who could have guessed at that idea? I bet you feel lucky it was Elizabeth who died first, eh?" Miss Mary said with a funny smile, part sad and part mischievous. Bridie barely stifled the guffaw moving up her throat.

The first thing Bridie hung up in the room was her mother's Celtic purse. On the dresser, she put her mother's little dish, its delicacy still unmarred, and her father's lamp.

Miss Mary, too, had brought a few treasures that shared space on the dresser. From a big box she had refused to let Bridie look into, she took out two small paintings.

"Oh, Miss Mary. I love those. They'll look lovely hanging in here. A little bit of home for you." She gave her a hug. "I still can't believe you gave up your whole house to protect my family."

Miss Mary smiled. "But, Bridie, you are my family."

Bridie nodded. "Yes, Miss Mary. We're all each other's family now, aren't we? What else is in the box?"

"Don't be so nosy, Bridie. You'll find out soon enough," Miss Mary said with a smug look on her face.

"Finn, would you bring in that box from our room, please?"

When he returned, Miss Mary continued speaking. "As Bridie can attest, my house was filled with paintings. When I grew up, it was important to have good art in your home. So, in thanks for taking me into your home, I've brought you two of my favorites. Landscapes, sisters to the two small ones I brought for our bedroom."

Bridie wondered at this little lady, born to wealth and ease. How had she become such a kind and generous person? Her sister certainly was not, and it didn't sound as if either of her parents were. Not for the first time, Bridie thanked her lucky stars that it was Miss Mary who sidled up to her that day outside Dayton's Employment Agency.

Miss Mary was the one to bring up money. "Thank you, Emily, for giving me such a good accounting of how you spent the money I sent you. Now Bridie and I need to know how we can contribute. We don't want to be a drain on your finances. When I sold the house, I made a bit of money, and I gave Bridie half. So, we can help you out."

Finn settled with his son on his knee. "Rent for a four roomer is a dollar a week, Miss Mary. We would accept twenty-five cents from each of you. We'll put it in a kitty for food and sundries."

Miss Mary said, "It doesn't sound like enough. I feel like we're getting off too easily."

He laughed and took Emily's hand. "Well, it's extra for us. I don't know about you, Em, but I feel downright rich right now."

One June day Bridie stopped in to see Ian. Having already seen him at the boarding house took away most of her nervousness. The large sign on his building read Courtenay Manufacturing—Lumber company, and below, in smaller lettering: *Manager, Ian McManus, Master Carpenter.* He rushed up when he saw her, giving her a big hug, while the men inside looked on with curiosity.

Ian seemed more mature, but he would, wouldn't he? Now that he was a man in charge of a business. He took her around the shop and introduced her to his employees. She could tell they liked and respected him.

On the walk back to the house, they fell to talking like the good friends they were—a natural, amiable kinship. "Those issues you thought the workers might have with you as the new boss are in the past, I see," said Bridie. "I'm not surprised. I knew you'd have no problems."

Despite the naturalness of their friendship, Bridie found herself overly aware of his physical presence near her. Where did that come from? She'd certainly never felt it before. It was because of all those people who'd told her they should be together. She wished they'd just kept their thoughts to themselves.

Bridie fell naturally back into the role of housekeeper, caretaker to Miss Mary, and now nanny to Charlie while his parents were working. That's if she could wrest him away from Miss Mary, who was delighted to find she had a way with a baby. Every time Charlie gurgled at her, she teared up. "I can't help it, Bridie. How lucky am I to still be alive and have an old dream come true?"

The house might have been small, but for Bridie, it was more work. There were four adults, one of them dirty and linty at the end of every day, and all were hungry. But the noise and confusion and being around young people was like a tonic.

From the beginning, Finn had taken to helping Bridie clean up after dinner. "You know you don't have to do this, Finn," said Bridie.

"I know, Mammy. But I like to. I did it for Emily too." He looked at her wistfully. "Mostly it's because I'm so thankful we're together. All that bad stuff was like a bad storm we went through, and now it's over."

"Yes, luv, it certainly was. And I love you helping me in here."

⟡

Bridie bought a pram at the store and took daily walks with Charlie. Newry was certainly no Charleston. It was only about one square mile, but each day was a new adventure. Most of the businesses were on Broadway: a barber shop, a milliner, the mill offices, the livery stable, a cotton gin for local farmers, a corn mill. And of course, the store, where they'd sometimes visit Emily. Before school let out for the summer, she watched the children running back and forth from the schoolhouse to their homes for lunch.

Sometimes she walked up the hill past the school and past the Courtenay mansion, about a quarter mile away from the mill. It reminded her of some of the mansions in Charleston, though this one stood apart, looking down on the town with a lofty air. It was called Innisfallen, named after Mr. Courtenay's family estate in Ireland.

When she was up there, just as the driver had pointed out to her, she always looked north to see the mountains far in the distance. So far away, they were in another state, for goodness sake. They were blue, but, depending on the light and the air, they exhibited multiple variations of color. She never tired of looking at them.

In addition to the bell, there was one other thing she thought she'd never get used to—The Dummy. It was a steam-powered locomotive that pulled one open freight car; a hopper-car, they called it. It ran on a single-track line from the Courtenay Depot at the top of the hill, down through woods, then along the tracks on Broadway between the street and the line of houses, ending up at the mill.

Big, black and belching smoke, The Dummy was a monster. It was also the workhorse of the mill, bringing raw cotton and supplies downhill for the mill and the town and exporting the finished mill products, woven cloth, uphill to the depot and a mainline track. There, the bolts of cloth would be transferred onto regular trains going elsewhere around the country.

The cursed engine created problems coming and going. It was a steep grade, and occasionally, the brakes wouldn't hold. Then it would begin to slip down the track towards town. Once the train ran totally amok with people jumping away from it on both sides of the track. Miraculously, it stayed on the rails, going between the mill office and a house, until it stopped with its nose off the rails.

Sometimes the brake failures were due to children greasing the tracks, then hiding to watch the mayhem. They were fascinated by the train and lined up alongside the track, leaning in to touch it or jump on it for a quick ride. Bridie gave herself fits, imagining all the possible accidents just waiting to maim and murder children.

⁓

"There are a lot of good things about a mill town, and for us, being gone from the Sweeneys sure is a major good reason," Finn said. He and Bridie were cleaning up after dinner. Both Emily and Miss Mary had gone to bed early.

"But there's a lot of not so good too. The company owns and controls everything—the mill, the town, the businesses. And they regulate all the affairs of the town and our living conditions. Basically, they own us. And if you get behind at the store, they just keep deducting until you only have a pay stub telling you how much you owe. Even if you wanted to leave, you couldn't. Sometimes it just makes me really pissed, you know?"

He smiled at Bridie. "Back in the old days, when I was so mad at everything, I'd have probably said something and gotten myself fired. Don't worry, Mam," he said to her worried face. "I have no intention of ruining what we have here. Certainly, not by some stupid remark about management. Having you here to help out, and Miss Mary, too, Emily and I have an easy time. A lot easier than many. I know I'm lucky." he said emotionally. "All I have to do is think about Charlie."

"You've earned your luck, you and Emily. I'm really proud of you Finn."

"It makes me think of Da. I think of him a lot, you know. Got himself all riled up about the Brits. God knows there was reason to be pissed at them, but he kind of messed it up for us, his family, didn't he?"

Finn was the most like his father, and Bridie knew he chaffed at the control the company had over everyone. When he said he knew how lucky he was, she breathed easier. Newry was safe and offered a decent living for him and his family.

Rory snuck into her head. It no longer frightened her to remember him. It saddened her but it consoled her also; it would be horrible to never think of him. If he was alive, was he doing something he was proud of? Did he have fun? Did someone love him?

As the weather improved, Ian and his dog Archie often joined Bridie and Charlie on their walks. Charlie broke out in loud screeches whenever he saw the little dog, and Archie replied by barking and licking the boy's chubby fingers and face.

Once when Ian was with her, a fancy car drove by with luggage tied into the open trunk. Bridie stopped to let the dust settle behind it.

"I bet those are the Courtenays," she said.

"Yep," Ian said. "Heading off to the depot, I'd guess. They travel a lot." He laughed. "I don't know, of course, that's just what I hear."

"Are most of your workers from Newry?" Bridie asked.

"Yeah, most of them worked in the mill. I hired one guy I used to work with from Charleston, and he brought his brother, a painter. We're kind of in the middle of nowhere up here, so when I have to hire, it's from the mill.

"This used to all be Cherokee Indian land. My best carpenter, Inola, is Cherokee. His name means Black Fox. He is an artist with detail work; intricate stuff the other men don't have the patience for."

"Are there many Cherokee here?" She had only a vague idea about the people who'd lived in this land before the Europeans came.

"Inola doesn't talk much. But between him and a couple of the old timers here, I got some of the story. A very sad story. We threw them out of their land, which they had lived on for thousands of years, here and in Georgia, Tennessee, and Alabama. Gold was found on their lands in Georgia, and that was it for the Indians. The government passed the Indian Removal Act, and over the next years, the Cherokees, and other tribes too, were marched out west to Oklahoma. 'Indian Territory' the government called it."

Ian shook his head. "That's over 900 miles! Imagine. Men, women, children, old and young walking through all the seasons, including blizzards. Sometimes it took up to four months to complete. They call it 'The Trail of Tears,' and I'm sure that's not an exaggeration."

"Why can't people just be left alone? It reminds me of back home in Ireland. Though the Brits didn't force us out, just tormented us. And killed some of us. And my husband wanted to kill the Brits. Humans are not very nice to each other, are we?"

"No, Bridie, sometimes we're not."

They walked in silence until Archie's and Charlie's antics distracted them.

"Nothing like a bit of foolishness to take your mind off serious things," said Ian.

Shortly, Charlie started squirming his way out of the pram. He grabbed the toy Bridie had tucked in beside him and tossed it away. She picked it up and handed it back. He tossed it again and laughed.

"Oh no, that's his devil laugh. I'm going to take him home. Once he starts chucking things, even though he's laughing, he's tired, and the next thing I know, he's rubbing his eyes and screaming. It's like a switch goes off in his head. Finn was the same way."

"I'll see you later then. Might I come by one evening to see Miss Mary?" Ian said, patting Charlie's head.

"Of course, Ian. You don't have to ask. She'd be delighted."

Bridie watched him as he walked away. She felt a little flip in her chest. Jaysus, what a fool. She's a granny now, for goodness' sake. Charlie let out his first scream, and she sped for home.

Chapter 30

1913

Bridie was happy. Both her boys were now in Newry. Brendan had graduated, and with honors. Bridie had a moment of regret that she couldn't be there for the ceremony—a son of hers graduating from high school! But it was only a moment. Her life was too full to spend time regretting things.

There had been no further activity from the Sweeneys, but just to be on the safe side, Bridie and the Beckers arranged for Brendan to be secreted out of town. Two days after he graduated, Hanks Livery left Charleston in the early morning darkness, bringing up another member of Bridie's family to Newry. Ian hired Brendan for the summer, giving him the extra room in his apartment over the carpenter shop. He'd go back in September when classes began at College of Charleston.

Mill baseball season was in full swing. Newry, Anderson, Issaqueena, Pendleton, Greenville,

Spartanburg, Cateechee… All the mill towns played each other in rounds. Newry had a good team this year and hoped to be in position for the Mill League play-offs in September.

Most of the mills closed for two days over the Fourth holiday and the workers enjoyed the time off. Bridie had never known a vacation or even more than a Sunday off from work, so she too felt the change in the rhythm of life.

"You'll see, Mam," Finn said. "It's a good party."

"And," Emily said, "the cake bakers are as competitive as the ball players."

Bridie had talked to the neighbor ladies and learned that they would all bring food, and the whole town ate together after the game. She was almost giddy as she made her version of potato salad: a cold *colcannon*.

"What's colcannon?" asked Emily, who was busy making pans of krapfen.

"I can't believe I haven't made it for you. It's just mashed potatoes with cabbage, and lots of butter of course. This is the same, but I won't add the butter or mash them. I'm adding pickles and vinegar."

On July Fourth, Newry beat their archrivals from the Issaqueena Mill, but all team rivalry was dropped afterward to enjoy the party.

Ian and the boys came over to Bridie, sweaty, dirty, and grass-stained. "Look at you all," said Bridie. "Your da would have been proud—both his lads playing ball."

Finn grinned at her. "Da taught me to kick a ball. Ian taught me baseball."

"I don't know about that. You're a natural. And so are you," Ian said, nodding to Brendan. "Those Thorpe boys taught you a lot. By the end of summer, you'll be good enough to try out for the school team in the spring."

Most of the townsfolk had staked out places at the picnic tables and were going through the lines at the food tables, where the proud housewives served their specialties.

Ian pulled out a brown jug. "My homebrew. I kept it on ice, so it's nice and cold."

"Oh no," said Emily. "Be careful, Bridie, it's his locust beer. Finn always acts like a complete fool if he's had more than two glasses."

"Oh, now, now. Don't go insulting my beer, Emily. You said you liked it last year. Here, Bridie, try some. It's good."

Bridie took a drink. "You're right. It is good and not too sweet. How do you make it?"

"I use the pods from the honey locusts, and when the pods are ripe, the pulp inside is very sweet. I cut them in half, lay them on the bottom of a barrel, add some sliced apples, two cups molasses, and cover with boiling water. I let it sit for three or four days, and then I've got beer and … and, well… there you go."

"I wonder if the Courtenays will be here again this year," Emily said.

"Do they join the party?" Bridie asked. She'd not yet seen anything of them but the back of their car and its dust.

"They used to always come on the Fourth of July," Ian said. "In the old days it was in their horse-drawn carriage. The older folks still talk about it, especially how impressive the horses were, a team of bay horses prancing and tossing their heads. Now, if they come, it will be in their cars. They'll hang around for a bit, chatting people up, then head back up the hill."

Finn muttered, "It's like they're royalty, for God's sake, and we're their loyal subjects."

Looking embarrassed, he said, "But I do like those cars; I just can't help it. I'm a mechanic, and those cars are the most beautiful things I've ever seen. One's a Hupmobile and the other's a Pierce Arrow, a 1905 Great Arrow." His voice trembled with awe and envy.

"Well, no one's perfect," Ian laughed. "We all have our weaknesses."

"I asked the chauffeur if I could help take care of them. When I told him I used to work on the trolleys, he said yes. I can't wait."

"Did you ever go into their house, Innisfallen?" Bridie asked Ian.

"Twice," Ian said. "Once to repair the staircase and once to meet the architect who designed the house. Campbell Courtenay, the son who's running things now, knew I was interested in architecture and invited me. It's quite grand."

Ian's face broke into a big smile. "I do have some news. I bought a piece of land up on the hill, near the schoolhouse, where I'm going to build a house—a grand little house just to suit my needs."

"Here's to you," Finn said patting him on the back. "Pass around that jug so we can toast you."

Bridie nodded. "That's wonderful, Ian. I'm sure it will be the best house in town. Innisfallen doesn't count. It's too big and fancy, faraway on its hill."

These days, Bridie allowed herself the luxury of looking back on her life, and thoughts she had pushed away came to her. She remembered wondering if she could ever again have good thoughts of Charles and Ireland.

She had forgiven Charles long ago; in place of her anger was a terrible sadness. He had done what he believed in, but it meant he chose Ireland over his family. Finn was right; he messed it up for his family.

But her memories of the excitement of their early love, their babies, his tales of Irish history, his humor… She could remember him fondly now.

Ireland was lost to her. While they were living in Charleston, Miss Mary brought her attention to an article in the paper about Ireland. That age-old enmity continued between Ireland and England, now with the "Irish Volunteers," a new name for another nationalist group, carrying on the old battles. The Brits still ruled, and the Irish Catholics still starved and got themselves killed doing stupid revolutionary skirmishes.

She would never go back there, even if the opportunity arose. The thought of another ship passage made her sick. The chances of finding Rory (or his grave) were slim to none. Where would she even start? Instead, she chose to dream that Rory, if he was alive, had found happiness. It wasn't impossible. Who knows?

She had made a pledge to only say prayers of thanks, never to be greedy and ask for anything else.

Except for Rory. Surely, that wasn't selfish.

One morning, Bridie took Charlie for his stroll, the same as she had almost every day. She looked over and saw the open framework of Ian's house. It was beautiful, the fresh light making the particles of cotton lint that floated all over town shimmer. She gasped at the unexpected beauty. And from nowhere came the image of Ian. Tears welled in her eyes. She was astonished at the sudden feelings she had about him: his steadiness, his kindness, his care for details, for people.

But what really knocked the wind out of her and caused her to nearly fall to her knees was the recognition of her own affection for him—much different from how a friend cared. It was a deep, safe love she felt. A feeling she hadn't known since Charles.

Was this a true feeling? If it was, how could she have hidden it from herself? Was it willful ignorance on her part that she shut her eyes to this good man? She had tucked these thoughts away, deep inside herself. It was foolish to have such thoughts about someone she thought of as a brother.

How could she trust her feelings? She, who had allowed herself to be with someone like Daniel. She shuddered each time she remembered him and their sordid meetings. What they did, how he treated her, and how degrading it was. She had risked so much and all for naught—Finn came home on his own. If she could stoop so low as to be with someone like Daniel, how could she expect a decent man like Ian to feel any respect for her? Her face grew hot as she remembered that last conversation before Ian left Charleston, when he told her he knew she was seeing Daniel.

Now, though, here in Newry and knowing she and her family were safe from Daniel, maybe it was time to stop being so harsh on herself.

After all, what she did wasn't that awful. She hadn't killed someone or robbed them. She'd had an affair with a dreadful man. She was lonely and stupid and in fear for her son. She certainly wasn't the first woman to make a bad choice in a man. It was time to get over her mortification and regret.

Even though she forgave herself, she couldn't just jump into something with Ian, who she suddenly seemed to have unsisterly feelings for. It wasn't fair to tempt him with her fickle heart. A heart that couldn't be trusted.

Apparently, her head couldn't be trusted either. It refused to stop thinking of Ian. She remembered the many instances with Ian and all the little things he had done for her; was still doing even now.

Despite her best intentions, her feelings for Ian grew. She felt like a silly schoolgirl. Oh, what she would give to be able to talk to Kathleen or Shirley. Was she just a flighty woman—an aging, silly one—wanting to love and be loved after a bad affair? She couldn't lead him on. God, she would never want to hurt him that way. Better he never found out she was dreaming about him.

Bridie, and Charlie in his pram, became a common sight in Newry. Archie seemed to know their schedule, often coming along without Ian. When Ian did join them, she was keenly aware of where their bodies were or when they accidentally touched. Was it just her? Sometimes it seemed Ian was accidentally bumping into her, taking her arm, touching her hand. Who was initiating it? They looked and sounded normal, she hoped. But she knew there was an electricity within her. Was it in him too? Dare she make the first move? Her heart fluttered. God, but she was ridiculous.

One day in September, Ian invited Bridie for a picnic at his house, still a shell, but now partially framed in.

"You don't have to bring a thing," he said, refusing her offer to bring the food. "You always take care of the food. I might be a bachelor, but I can cook and bake. I'll make egg salad sandwiches and an apple pie."

The invitation was for Sunday, so Bridie left Charlie and Miss Mary in the care of Emily and Finn. As she walked away from the house, she thought she saw Finn and Emily nudging each other and smiling.

God, now she was seeing things. Were her feelings that obvious?

Ian took Bridie for a tour of his house. "You'll have to use your imagination," he said as he took her hand.

"This is the front hallway and…" His descriptions allowed the house to appear in Bridie's eyes. "Nothing fancy. The usual living room, dining room, kitchen, and bathroom downstairs. But they'll all have two or more windows. I love having light, the more the better," Ian said. "And high ceilings to let in even more." He showed her where the stairway would be. "There will be two bedrooms upstairs, and another bathroom."

Bridie was impressed. "Two bathrooms. It's almost as grand as the Fleming house."

"Are you making fun of me, Bridie? Well, go right ahead. It's mine, and I can make it whatever way I want."

"Yes, you can. And you should. You're a great carpenter," she said with enthusiasm. They both looked a little embarrassed at her fervid compliment.

After the tour, they sat on a blanket Ian had spread on the ground, chatting the way they always did, lunching on his sandwiches and sipping sweet tea.

Then a lengthy pause drifted into a charged silence.

"Bridie," Ian said, almost in a whisper. "Bridie, I have to tell you something that I can't keep to myself anymore. I love you." He sat back and waited.

She took a deep breath. She could not look him in the eyes, so looked down at the blanket. Her hands trembled.

"I think I love you, too," she said. "I think I started to love you way back, when you did the work on my little cottage at the Flemings'."

Now she did look him in the eyes. "I stuffed those feelings away somewhere. I was poor and busy with two lads. And still in mourning for my husband and my lost Rory. You were so young and just starting out… I couldn't admit to those feelings, and I hid them away somewhere in the back of my brain. And I made some terrible mistakes."

He stared at her full on, unable to speak. Suddenly, laughter rose up, and he elatedly fell back on the blanket, where Archie promptly leapt on him, barking.

Bridie hadn't expected this reaction, but his joy was unmistakable.

"Bridie, love. Oh, my dear, dear Bridie." He sat up and pulled her down, wrapping his arms around her while Archie happily jumped on them both. "I love you. My God, how I have wanted to say those words to you. From the moment I first saw you on the ship and through all your ups and downs." He suddenly stopped talking. Even Archie was quiet, moving off them to the corner of the blanket.

They were lying inches from each other, body to body, face to face, eye to eye, mouth to mouth. They inched their heads even closer. With a slowness that made her ache, their lips met—so softly and tenderly it could hardly be felt.

Then the heat rose and flowed through her body, making her suddenly breathless. She paused, just enough to catch her breath. Her eyes were still locked on his; she didn't dare close them for fear he might disappear. Then he leaned in, and their lips met again. Finally, they parted. "Bridie. Marry me, please? Make me part of your life."

"Oh yes, Ian." Bridie sighed; her whole body flushed with the feeling those words gave her. "Oh yes, yes, yes."

Ian leapt up and ran to his house. He kept a jug of his locust beer in what would become the root cellar. He poured them each a glass, and they toasted, their words and their faces displaying all that they felt for each other.

"Lord, Ian. That beer is quite breathtaking."

Chapter 31

1913

In September, Rory said goodbye to Tim and a now busy Belmont Racetrack. On May 31, 1913, Belmont Park reopened to an enthusiastic crowd, the second highest number in attendance since 1906. The large crowd sent a loud statement that racing was back. Gambling was still illegal, but bookmakers found ways through the loopholes. Horses and betting were interwoven, and if a race was run, someone would find a way to place a bet.

Tim asked Rory to stay on a few months. "I haven't had a vacation in years, and the missus is getting cranky. The owners agree I'm overdue for some time off, and they're giving me two months of paid vacation in August. Unheard of, but who am I to question their logic? They want you to cover for me. Apparently, I'm not the only one who appreciates your work. If you change your mind about going to Charleston, they'd hire you permanently. For someone so young, you sure do have what it takes to run a stable."

Rory was glad to help Tim out. He was a good man, like Devlin. Rory would get to Charleston soon enough, and in the meantime, he could build up his reputation, especially now that the track was open. He had reference letters from Tim to add to Devlin's and Sean's, as well as the name of a track in Charleston where he planned to seek work.

∽

When Tim returned from his well-earned vacation, he gave Rory an envelope. "Consider it your bonus," Tim said. "I've never given anyone a bonus before, but you've earned it. Don't let it get out or my reputation will be ruined."

Rory opened the envelope and found two train tickets.

"The first ticket takes you past Charleston to Savannah," Tim said. "From there you'll take another train back up to Charleston. It's a bit out of your way, but it's through totally different country. You've probably never seen country like it before. You, bein' an artist, I thought you might want to see it."

They were standing in front of the stables, Rory's bags around his feet. "I have something for you, too," Rory said, reaching into a large canvas bag filled with a number of rolled canvases. He unrolled one and held it out, his arms spread wide. It was an oil painting of Sir Samuel. Tim shook his head, but Rory insisted.

"No, I want you to have it. You deserve it. You gave me a job and a chance. Plus, you'd heard of him."

"Well, thank you. I'll treasure it, and it will remind me of you. You're going to go far in the horse business. Now, you'd best get on your way," Tim said. "You don't want to miss your train."

Rory gathered his bags of clothing, artwork, paints, and canvases and, feeling a bit like a beast of burden, walked out between the stone pillars that had come from Charleston. At Queen Station, he took the Long Island Railroad Extension into Manhattan, where he boarded the train leaving for Savannah at 12:25 p.m.

A conductor helped him find a seat and stow his gear above. "The seats on this side of the aisle don't convert to bunks, but they're comfortable. You won't have any problem going to sleep."

Rory sat down, trying to look like he took a train every day. Opening the brochure the conductor had given him helped. The cover showed a pretty woman in a white dress holding a string with a weight in front of a map of the eastern United States, grandly touting: "*Straight as a Plumb Line to the Winter Resorts of the Carolinas and FLOR- IDA … A Magnificent all Pullman electric lighted train…*" Pretty posh, boyo … *magnificent resorts*. He laughed. If Devlin could only see him now.

The total trip was scheduled to take twenty-one hours. Rory glanced at the cost of the tickets. Tim's generosity had preserved almost a third of the money he had saved for the trip. He was glad he had insisted on Tim taking the painting.

For the first several hours, Rory sat in the comfortable car. Initially, he could only stare out the window in awe as the train moved out of the city, through towns, and on into country. Then he remembered his sketch pad and began to draw quickly, just bits and pieces to remind himself later of all he was seeing.

When his hand cramped and his back began to complain, he got up and walked through the train, an adventure in itself. Sitting in his seat, he hadn't realized how much the train bumped and swung side to side. He felt the fool, lurching around, nearly landing in someone's lap more than once. At the end of his car, he debated opening the door, when another passenger came up behind him.

"Here, let me open it for you."

Rory jumped back at the whoosh of air and the clacketing of the wheels.

"Pretty amazing, isn't it?" said the man. "I'm guessing this is your first trip, yes?"

Rory gulped. "Yes." It was all he could say. He felt nauseous watching the rushing ground passing underneath.

The man moved through the door and shouted back to Rory. "The easiest way to get used to it is to stand outside on the gangway connection here and watch the world go by."

Rory doubted that, but the man looked comfortable standing outside, so he took the step. Samel came to his mind. He remembered how he and the other horses panicked when being trained to go into the starting gates. They got used to it.

He smiled at the man. "You're right."

He lurched less than before going back to his seat and promptly fell asleep. When he awoke, it was dark outside and his stomach was complaining. He made his way to the dining car, now walking almost normally, and arrived just before it closed. He was the only diner, and the kitchen had run out of some things on the menu. The waiter made him feel at home and helped Rory choose roast beef, mashed potatoes, squash, and rice custard for dessert, all for one dollar. Rory felt like a king. The menu reminded him of the ship to New York, but they had a big kitchen on a giant ship. How could they cook such meals in the car of a train?

He bade the waiter a good night and went to the lounge car, where he found the man he met earlier— name of James, he learned— with a group of other young men, all in high spirits. Waiting for his beer, he was reminded again of the ship and his bunk mates. They had all kept in touch and would be interested in hearing about his new adventures.

After two beers, exhaustion kicked in, and he headed back to his seat. While he'd been gone, the cars had been transformed into dimly lit sleeping cabins. One side of the aisles still had the upright seats, where passengers whispered to each other or read under dimmed lights while others dozed. The other side of the aisles had been converted into the famous Pullman sleeping berths with curtains draping them off. He could hear the sounds of passengers nestling into their hidden beds. He was in a strange, cozy world hurtling down the tracks. He found his seat and was asleep in minutes.

The next morning, he had a hearty breakfast of eggs, bacon, biscuits, and grits, the latter new to Rory. "Welcome to the South, sir. Just put a lot of butter and salt and pepper on 'em," his waiter said. At 9:20 they disembarked in Savannah, where he then boarded the train to Charleston.

He was transported to a new landscape. New, but strangely familiar. Palm trees! He knew them only from illustrations in *Robinson Crusoe*. Large birds swooped over open plains of water and grasses. Other trees, tall with large spreading canopies, had strange tendrils hanging from the branches, shaggy like Finn McCool-sized beards.

Finn McCool. He flashed on a dim memory of his father's old stories of Ireland, and of his brother named for a hero of legends. He fought the tears that suddenly threatened to fall. How did he ever remember that?

His talkative neighbor told him the land was called the Lowcountry, the palms were cabbage palms, the large trees were live oaks, and the dangling stuff was Spanish moss. Sometimes, in the distance he saw lighthouses. He sketched feverishly until they pulled into Charleston three hours later.

Rory stepped down from the train. He felt he should celebrate somehow—fall to his knees and kiss the ground or raise his arms in jubilation. He did neither, his feelings overwhelming him. It was September 15, 1913. Fifteen years it took for him to get here.

He picked up his luggage and started off. The first things he noticed were the heat and the humidity. The noonday sun beat down on him, and the dampness made it hard to breath. Even if he found a job in a stable, how could horses run in this weather?

He looked at the faces seemingly unbothered by the heat. So many faces. Would he even recognize any of his family if he saw them? Would they recognize him? Were they here? Were they even alive? How long would it take? Months? Years?

He was driving himself crazy. As much as he wanted to find his family, he couldn't spend every day looking for them. It was best to find a place to stay, get a job, and become more familiar with the city. He'd gone this long without them, he could go a little longer. In the back of his mind, thoughts flickered about bad things that could have happened to them, and he wasn't ready to face those yet.

One of the lads he'd met the night before on the train had told him about a boarding house only a half mile from the station. He checked into his room, comfortable and well-lighted, and went for a walk in Charleston.

After living in dark, dank Belfast, he was almost blinded. The Charleston sun seemed to shine hotter and brighter here than up north. Certainly, it was the most picturesque city he had ever been in. It was a city made for artists, and there were many, stationed everywhere on sidewalks and parks, some alone, a few side by side. At first, he just glanced at what they were painting, worried they might think him rude. But then he remembered how passengers on the ship watched him and how he hadn't minded it. So, he stood near them and watched. Most ignored him, but some smiled and nodded. He restrained from talking with them. For now. He had to get a job and start the search for his family. But he was itching to set up his easel when he had time.

When he had checked into the boarding house, he'd told his landlady he hoped to find a job working with horses. She suggested he go to a local bar nearby called The Last Race.

"It's owned by Roscoe. I don't even know if he has a last name. But he's an old jockey and raced in the last race run at the Washington Race Course. If there's anything to do with horses, especially racehorses, he would know."

The Last Race looked as old as the little man behind the bar, who glinted up at him through his glasses.

Rory introduced himself and asked if he knew of any jobs at racetracks.

"Glory be," the man squeaked. "You're in Charleston and looking for a job with horses at a track. If youda came two years ago, youda been out of luck. But there will be a race again this year in November, at Palmetto Park during the fair."

Rory let out a big breath and grinned. "That's great."

"You're lucky. Racing in Charleston pretty much faded after the Civil War. But back in the day, before the war? Those were the glory days for horse racing here. I don't know if we'll ever see anything like that again. Still, folks are trying. Palmetto Park will be racing its second season in November during the Charleston County Fair. I'll take you there when I'm done here at four. They know me, and my word might still have some weight around there."

It was already two o'clock, so Rory continued wandering around the city. He was taken by the designs of the buildings, most made of brick, many whitewashed, others painted stucco. Many were quite majestic and ornate, with arched windows and columns, while others were simple brick or clapboard.

One impressive building, the South Carolina National Bank of Charleston, its brick walls covered with glaringly white stucco, had a gold eagle adorning its grand front gable. There was an abundance of churches. The First (Scots) Presbyterian Church was big enough to be a cathedral, with four grand pillars in front and two bell towers rising above its roof. He wanted to paint everything he saw.

At four o'clock, he returned to the bar, where Roscoe waited for him out front. They took a trolley to Palmetto Park. "This used to be all pastureland, but last year, they used it for the fair and built a new track for the horseracing. They say it's better than the Washington course was."

They went straight to the stables, where the familiar horse smells calmed Rory's nerves. The racetrack manager gave Roscoe a bear hug that Rory thought might crush the little man. When he was released, Roscoe introduced them.

"Dave Johnson, meet Rory Murphy. He's looking for a job. He told me a little of his history on the way here. I was impressed. I'm gonna wander and get my fill of horseflesh."

Mr. Johnson was a short, fat, red-faced man with a dead cigar gripped between his teeth and an old hat atop his bald head. He read the letter of recommendation from Tim, nodded, then stared at Rory for seemingly a good minute.

"Good God, man. You're a prayer answered. It's already September, and the fair opens in two months on November seventeenth and we'll have races on all seven days, weather permitting. We've got one of the largest racetracks in the South, and the Fair Association is promoting it by saying this year we can accommodate eight hundred to a thousand horses. *Accommodate!* Jesus, I love that." Somehow, he rolled the cigar to the other side of his mouth and shook his head in disgust.

"C'mon, let me take you around. Last year we didn't even have close to a thousand horses. Now we already have seven hundred reservations."

They walked the grounds, most of it pasture, with a number of training and cool down paddocks. The track was well maintained, and the grass infield had a number of low trees and shrubs. The grandstand along the north side of the track was white with three levels and blended nicely with the white barn behind it.

The center section of the barn was two stories, with one-story wings extending on each side. "Offices, storage, feed, and housing in the middle, and the two wings house the stables," Dave said.

The doors to the stalls all opened to the outside. Rory thought if he were a horse, he'd like to hang his head out and see and sniff the outdoors. He stopped and petted two big draft horses doing just that.

"Tom and Dick," Dave said. "Harry's out in the pasture. They do all the heavy work." He stopped to relight his cigar. "I wasn't in charge last year, but I was second in charge. That poor guy had no idea what he was doing, and no one was fired at the end. I was stupid enough to accept the offer to replace him.

"I should have insisted on keeping the facilities open and getting the work done over the winter and spring, but the powers that be didn't want to spend the money and kept it closed until August. So now, not only am I playing catch up trying to get the place ready, but it's the hottest time of the year. Those three boys have earned their feed and more, dragging the two chain harrows getting the track ready. On October 15 we'll open the stables to those early bird trainers who want to get a head start working the track."

Dave led Rory away from the barn to what looked like a heap of rubble. "That is what's left of the temporary stalls they built last year. Just wooden frames with tarps, but they did the job—once. The Fair Association won't spend for permanent stalls, so we'll use what's in that pile and add more if we have to. They'll be up by October. I'm hard pressed to figure out how to do it all. It's a damned mess."

"I know you're a trainer, Rory, but right now, I need someone to oversee the stable and the logistics of putting up so many horses and all the crap that comes with them. I bet Belmont Park knew a thing or two about organizing for a big crowd."

Rory was thinking the same. He was lucky he'd had the experience of converting Belmont Park to an airfield and then back to a racetrack for that race in May. He was worried about working for this guy though; he looked a little rough around the edges. But he could see it through to the fair, anyway. It was a short-term job he could do, while still looking for his family.

The next day he moved into the room reserved for the stable manager on the first floor. Rory was young and a foreigner, but there was little resistance from the other employees. There were only three; more would be hired as needed. It was obvious Rory knew what he was doing and no one else wanted the responsibility.

Rory wrote to Tim and Devlin for advice. Both were generous with their suggestions and opinions. Devlin's last letter had sad news.

Mistress Campbell died from lockjaw. Tetanus, the doctor called it. And from a trip to the barn, of all things. Can you imagine? One of her society big wigs wanted to see the stable, so she arranged a tour with Oliver. For whatever reason, the mistress came down too. Just as they were leaving, she tripped and fell, catching her hand on a nail. It got infected and she got very sick. You could hear her screaming down at the barn. It was awful. God, it makes me shudder still. Of all the things, right?"

Samel is still tearing up the track. Oliver and I think we'll let him race one more year, then put him out to stud. Rough life.

I know you'll find your family, someday.

With fondness, Devlin

Rory sat in a daze. Of all the things… She never went to the stables. He had only seen her that one time, at the stables then, too, but he remembered her clearly. Her dislike for him came at him like an arrow. Why? he asked himself then and now. Just one of those things that have no answer, and he'd never find out now anyway. Poor Oliver.

⌒≈つ

On the first afternoon he could steal some time away from the track, Rory visited the Irish section of town and went into the Catholic church, St. Mary's. The priest saw him standing in the narthex.

"May I help you, son?"

"I'm new to Charleston, Father, and I am hoping to find news of … of my family." He took the old picture of Mam from his pocket and unfolded it. The light was dim, so the priest led him outside into a patch of sunlight.

"It's my mother," Rory said. "I drew her from memory—I'm not sure how good a likeness it may be. Her name is Bridie Murphy. Do you know her?" His voice shook.

"I'm sorry, son. I've only been here a short time, but I don't know her." He folded the picture again, smoothed it, and handed it back. "You should come to Mass on Sunday and then go to Hibernian Hall. It's where your countrymen gather, both newcomers and those who've been in Charleston for years. That's where you're most likely to have success. God bless you."

Many times over the years, Rory had let himself imagine finding his mam, his brothers, and just as many times he'd thought it would be impossible. They could be anywhere in this huge country. All the way to California, or back in Ireland. The priest was kind but unable to help beyond a blessing and a suggestion that seemed vague.

Not sure what he was feeling or what to do next, Rory walked on. He passed a bar. Sweeney's the sign read. A young man around his age was sitting outside. On impulse, Rory stopped. The man looked up with a look Rory knew—ready to be friends or foes, one as easy as the other.

"Good afternoon," Rory said. "Is this a good place to have a pint?"

"Not bad." Not a man to commit in a hurry then. "My da owns it."

"Then it must be grand. I'm new in town, glad to know the right places to go. Ask you something?"

The man shrugged. "Up to you."

Rory took out the picture once again and offered it.

"My ma, name of Bridie Murphy. She has two other sons, Finn and…"

Before he could say more, the man grabbed the picture and stared at it. "Brendan. Yeah, I know. So, you're …?"

"You know them?" Rory asked.

The man blanched. "Jaysus." He stood up, knocking his chair down. "Follow me."

He almost ran down the block and behind a building. When Rory caught up, they were in an alleyway. This man could have lured him there to rob him. Rory felt his blood rise.

"Whatever I say," the man whispered, "you didn't hear it from me." He looked around, fearful.

"My name is Jimmy Sweeney. I met Bridie Murphy when I was a kid. I was a friend of Finn's, and she caught us doing stupid stuff in the house she worked in. Anyway, Finn and her had a row, and he moved in with us, upstairs above the bar. He stayed for a few years. His mam came around askin' about Finn, and my da started seein' her. I think he might have roughed her up some.

"Next thing you know, Finn moves out and no one can find him. Then someone sics the feckin' police chief on Da and all hell breaks out. He still hasn't got out from under the chief's eye. Comin' around all times makin' life miserable for him."

Rory's throat had tightened the minute this Jimmy said Mam's name, Finn's name, Brendan's. His heart pounded against his ribs. He felt he might faint or throw up. The hell with the man's father and whatever his trouble might have been.

Speaking as calmly as he could, he asked, "Are they alive? Do you know where they are?"

"I know nothin'. They just vanished. But if you find Finn, will you put in a good word for me? He was my best friend, and I miss him. I know my da can be an arsehole. Tell Finn I'm sorry about everything, and I hope he got away from here. And that he's livin' a good life."

He turned away and hurried back to the bar.

The next day, Rory went to the Hibernian Hall right next door to the St. John Hotel. It was large and white with six huge columns in front. It looked like one of the Greek temples in his teacher John's art books. Pretty impressive meeting place for a bunch of Irish immigrants, Rory thought.

His knocks on the massive front door got no response, so he made his way to the back. He found a door unlocked, opened it, and called, "Anybody here?"

A man in an apron appeared at the end of a passageway. "Nobody but me. You are you looking for?"

"I've just recently come to Charleston, and I'm looking for my mother and brothers. They came from Ireland years ago."

"I'm only recent here myself. Come back on Sunday for breakfast. The place will be full then. You're sure to find somebody who knows them."

The man disappeared again. Rory wondered for a moment, had he been real? Jimmy Sweeney had at least known Mam and the boys. Maybe Sunday would be the day someone else could tell him where they were.

He was glad to have work to do, to make the days go faster.

Despite the ever-present cigar moving up and down in Dave's mouth, the man wasn't as bad as Rory first thought. He had been given a huge job he wasn't prepared for, and Rory's experience was a godsend. Between them, they made headway on the many problems they needed to solve before the onslaught, all of which needed to be approved by the Charleston County Fair Board. "Slow as molasses, and so tight their shoes squeak," Dave said, giving an extra chomp on the cigar.

November was fast approaching, and both Dave and Rory were feeling the pressure. The temporary stalls were finished. Assorted barn workers were living in the rooms adjacent to Rory. Horses were arriving daily from all parts of the country in their horse trucks, with their trainers, grooms, jockeys, track ponies, food, tack… Schedules were made for practices on the track and for workouts in the fields. They were working round the clock each day. As much as Rory wanted to find his family, at this time, his obligations were to Dave and the horses. The Hibernian wasn't going to shut down any time soon. He kept telling himself Mam would still be here when the fair closed.

All their work paid off. The races went off without a hitch. Afterwards, Dave, Rory, Roscoe, and the barn workers sat around with a few beers, telling stories. When the fireworks began, Rory walked out to the pasture to see them better. Tom, Dick, and Harry nickered at him. He climbed up onto Harry's wide back and laid face up to watch the fireworks. It was almost magical, and the sight filled him with hope. Tomorrow was Sunday, and he would finally go to the Hibernian. His heart jumped. Tomorrow.

Chapter 32

1913

The inside of the Hibernian was a crush of people. Rory guessed maybe a hundred. How in God's name could he find Mam in such a crowd? He backed up and leaned against a wall to get his bearings.

It was a lively crowd, noisy and jovial. Some tables looked to have families, others had women in their Sunday dresses, others had men sitting with ties undone and collars loosened. Children ran about; babies sat on laps. The sound of Irish accents, though loud, was soothing to Rory. He was unsure who to ask. Trying to look normal, he walked to a tableful of women he guessed to be around Mam's age, but turned away, bashfulness overcoming him.

Even though it was a Sunday and the bar was closed, many of the men hung around it as if from habit. They were trying to be subtle as they took nips from flasks, and they eyed him suspiciously when he neared them. He almost turned, but one of the men spoke up.

"Can I help you? I've not seen you here before."

Rory coughed. "I'm looking for my mother. Her name is Bridie Murphy. She and I got separated when we left Ireland. We were coming here to Charleston."

He showed the picture to the men. "I drew this from memory, so she could look different now."

"No, can't say I've ever seen her. I'll get Hugh. He's one of the old timers, and he might know her."

Rory stood at the bar, trying to control his emotions, trying not to allow his hopes to rise or to sink too low. In a few minutes, he saw the man coming back, another man following him.

"I'm Hugh Brady. I was told you were looking for Bridie Murphy. Who's askin?"

Rory's heart thumped. This man knew her, or he wouldn't have asked. The hall was crowded and noisy, overly warm with so many bodies pressed into it.

"Can we sit down, please. I'll tell you all about it."

Hugh nodded and motioned for Rory to follow him. It was slow going, but finally, Hugh showed Rory into an alcove with a small table and four chairs. "Give us a bit of privacy." He got them each a glass of water. "So, tell me why you're askin' about Mrs. Murphy?"

Now that he could breathe again, Rory found himself becoming irritated. "I just want to know if she's alive. If she lives here, in Charleston. I'm her son, Rory."

A woman came into the room in time to hear what he said.

"Bridie's son?" She sat heavily, as if stunned, on the nearest chair. "Can't be."

Hugh drew a chair nearer to hers and sat down too. He put a hand on her shoulder, protective.

Rory was sure now these people could tell him what he wanted to know. Why didn't they? Once more, he took the drawing from his pocket and unfolded it. He laid it on the table and looked at them both.

"I'm Rory. I was lost from her years ago. I've come from Ireland in hopes of finding her."

The woman touched the image of Mam's face, looked to Hugh, then to Rory with tears in her eyes. "That's Bridie, for sure. My name is Shirley Brady, though she knew me when my last name was Ames. Bridie was my best friend."

Why did she say *was*? "Is she—no longer living?" His mind was screaming. "Please say she's alive."

The woman paled and took Rory's hand. "She told me about her Rory, her lost boy. Aye, lad, she's alive and in South Carolina, but not in Charleston. I don't want to talk about it here. Let's go for a walk." Hugh started to get up, but she gestured for him to stay. "It's all right, Hugh. I'm going to take him to the Beckers. We'll be fine, dear."

"Let me walk with you both. It will make me feel better."

Rory took the drawing from her. If he folded it many more times, the paper would fray. Well, he'd make another if he had to. Then the three of them went out to the street.

On the way to wherever they were going, Shirley told Rory about Bridie. "A man named Daniel Sweeney tried to kill your mother. And Finn too. He's a bad, bad man. That's why Hugh was so cold with you. We still try to protect her."

Rory said, "I met a man yesterday named Jimmy Sweeney. Does that name mean anything to you?"

Shirley looked like she might get sick. "That's Daniel's son. He was friends with Finn. He probably still wants to be friends, but that monster Daniel won't let him. Just as well. You have to make a clean break from people like him, and that's what Bridie did. Once Finn and his wife got settled…"

"Wait, Finn is married?"

Shirley laughed. "So much you don't know. I don't know how to tell it all. Yes, indeed. To Emily Becker. Her parents own the coffee store we're goin' to now. And Finn and Emily have a baby, Charlie."

Rory stopped short, staring at Shirley. Then he broke out in laughter. "Finn is a father? I'm an uncle? I'll be. And Mammy moved to wherever they are?"

"Yes. Finn left town durin' the night, about a year and a half ago, and Bridie left recently. Daniel and his hooligans are still here, though they've been taken down a notch or two, thanks to Bridie."

Shirley had brought Rory into a part of town he'd walked through when he first arrived. He'd liked the neighborhood of small houses, mostly two story. Many had businesses downstairs—a milliner, a seamstress, a candlemaker, artists. Most of the residents appeared to be immigrants, but not just Irish. He'd heard a variety of accents.

They stopped at the glass door with *Kaffee Store* painted on it in black letters.

"Here we are," Shirley said, "at Emily's parents' place."

Rory laughed. "That's funny. I saw this store on one of my walks and came in for a coffee and a pastry. I was tempted by the smell of baking."

"And for good reason," said Shirley. "Ingrid, I have someone you need to meet. Karl too. Maybe we could go upstairs when he gets here?"

A small, middle-aged woman behind the counter gave Shirley a puzzled look. "Not sure why we need to go upstairs. We're crazy right now. For now, take that table over there. The other counter woman will be here to relieve me in a bit, and I can chat. In the meantime, I'll put in your usual order. For three?"

Rory looked around the little store at all the people patiently standing in line at the counter. He looked at the bounty in the display cabinet and hoped there would be enough for him, maybe even seconds. His senses were overwhelmed.

"Everyone's coming in for their Thanksgiving orders," said Shirley as she motioned Rory to a table near a window. "I don't know how she does it."

A waitress came over with their orders. Rory took a small bite of his pastry and smiled broadly at Shirley.

"I told you, didn't I? The coffee might be a bit bitter, but I add lots of cream and sugar." She took a sip. "So, Rory, tell us about yourself and how you've survived all these years."

Before he could start, Shirley began giggling. "God. Your mam is goin' to go crazy when she hears you're alive."

"But you haven't told me where she is. I want to go there as quick as I can."

"You have my thoughts scrambled, Rory. She lives in a town named Newry…"

"Newry? I thought you said she was still here in South Carolina."

"She is. There's a Newry here in South Carolina."

Rory was dumbfounded. Another Newry. Who'd ever guess?

A new woman was now at the counter, and Ingrid came to their table. "Let's go upstairs to our apartment. Karl's already up there, with coffee for us all." She looked at Rory, who was trying to stuff all the pastries into his mouth. "Just bring your plate with you."

Once they were in the apartment, Shirley introduced Rory. "Yes, it's Bridie's lost son. I didn't want to say anything in public, just in case."

"Karl!" Ingrid almost shouted, looking at him urgently. "You've got to go…"

"I'm going." Karl slammed down his cup, jumped up, and ran to the door. "I'll get Josef to drive me. He hasn't finished unloading the truck yet."

He looked at Rory. "Please excuse me, but I'll be back shortly."

"Go on, Rory," said Shirley. "Keep on with your story. It's unbelievable, Ingrid."

Ingrid listened with interest, though she and Shirley took turns getting up and looking out the window. Rory was too busy talking and trying samples of pastries to notice.

Suddenly there were the sounds of feet on the stairway. Rory hardly noticed the noise, but the two women sat down.

Karl entered the room looking at Rory while motioning behind him. "I think there's someone you might want to meet."

A young man with red hair stood in the doorway. He eyed Rory nervously. "Mr. Becker told me your name is Rory Murphy. Is that right?"

Rory looked around at the faces staring back at him.

The lad began to smile, and there was something Rory recognized in that smile. His mother's smile? His father's? How to know? They were so dim in his mind.

Slowly, he took the wrinkled picture of his mother from his pocket. He stared at it, praying this would be the last time he would ever have to use it. Then, he unfolded it and laid it out on the table, face down. With great care, he ironed out the wrinkles. He felt as if he was giving up a part of his body, he'd carried it around so long. He turned over the paper and watched for the lad's reaction. Please let this boy be my brother. Please lead me to my family.

The lad stared at the picture, then gently touched Mam's face. "It's Mammy. Oh, that is her," he whispered. "Rory? Can it really be you?"

Afterword

My husband, son, and I moved from Miami, Florida, to Salem, South Carolina, in 2016 after I retired from nursing. We lived in Keowee Key, a small community on Lake Keowee. It was pretty much in the woods, and Seneca, the closest big town, was eighteen miles away, usually a thirty-minute drive. But it was a beautiful drive, with scenic views of the Blue Ridge Mountains in the distance and Lake Keowee along the side of the road. The lake was created in the early 1970s, when Duke Energy dammed the Keowee River and the Little River for its Keowee-Toxaway hydroelectric project. In the winter, when there were no leaves, I could see a tall brick tower in the distance. A short distance after, there was an inconspicuous sign and arrow saying NEWRY. What was that?

One day there was an article in the paper about Newry, an old mill town, and my husband and I took a drive to Newry. Initially, I thought the town was abandoned. Houses, some brick, most two-story white, now grey, clapboard, with trash, debris, and old cars in the front yards. We did see some people around, all looking as tired as the town. When we got to the end of Broadway Street (yes, that's the name) there was the tower I had seen through the trees. Even in its dilapidated state, it loomed over the abandoned mill buildings. Ivy and graffiti covered its brick walls, much of which had fallen to the ground. Its windows stared out blankly, only shards of glass glinting out from the inner darkness. I imagined how it must have ruled the town back in its heyday. Now, it was sad and scary, and I was glad I was in the truck with my husband.

It took me a while to get around to writing the story I hoped was there, but I was still writing my first book, *Deplorable Tragedy*. In 2022, I started to write *A Town Named Newry*. I wondered if there was a story there…

Newry lingered in a state of disrepair, although each time we drove through, there were incremental improvements to the houses. Rumors of redeveloping the town were met with conflicting responses. In 2020, work began, and in 2023, after an investment of more than sixty million dollars, the Newry Mill opened to the public with improvements: 197 apartments, revitalization of the company store and post office, nature trails, wildlife restoration, a kayak launch.

The Newry General Store and Café opened in 2024. On my first visit, I walked up the steps to the front doors under the awning, the same as the old one.

(Could it be the same?) Inside, I sat in a daze, realizing I was in the store that Emily ran, now primped up with white paint, clear bright windows, and modern furnishings, with the smell of lattes and fresh bakery goodies wafting over me. I think she would have approved.

Fud Cater, who I mention in the Acknowledgements, was requested by the development company to act as an adviser. I asked him how he thought his father would have felt about what they were doing to the town.

"I think he'd be grateful that the town would still exist. That they didn't demolish everything. The mill and the tower were rebuilt, the store was refurbished... It's still Newry."

Acknowledgements

I self-published my first book, *Deplorable Tragedy: A Family's Mystery Answered* in 2020. I had taken a Zoom class with Nora Gaskin Esthimer on self-publishing through the Flatiron Writers Room in Asheville, North Carolina. It was very worthwhile. Then.

That was five years ago, and I swore I would never do it again. I looked Nora up again, and lo and behold, she is an editor and a publisher: Lystra Books & Literary Services. She and her copy editor and book designer, Kelly Prelipp Lojk, pulled and squeezed and molded my book into a polished novel. I can never thank them enough.

I couldn't have written this book without the support of my husband, Steve Carney. A writer himself, albeit scientific, he proofed multiple iterations and had many suggestions. My sister Genii Cockshutt, an English major, did two readings. (I think they might want me to stop writing.)

When I started writing the book, I was still living in South Carolina and my writers' group, Writers' Ink, which now has more than a few published authors, offered the same wise suggestions they had with my first book. They are a motley crew of really good writers not afraid to tell me the truth. I miss them.

The town of Newry was my inspiration, and living down the road allowed me to get information from people who had lived there. I had come upon a book, *Newry: A Place Apart* by Michael Hembree, that introduced me to Newry's history. I contacted him about the book's photos, which he told me were taken by Henry Cater, who had long since passed away. But Hembree thought Cater's son might be able to help.

He did indeed. Fud Cater grew up in Newry and now lives in Seneca. Not only was Fud a gold mine of information, he gave me a thumb drive of photos. (As an aside, when I told my friend Kaye King, who grew up in Seneca, that this wonderful man gave me the photos, she said, "I went to high school with him." She's also the one who insists, in her southern accent, that I should pronounce the town's name *NER-ry*, not *NEW-ry*).

Wayne Richard, a friend, had rented a house in Newry during the 1980s. He shared with me many of the old timers' stories he'd been told. He and his wife Lauren, Steve, and I went for a walk to see Innisfallen, the abandoned mansion built by the mill's builder and owner, William Ashmead Courtenay, as his family home. Walk is a misnomer. It was a laborious trek through the woods, bamboo forests, and wisteria that fought us every step of the way. In the end, we found the mansion reduced to crumbling chimneys and stone walls, a sad reminder of its glory days.

ALIX CRAWFORD CARNEY published her first novel, *Deplorable Tragedy: A Family's Mystery Answered*, about the mysterious deaths of her maternal great-grandparents in 2020.

Born and raised in Massachusetts, Alix then moved to Miami, Florida, where she lived for some fifty years. She worked as an operating room nurse, traveled to Europe, cruised the Bahamas on a sailboat, renovated an old farmhouse in France, and wrote stories.

When she retired, she and her husband, son, and their cats, moved to Salem, South Carolina. It was there she wrote *Deplorable Tragedy*. In 2022, she began writing *A Town Named Newry*.

In 2024, she and her family moved to Vero Beach, Florida.

www.ingramcontent.com/pod-product-compliance
Lightning Source LLC
Chambersburg PA
CBHW030227120726
47903CB00005B/1395